MIDNIGHT IN THE MORGUE

CAINE PRIZE ANTHOLOGY 2024

Edited by Femi Kayode and Karen Jennings

Foreword by Chika Unigwe

Abuja - London

First published in 2025 by Cassava Republic Press
Abuja – London

Editorial Copyright © Femi Kayode and Karen Jennings
Copyright of the text © of their authors, 2025
Copyright in this collection © Cassava Republic Press 2025

A CIP catalogue record for this book is available from the National Library of Nigeria and the British Library.

ISBN: 978-1-913175-68-9
eISBN: 978-1-913175-69-6

Book design by Abdulrahman Osamudiamen Suleiman
Cover & Art Direction by Jamie Keenan

Printed and bound in the UK by Clays

Distributed in Nigeria by Yellow Danfo

Distributed worldwide by Ingram Publishers Services

Table of Contents

Foreword

A while ago, after learning I was a writer, my cab driver asked if I feared being made obsolete by AI. My answer was an emphatic no. There's something inherently human that machines lack—a heart, a soul, a pulse. Machines haven't lived. When writing truly moves us, it does so because life is coursing through its veins. Yet, it is a fact that fiction writers face competition from technology in other ways. Readers today are inundated with options—social media, podcasts, TikTok, endless content just a click away. Content creation has become a lucrative profession, and there's a sense that people now prefer quick, easily digestible pieces over the slower, more immersive experience that traditional fiction provides.

Ironically, when the cab driver asked me that question, I was in the midst of reading for the 2024 Caine Prize, trying to narrow down over three hundred eligible stories from twenty-eight African countries—many of which were very good—to a manageable top twenty for the judges' initial meeting. I struggled with which stories to let go. The ones that stayed with me, that ended up on my list, were those that held my undivided attention. Despite the many distractions technology offers, a well-written story will always captivate, transcending the noise of modern life.

For the past twenty-five years, the Caine Prize has celebrated the best fiction by African writers published anywhere in the world in the preceding year. This year, I had the privilege of serving as chair of the judging panel alongside a remarkable team: Zimbabwean writer, scholar, and filmmaker Siphiwe Gloria Ndlovu, Sierra Leonean poet, artist, and filmmaker Julianknxx, South African hip-hop artist and lyricist Tumi Molekane (aka Stogie T), and Ghanaian writer Ayesha Harruna Attah. We read, we debated, we laughed, we re-read, and together we whittled down the stories to a shortlist we are immensely proud of.

Uche Okonkwo's *"Animal"* (Nigeria), Samuel Kolawole's *"Adjustment of Status"* (Nigeria), Tryphena Yeboah's *"The Dishwashing Women"* (Ghana), Nadia David's *"Bridling"* (South Africa), and Pemi Aguda's *"Breastmilk"* (Nigeria) have earned their places on the 2024 Caine Prize shortlist. These stories are compelling. They carry the weight of personal, cultural, political, and emotional truths. In a time when technology threatens to drown out the nuances of individual experience(s), these stories remind us of the irreplaceable value of storytelling. They reflect our shared humanity, offering diverse and profound perspectives. They are also, above all else, masterfully and beautifully written. These are writers of superlative talent.

In Okonkwo's story, a husband struggles with his (idea of) masculinity, his wife with her unspoken wants, and their child with eating the aptly-named Otuanya, a one-eyed chicken that, despite being elevated to the status of a family pet, is doomed for the cooking pot. Kolawole's protagonist is an undocumented immigrant who suffers indignities abroad and returns home to Nigeria, yet cannot face his family—until tragedy forces his hand. Yeboah introduces a domestic worker who hatches an audacious plan for revenge on the powerful family she serves. Davids presents a somewhat surreal story of an exacting male theatre director and the rebellious women who eventually challenge his vision. Finally, Aguda's protagonist struggles to be the mother she wants to be for her infant son until she confronts the truth about her feelings regarding her husband's infidelity.

However, a good story is never about just one thing. These works also explore feminism, gender roles, class, exploitation, and patriarchy. They are the product of writers who are astute observers of life.

We sometimes hear African literature spoken of as though it were a single, easily identifiable entity. Reading for the Caine Prize is a reminder of its vast and varied nature. It is sci-fi, horror, experimental writing, realism, fantasy. It is both local and global. Both domestic and political. These five shortlisted stories—witty, serious, thought-provoking, sad, utterly brilliant, compulsively readable, and unique—are all African literature. This anthology is a generous offering, a feast of diverse, delectable narratives, with something for everyone. Bon appetit!

Chika Unigwe
2024 Chair of Judges

Preface

In *Home and Exile*, Chinua Achebe describes the writing process as a term of imprisonment – "one you will have to endure to bring [the work] to fruition." Consider having an idea for a short story and being told that in order to write it you will be imprisoned for two weeks. Only two weeks! How wonderful, two lovely weeks in which to write at one's leisure. Even better, instead of a dank cell, you have a room in a beautiful resort in Malawi, right on Lake Malawi, with a comfy double bed all to yourself, a desk, a chair, all the food you can eat, and friendly staff to serve you. Ah, idyllic!

You go to sit at that lovely desk and you turn away from the beautiful view, and suddenly your smile fades because in front of you is your open laptop or notebook and the blank page stares at you, daring you to deface it. Now you remember the truth of your prison sentence. It is that you have been condemned to writing – which is gentle shorthand for delirium, torment, suffering, for being struck by one's own awful inadequacy and knowing before you have written a single word that you will fail, fail, fail, and you are all alone in this, quite alone.

But then you remember that this is not solitary confinement, that there are, in fact, others who have been sentenced alongside you, each of you trying to bring to life some truth, some real feeling, a view of the world that can speak to those beyond yourself. You leave your room, knock on doors, call the others, all of you from different backgrounds and cultures and ages, with different personalities, tastes and skills. At once the delirium, the torment lifts. You share your ideas, your frustrations and fears, you show your work in progress to one another, give one another feedback, encouragement, inspiration and support. Sometimes there are tears or anger, or frustration or disagreement. Because tensions do arise. How can they not? When everyone feels this enormous pressure, mostly from themselves, to do their best, to get up each day and to write and write and write, to write flawlessly, brilliantly, writing in the frenzy that Flaubert once described as "bellowing like a fiend, in the silence of my study" and joked that he would one day "explode like an artillery shell and all my bits will be found on the writing table."

There is a reason why writers speak about the writing process in this way, about exploding, bellowing, prison sentences, pain and turmoil. It isn't for dramatic effect. To create something of value, to put oneself into it and bring forward something that has meaning, is not easy, far from it.

This is part of the reason for writing workshops being so important and why they continue to be popular as places of community and nurturing. All writers – whether they write fiction, non-fiction, academic essays, memoir, biography, maths textbooks – all writers want to do two things: to understand and to share. This is precisely what the Caine Prize Workshops allow. Yes, there are important life skills, like writing to a deadline, writing under tension, having various requirements placed upon one in terms of word count and participation. But the process of doing all of this through mentorship and community means that beyond the learning and understanding is the incredible opportunity of sharing. Sharing with mentors, sharing with fellow attendees, sharing with the anthology editors at Cassava Republic, and now, here, the opportunity to share with you.

As you read these short stories, think of the writers, think of their lungs bursting as they bellow into the night, as they writhe in torment, but think of them too, coming together, eating cake, gossiping, laughing, giving advice and support. Think of them as wonderfully human, both flawed and brilliant, and bringing that humanity to you. Can there be any greater gift?

Karen Jennings
Editor and Workshop Facilitator

2024 SHORTLISTED STORIES

The Dishwashing Women

Tryphena Yeboah

Originally published in *Narrative Magazine* (2022)

At first there was one of them, and then two, and like a child that isn't planned but also isn't an accident, there was a third. They lived in a small kitchen inside a big kitchen. They imagined their place as some kind of pantry—only rather than a cupboard with shelves, it was an entire room, with a door and a window (that quickly steamed up when there was a lot of cooking in the big kitchen, which was often the case) and even a tall wooden cupboard in the corner where they kept canned foods, chipped plates, colorful scarves, woven straw hats, and a million other unnamed things. Adoma, the newest addition to the kitchen staff, did not want to believe it was the room assigned as the maids' quarters. It was a tiny room compared to all the other rooms in the house. But the maids made a home of it, and when she would look around, Adoma was indeed surprised by their possessions—a stained velvet curtain that hung on the wall, a side table with a lampshade that had no bulb in it, old newspapers to wrap smoked fish in or fold in two as a hand fan when the heat was unbearable, a basket filled to the brim with aprons. So much of it secondhand treasures, and so many times their hands did the digging and salvaging from what would soon be discarded as worthless.

Adoma was the youngest of them all, and at twenty-nine she did not want to accept that well-meaning people designed their homes to include small rooms of this kind for other humans. It seemed strange, the disparity; reckless, the thought of it.

The mansion belonged to a diplomat, his wife, and their two children—Samantha and Ben. At two years old Ben was a precious and often abandoned boy walking and throwing two-word sentences all over the place. When the women first moved in, he would poke his head into the kitchen, cackle, and turn around and head back to the other side of the house. It was almost as if he knew where the territory ended for him, to which side of the building he belonged. After a few weeks, though, and this might be because of all the aromas of food, or their singing and chatter, Ben crossed the gray marble tiles that separated the hall from the kitchen. His mother didn't mind and was perhaps pleased to have him off her hands, and so he kept coming—only on condition that he stayed in the main kitchen. The women had come to wash dishes (that was the initial arrangement), but with all the gatherings and parties the family had been having, extra hands were needed to assist with the cooking. Soon enough, with their secret recipes and many whispered recommendations to the cook about what local spices to use and the right amount of time to keep pastries in the oven, they had more to add to their workload, while their payment stayed the same. And with Ben wanting no other place to play with his toys than on the kitchen's wooden floor—surrounded by women who saw him, tickled him, stuffed a tiny cornbread muffin into his small mouth every now and then, and threw him up in the air and caught him in their firm hands—they quickly became nannies too.

As for Samantha, or Sam, as her parents called her, she watched them from a distance. Sometimes she was envious of the affection her brother received, but most of the time, her eyes were cast down, the anger visible in her slumped shoulders. She did not want to be there, away from her friends and her private school and paved roads back home. She sat in the next room journaling, sometimes writing letters to friends, complaining about the scorching sun. When her father would walk by and say, 'You have to make a conscious effort to make yourself feel at home, we will be here for at least two years,' she would sulk and shake her head, her red pigtails swinging on both sides of her face. 'This is not home, and it will never be.'

To the women, home was never explicitly defined, but they knew they were seen by each other, that they could stretch their hand in the dark and another would reach out to hold it, that the unspoken rule was to keep watch and take care of your own, wherever they may be. Every job they did, they did well, talking among themselves, latching on to a tune when one started a hymn, working and praying and stretching their strength into the night. They were aware of each other's sighs and lifted spirits, nursed one another when there was a new burn on the hand from a boiling pot or a deep cut on the finger from the endless chopping of carrots or peeling the skin off plantains, and ended each day looking forward to the next—not so much the labor of the new dawn, but that they could partake in the living again, could strum the chord of being alive, regardless of what it looked like, and what it stripped away from them.

There were empty rooms on the other floors. Adoma knew because she counted them each week when she went up to change the sheets, even when no one slept on them. Six empty rooms. Surely one could be given up for them? She fantasized about sleeping in one of the beds. To just walk up those stairs one night and throw herself onto the soft mattress and feel her body sink into its padded layers of cotton and wool. What's the worst that could happen if they found her in the morning—she'd be sent back to the small kitchen shelter? Well, that wouldn't do much. She imagined the shocked faces of the master and his wife, how they wouldn't know what to say because they hadn't anticipated a day like this would come when somebody they did not—and would not—consider one of them crossed that threshold and made herself feel at home. And perhaps along with the shock would be fear—how did they let this happen? When did they stop being in charge? They would be quick to question: How is it possible that this shy twenty-nine-year-old kinky-haired, soft-eyed, kitchen-bound lady could do this brave, unacceptable thing? It made Adoma laugh whenever she thought about such things, and she thought about them a lot.

Esiha, the oldest and first to arrive at the house, couldn't stand the young lady's absentmindedness and giggles. The whole act was strange, and to Esiha, even impolite. They would be washing and slicing vegetables for an evening gathering, and there Adoma would go, half a tomato in hand, laughing and covering her mouth; or they would be sweeping and mopping the floors and she would stop and nod and chuckle, as if someone had just appeared to her and whispered a joke in her ear. In so many ways she reminded her of Helen, her daughter, who was away from home, from her care, and in the faraway wildness and strangeness of a foreign land. It had been two years since she left to study psychology, and now during every phone call, the girl had questions, she wanted to know everything. How was her mother coping, was there anything from her past holding her back, if she could go back in time, what would she change about her life?

Sometimes Esiha shook her head and smiled, amazed by how smart her girl sounded, how she was confident enough to ask her these big questions. When Esiha was Helen's age, her own voice was unfamiliar to her, and when she did speak, she was meek sounding, uttering the words with fear and uncertainty, unsure of herself. Often swallowing them down before she could even string the words together to articulate them. Her daughter's questions wore her out. She had no complaints, she would say.

'Life is good, there is nothing to change. I wake up, take what I can get, and hope to God I live to see another day.'

'And what happens then?' Helen always knew what to say, how to steer the conversation back to what she really wanted to know. 'What happens when you see another day? How are you walking into tomorrow, Ma?'

Esiha did not know what to do with her and all this newfound and disconcerting curiosity.

'Ach! Why are you bothering me with all these questions? When tomorrow finds me, I know what I want to do with it. Tell me about you. Have you found a church? And how are you doing in the weather? Don't let the cold get into your bones. It'll stiffen up your veins and cripple you!'

Helen told her not to worry about the cold; there were clothes to keep her warm. She was concerned about her mother, how her work in the house was going, if they were treating her well. They went back and forth like that, each not saying much of what the other needed to hear but still asking enough questions to keep the other talking until one of them had to go. It was often Helen running off the line, her voice suddenly taking on a sense of urgency, as if she were going to miss her train if she didn't get off the phone that instant, but it was always to the library or a café or some department meeting, and none of those things could wait.

After every phone call, Esiha shared her diagnosis with Nkwa-daa, her quiet and observant friend. The one who wouldn't let her do this job all by herself, the one who, despite all of life's misfortune, got back up on her feet every time, humming as she cooked and cleaned and moved about. No one ever embodied the meaning of their name like she did, *life always*. Esiha and Nkwa-daa had been friends for more than twenty years, and when Helen was born, Nkwa-daa was right there to pick up Helen's small wailing body and shush her in the middle of the night, urging Esiha to go back to sleep after the baby had had some milk. But Esiha mostly stayed by her friend's side, dozing off a few times, while the image of her dearest friend cradling her baby stayed with her, made her heart heavy with gratitude and at the same time light with relief, for how could she survive these nights all by herself?

'She is well, by grace. But her voice . . . maybe she has a cold,' Esiha said, looking at the phone as if expecting Helen's call to come through again.

'Did you tell her to drink some herbal tea?'

'Well, no. But when does she ever listen to us?' Esiha started for the main kitchen.

They were cooking yam and kontomire stew for dinner and some chicken soup too. There were guests coming, foreign people who had slowly trained their palate to enjoy unfamiliar foods. There were, of course, the days of mashing potatoes upon request, when they'd rather fry them, or throwing mixed fruits into a blender when they'd rather pop the solids in their mouth, feel the textures of pineapples and mangoes on their tongues. But rarely did they do anything in the house for their own pleasure. They followed orders for no reason other than it was what they were for.

'She listens to me,' Nkwa-daa said, playfully poking her friend in the ribs with her finger. 'Next time let me talk to her.'

Helen was Nkwa-daa's daughter too, and some days, when the girl was not in a haste and remembered her manners, she asked of her aunt and even spoke to her on the phone sometimes, but of course the woman sounded no different from her own mother. They had the same thoughts, worried about Helen's life abroad, if she was eating well and filling up her Rawlings chain—the visible and protruding collarbones of starving Ghanaians under Rawlings's rule—and if she was staying warm and remembering their God. They whispered the same prayers over her life, lived as if tied to each other by a string. You tug on one end, only to find the same at the other.

Helen's first year on campus, she had secretly yearned for a friendship of this kind, and that had meant saying yes to parties or going on a group hike or enrolling in the same classes as her colleagues. She didn't expect it to be hard—to find someone who brings your presence an ease, an ease that comes from years of knowing and understanding, of paying attention to another. She was wrong and it had been lonely, even lonelier after these gatherings where one is somehow reminded of her own isolated existence while surrounded by happy, dancing, drunk people. Helen wouldn't admit this to herself: if she stayed on this quest of finding a sister-friend, wishing so desperately for what her mother and Aunt Nkwa-daa had, she might indeed miss out on other kinds of friendships, even ordinary delights in being with someone. It need not be what they had, nothing of this strange devotion, this rare unrelenting bond.

It did not surprise her that Aunt Nkwa-daa always asked about her safety and whether she walked home alone at night. Helen said yes, she was being careful and no, she never walked home at night by herself.

Since her daughter's disappearance five years earlier, Aunt Nkwa-daa had a way about her. She was fearful and untrusting, always looking over her shoulder, double-checking locked doors, sitting up in the middle of the night to see whether the sound she heard was the wind blowing things around or somebody in the dark, closing in on her. Helen had to leave behind the pepper spray her aunt gifted her at the airport, although she had tried convincing Nkwa-daa that she wouldn't be allowed to take it on the plane with her. But the woman had pleaded, pressed it firmly in her palms, and wrapped her fingers around it, saying, 'Take it, please take it. My heart hurts, take it with you everywhere.' And yet, Helen remembered, she is also the woman with so much love in her eyes, so much patience to give, a vessel of flesh that takes on whatever burden is laid on her without so much as a murmur. And of course there was her mother, ready to strike anything that threatened them, and Adoma, the new girl her mom talked about. Helen knew exactly why she was there and what she'd have to give up to get what she wanted. What they all wanted, she believed, was an escape. When she was home, Helen had only wished to be away, and she couldn't exactly say why other than everything about her life in that place was small and stifled and ordinary. She wanted out and wanted more, and she now convinced herself that she had it. The new girl, who her mother said ought to be in school but wasn't, wanted to live the promise of this new life too, at whatever cost. Helen did not blame her; it is the kind of scholarship and good fortune that could change one's life after all. It's changed hers.

Three times Adoma had tried to speak with the diplomat, and three times Esiha had stopped her, pinched her waist on their way out from the dining room.

After all the guests had left, they pushed a cart around to collect the dirty plates. So much food left untouched, so much waste. As soon as they were out of sight, Nkwa-daa grabbed a plastic bag from their cupboard and scooped the leftovers in, stealing glances at the door to be sure the Madam was not walking in. Once when she discovered the women were packaging food and giving them away to people, she told her husband first, who told her to deal with the maids directly and not involve him. So she called some kind of meeting, warning them in a tone she might have used to address fifty people rather than the three tired faces that looked back at her. They nodded their heads yes, they understood her, and it wouldn't happen again.

Nkwa-daa had been restless that night. 'How can we throw away all this food? She won't ask us to reduce the quantity, and she won't let us share what's left of it. And they won't eat anything that isn't fresh the next day. What is this life?'

But Esiha had told her they didn't have to stop, they just had to be sure not to get caught. They found a way to make it work and managed to stay out of trouble.

That night they were surprised that Adoma brought it up when they confronted her. It was very clear to both of them how much she sought the diplomat's attention, how she leaned closer than was usual to refill his glass and how even her fragrance was different when the man was around. Some kind of fine perfume mist with notes of vanilla bean and fresh orange blossom filled the air when she walked past them. She wanted so badly to be seen and did not care to hide it. The three of them had a pile of dishes to clean and a conference room to set up for the next day's event before it got too dark, but Esiha's temper was fiercely pressed against their waiting duties. She grabbed Adoma by the arm and pulled the girl face-to-face with her. She made sure her grip was firm, firm enough to send Adoma whimpering and trying to wrest her hand free from Esiha's grasp.

'What's the matter with you? What is it that you want from the man, eh? What do you want to tell him?'

'Ach! I've done nothing wrong. Let me go!'

'Nothing, eh?' Esiha chuckled and shook her head, still holding the girl's wrist. Foolish and ignorant, these young ones. 'You're walking around stinking with all these wants. Craving so boldly, throwing yourself at him, having no shame, no dignity. You think no one sees you? You think no one sees those pitiful, pleading eyes?'

'I'm not the only one going against the rules here!' Adoma finally yanked her hand free and fumbled with her apron strings. She was shaking all over. It stung to hear the words because she did feel unseen, and she hated it.

'You and her,' she pointed a trembling finger at Nkwa-daa, 'have been giving away food. And sometimes, sometimes, I know Ben goes in there to play and he's not supposed to ever be inside that small kitchen.' She said the word *small* with such disgust, such spite, that both women looked at each other, unable to hide their shock. Such disrespect.

'What do you want from the man?' Esiha was so close to the girl now and she saw it in her eyes—that fire, that misplaced rage, that stubborn will that would not be shaken.

She had seen it in Helen too, just a few days before she came running into her arms with good news. She had been considered for the scholarship, and she, Helen, would be going abroad to study. The diplomat, together with the school, had picked her last but he had picked her. It was supposed to be good news, but Esiha could not shake off the feeling that something had happened to cause them to arrive at this point. Days before, Helen had sobbed quietly on the other side of the bed as her mother slept, her Bible held over her chest. They slept in an office by the church then, their own home having been submerged in a flood. Helen had complained to her mother about how she was so close, how her grades were good but not good enough, how an opportunity like this could save their family, and if only she could see the man, if only she could make an appointment at his residence and show herself and argue her case.

Esiha could barely follow what her daughter was going on about. Helen explained it over and over. The university had partnered with some ambassadors and diplomats to fund bright but financially challenged students. They announced the selected students in school and she did not make the list, but she was close. She was certain she was close because her grades were good and she could convince them, she could change their minds. 'Don't you see? I could be one of them!'

But Esiha did not really see. Yes, the girl was bright, but not so spectacular that anyone would be willing to pay for her to continue schooling. And besides, she hoped her daughter would join her at the market, help her rebuild their lives from all they'd lost in the flood. And so that talk about more school and much worse, Helen possibly going away from her, was unexpected and to her, implausible. Like all things she did not understand or care much about, she dismissed it—her daughter's hopes to meet the man, to change his mind and change her life, a fading noise in the background.

But Helen did exactly as she'd said she would, and she came bearing the good news a few days later. At first she wasn't in, but now she was. Just like that. She was going to America, and it was going to be the best thing that would ever happen to them. Esiha had looked up from the palm kernels she was pounding, settled her eyes on her daughter's body, and looked away without saying a word. Her daughter went on, saying that the diplomat had even offered her mother a job. She could wash dishes. But Esiha was no longer listening. She felt sick to her stomach. There was a burning sensation in her lower abdomen, making her nauseous, causing her to jump from her stool and hang her head over the toilet.

Something had happened to her daughter. Something had happened to her, and it had opened a door and it might just be the happiest she'd ever seen Helen, but something terrible had happened. Esiha thought this every day after the news. She couldn't shake off the feeling as Helen prepared for her visa interview, as she stood in front of the church to be prayed for, as people stopped by to drop off clothes and food items, half of which she would leave behind.

Esiha would take the job and later put in a good word for her best friend. She would hear the stories too—of what many of the girls at the school had to do for these scholarships, how much of themselves they had to give up in exchange for this dream. And she would think about her poor girl, walking down the halls of this mansion, her transcripts in hand, ready to fight and prove her worth. On the other side of the door was the greedy world Helen knew nothing about; the bloodthirsty hands, the wolflike creatures who, with a conscience long rotten, would snatch, deceive, throw a bone of promises to whomever was innocent and desperate, and like a dog, a girl chased after it, undressing herself in every leap. Afraid and cold and alone. Stubborn and prideful and determined.

When Adoma did not respond, suddenly subdued and visibly weakened by the interrogation, the question hung between them.

'What is it that you want from the man?'

A new life. Change. Opportunities. All that can be possible for a girl like me.

Esiha knew the desire as well as the cost, perhaps even more than the girl did. Her daughter's departure left her sick with numbness and a recurring malaria that dug at her bones. She stayed in bed, refusing to eat or bathe or clean the compound before church service. She would see only Nkwa-daa, and when her friend would come, she would sit quietly, watching her and saying nothing. If anyone understood grief and the illness that separation causes, it was Nkwa-daa. The first few days, Nkwa-daa gave her silence and the comfort of her presence, left a banana by her bedside. Then she would bring fresh wheat bread from the bakery along with soup, sit next to her, and feed her. The silence at that point was so familiar, even necessary, that Nkwa-daa did not bother to break it. And one day, as Nkwa-daa was getting ready to leave, Esiha began to speak. And the words, they rushed out like some force was pushing them out of her. Nkwa-daa thought her friend was praying under her breath, but she got closer and realized she was talking to herself but also to her.

She had failed her daughter, she said. Something terrible had happened and she should have been there to stop it. 'What kind of mother am I? And all this for what—a new country without me? How is this better? Tell me, Nkwa, how is this better?'

That night Nkwa-daa stayed by her friend's side, dabbing a cold towel on her forehead, for her friend was running a temperature, shaking with fever. A love illness, the terrible condition of the heart where it convinces itself of its brokenness, its deep, incomprehensible calamities. The whole body buys into the illusion and suffers it faithfully. Nkwa-daa held her friend then, as her friend had done in the past when she thought she was losing her mind, when she was so sure that at any point in the day, her own daughter, missing for months, would walk through the door. How she waited, how she hoped—all the while, Esiha was by her side, waiting and hoping, knowing very well no girl was coming home. Saying, 'Waiting is the easiest thing we can do, and we can do it for years. It demands nothing of us. Look at us. We sit and weep and fold our hands and look out to see who's coming. But to move on? To gather our breaking selves and plunge back into life after this misfortune, that is the hardest thing we'll ever have to do. And we'll do it, together.'

In the kitchen Adoma had turned her back to Esiha's intense black eyes and stood at the sink, furiously scrubbing the bottom of a casserole dish. Esiha exchanged a look with Nkwa-daa, who stood watching the dispute and appeared to be shut in her own despair, worn out from the noise around her. Esiha nodded as if to say 'enough,' turned, and headed for their place, and Nkwa-daa left the girl and followed suit, a limp in her walk from all the standing that seemed to weaken her knees and leave her feet swollen.

Time was running out. Whatever they had to do, they had to do it fast.

This is one way to say it: they had no plan and yet, the minute she took the job and walked through the towering, polished wooden doors, Esiha knew she couldn't *not* do anything. This was the same place. The same bloody tile, with its dramatic veining and glossy finish that Helen had walked on because the man wouldn't see her in his office, not for a discussion of that kind. They should go home, where he could be comfortable and take his time to listen to her. Esiha never saw the rooms in the house—it was Adoma's job to clean them, and she was partly relieved that nothing triggered her imagination, visions of her daughter vulnerable and naked on one of the sheets. Relieved too that the man had kept his distance from the kitchen altogether, coming and going through his wide office doors—his domineering presence lurking through the halls, always up to some official engagement.

He barely glanced at them when they served people at the table. He appeared so shut off, so indifferent about their presence and movements that it was as if he did not see them. Or rather, it wasn't that they were invisible to him—he could not, after all, miss the clinking of utensils as the women set them on the table or the fact that his bowl of lentil soup did not magically appear before him but was carefully set down by two hands—but did not find them worthy of his attention and time and in fact, of even registering their presence.

Anyway, Fridays were the days his wife took Ben to the park. With a persistent nudge from her friend, Nkwa-daa asked the madam if she could take her boy to the park this time. The madam declined politely, a little surprised about the unusual request; so far, the women's nanny duties had been restricted to feeding and changing Ben, collecting all his toys and scrubbing those that needed scrubbing, and simply watching him closely when he was in the kitchen. But she did think about it when she went to bed, turning in her silk nightgown for the empty side of the mattress; the familiar absence of her husband did not scare her anymore. She had grown used to it over time and treated herself to shopping sprees whenever the fear crept up on her. It was a good distraction, like so many of their properties had become over the years—a veil draped over their faces to keep them from ever coming to terms with their lives and what they'd made of them. Giving Ben to the maid would certainly give her more time to meet with a friend at the spa or spend some time at the public library. She'd always wanted to do that—to be away for a while and experience the town and its people, put herself out there. So she said yes to Nkwa-daa and agreed to go with her the first time.

They sat on the bench and watched Ben play with the other rich kids. Nkwa-daa wasn't sure what to do or say. Their closeness to each other in that moment was odd. Without it being said, each one's place had always been clear and both parties assumed their roles without thinking. One set the rules and insisted on what needed to be done, and the women bent their heads and lives low in subservience. All of it felt strange and Nkwa-daa hoped her uneasiness didn't show. She prayed she wouldn't have to speak. In fact, she hoped the woman would forget she was sitting next to her, which would not surprise her much. The madam wore a white lace pleated tank top tucked in her wide-leg pants. She had twisted her long hair at the back and kept it in place with a leopard-print hair clip—not a single strand of hair in defiance. Hanging loosely on both ears were sparkling silver earrings. She was stunning, an observation Nkwa-daa was sure no one was more convinced of than the woman herself.

'May I ask why you offered to do this? It's ... quite nice of you, actually. I see how Ben is fond of you folks in the kitchen. But I'm just curious, you know. Do you have any children? Where are they? You must miss them, slaving away in the kitchen like this.' She looked at her son as she said this, her eyes all dreamlike and distant.

Nkwa-daa fidgeted with her hands in her lap. They were dry and rough and in serious need of some lotion. They sat on the same bench; the woman's pumpkin-orange bag, the size of a small pillow, was the only thing that separated them.

The woman smelled of lavender and expensive oils. Next to her bright bag, Nkwa-daa was reminded of just how faded her skirt was. It was as if someone had stabbed a needle through the fabric and drawn out all its blue, just as life had dealt with her—sapping her of her very strength.

She wasn't sure which of her questions to answer first, so she said simply, 'Ben is a sweetheart. No, no children.'

The woman lit a cigarette and looked ahead as the sounds of children shrieking and chasing after each other rang in their ears. Nkwa-daa wasn't sure if the woman had heard her, but she liked it that way and hoped that would end their conversation. What smart words do you say to a wealthy woman with a fancy bag like that and skin so smooth, so soft you want to touch it? Nothing. You only watch.

'You like them? I got them for my birthday. Never worn them. Well. Until this morning.'

Her madam touched the earring on her left ear and her finger lingered on its sleek surface. She did not really look at Nkwa-daa as she spoke. She seemed to glance at the area around Nkwa-daa, to scan with her eyes but not really to focus on her. And so it took a while for Nkwa-daa to know she was being spoken to, and an even longer while to decide on what to say in response. But before she could think of anything, the woman reached behind one ear and took out the earring and then the other. They were pear-shaped, sterling silver. Nkwa-daa pulled back, both nervous and unsure of what was happening.

The woman, with the confidence of one who is familiar with having her way, grabbed Nkwa-daa's hand and placed the jewelry in her palm. The earrings were beautiful and sparkling, a glorious thing nestled in her coarse and dull hands, exposing the lumpy arthritic joints knotting her fingers. Nkwa-daa wished she could hide her hands or cover them with a handkerchief and then take the earrings. But she said thank you and like an afterthought, asked why. The woman looked at her with an expression that Nkwa-daa couldn't tell whether it was disgust or disbelief, but she recovered quickly, showing a tight smile that did not reach her eyes. Nkwa-daa thought she had ruined the moment. Now the woman would take back her earrings and walk out of the park and take her son with her.

But the woman appeared to give the question some thought before she said, lowering her gaze, 'I frankly do not know. I saw you looking and thought you might want them.' She spoke fast then, the words toppling over each other. 'But of course, that was a silly assumption. Silly of me too. Why would I think that? People are allowed to admire things without needing to own them. Not that you can ever afford these but . . . I don't mean . . .' Her cheeks turned red, and it fascinated Nkwa-daa to see how easily her skin filled with color, how one's emotions could knock past all walls of defense to intrude and ride on their flesh.

If Nkwa-daa thought it was unsettling to be sitting so close to her, it was even harder to watch the woman fumble for words. She was always so poised, so upright in her heels, not a strand of brown hair out of place on her head. Her face was beautiful, with eyebrows that were always drawn over and a very small dimple in her left cheek. They were utterly different women and yet, for a brief moment, one would think they had swapped places. 'Thank you,' Nkwa-daa said slowly, closing her fingers over the earrings, finally claiming them. 'No, thank *you*,' the woman said. Her voice trailed at the end, perhaps searching for a name, but when it wouldn't register, she said again, 'Thank you.' And this time, she looked directly into Nkwa-daa's eyes and clasped her delicate hands over hers.

They got rid of Adoma easily. Esiha only had to break a few pricey dishes—brought out for special occasions like fundraisers—and the woman was furious, a torrent of cries flowing out of her. They could get new ones, she said, but these were her favorites. How could this have happened? She even went down on her knees, picking up the pieces, taking one last look at the floral design that lined the broken rims of the plates.

The girl was absent-minded lately and moving very slowly, Esiha told the Madam. Adoma could use a break; she interrupted their operations in the kitchen and Esiha was confident she and Nkwa-daa could handle the work without her. The whole time Adoma stood there, in shock, a scalding wrath stirring in her. For some reason, she couldn't talk. Her mouth was dry and her words failed her when she needed them most. She was asked to leave that very night. The women filled up a sack bag with fruits for her, and because Nkwa-daa had heard her go on and on about the beds and the soft sheets upstairs, she had managed to find a sheet in the laundry pile and rolled it into a ball to tuck into the bag.

'There's some money tied in a sock for you,' Esiha told her, handing the sack bag to her. 'Find something to do. If your grades are bad, take that exam again.'

Adoma flinched when she heard the word *grades*. Her mission was not a secret after all.

'But do not come back here,' Esiha continued. 'Do not ask to see the man. I know you think this is what you want,' there was a quiver in her voice, but the woman held herself together, 'but you're wrong.'

'You think you know me,' the girl spat back, locking eyes with Esiha. Her eyes were burning, and maybe the women could tell her legs were shaking, but she was going to say what she was going to say, going to do what she was going to do, even if she had to find another way.

'I know Helen, old woman. I know your daughter and what she did here and her filthy—' The riot rising inside her was instantly stilled by a slap from a hand she was not expecting. It was Nkwa-daa's; she had stepped from behind her and struck the right side of her face. Adoma was shocked, betrayed, even; she had always preferred Nkwa-daa's gentle spirit to Esiha's hot blood and mistrust, which seemed to seep into everything she did. The side of her face stung, and her tears flowed freely now, from pain and also from rage at being let go like this, like she was expendable and unwanted. With one last dark look from

Esiha, the girl turned, picked up the sack they'd given her, and stepped out through the back door. But not before Adoma had noticed Esiha's sudden muteness; the woman seemed to stiffen and weaken before her at the mention of Helen's name. She had finally left Esiha with no words. It served her right, she thought. It served her bloody right.

They wasted no time and got to work the next day. It was a Friday.

'I will leave the house shortly after you leave for the park. We will meet at the train stop in Salaju. I will sit by the window. When you see me, come.'

'With the boy?' Everything about this plan scared Nkwa-daa to death. There was no way they were going to get away with this, and yet she knew her friend's mind was made up. Esiha was going to get back at the family, and Nkwa-daa was going to be a part of it. It was simple, and also the vilest thing she'd ever had to be part of.

'Yes. With the boy.'

They were in the small kitchen. Scheming. Looking at her friend now, the crow's feet tugging at her eyes, which seemed red from too much rubbing or crying, her sunken cheeks, the worry lines stretched across her forehead, Nkwa-daa knew she was exhausted and old and yet, after all these years, that fire in Esiha was not quenched. She was after something and by all means, she was going to get it. The whole plan made Nkwa-daa sick and restless. They were going to be caught. Thrown in prison. They would be all over the news, and everyone in town would hear about their abominable offence. They would be shamed and mocked. She knew she wouldn't be able to live with herself, but Esiha eased that thought with the assurance that they would still have each other. She would not have to go through it alone.

Weeks after her daughter went missing, Nkwa-daa would hear her voice in her head, clear as though the child were right in the room with her. She would turn, expecting to see her daughter behind her, but there was no one. The voice wasn't disturbed or filled with panic. It was calm, soft, the way her girl sounded when she was just waking up from sleep. *Mama?* When she called her, it was always in the form of a question, just throwing out her name in the void and expecting a response. *Mama?* Nkwa-daa told Esiha about the voices. How she wanted to hit her head against something, how she wanted them to stop but also didn't. Was she crazy? No, her friend said firmly.

Esiha was the only one who wouldn't mock her or tell her something wasn't right with her head. Or tell her it was nothing, that she was only making up the voice. Some days she told Nkwa-daa she heard the voice too. And so they spoke back to the girl—telling stories or jokes, and other days giving an account of how they spent their time, the new gossip in town, how different things would be with her. They lived through the grief like one wandering in a forest—taking all chances, clearing uncertain paths, clinging to the hope that there was an opening somewhere, that somehow, if only they kept walking through the woods, they would arrive at it.

Now Esiha wanted Nkwa-daa to have the boy. She would keep Ben. This baby that looked nothing like her. She would have another child and she could start all over. Yes, but only this time, the child wasn't hers, Nkwa-daa thought.

'What about you? What do you get from this?' Nkwa-daa knew the answer to this, knew exactly what had driven her friend to come into this house in the first place; she had played servant and surrendered everything for this moment. But still, Nkwa-daa couldn't believe what they were about to do, what Esiha was promising her. There was no way they could get away with this. The diplomats were powerful. How could Esiha be this resolute?

'All the satisfaction knowing how they're going to live from this day.' She did not look away from Nkwa-daa as she said this. Her eyes were cold, her voice sharp.

It did not take long for Esiha to pack all their belongings—which weren't much—into a bag and head out through the backdoor. As she walked, she thought about the house—its raised walls, all the useless antiques placed at every corner, their class of people and their expensive wines, their money, clothes, and shoes, their eyes, oh their eyes: unseeing, dismissing, looking down at you and pressing you to the ground without the need to even say a single word. She was leaving it all behind and taking away the best and undefiled part of them.

On the train she thought of nothing else but Helen so far away from her. Sitting somewhere in a strange land, reading a book or eating some new dish. Her daughter walking around campus, acting normal while her life was falling apart when no one was watching. For one did that forget a thing like this, even when they prayed for relief and wished it away with all their heart. The damaged past is a plague that attacks at all times. There are days it sneaks up on you like a thief and plunders your very being. Even when you have nothing left, especially when you have nothing left, it finds you and persists in its merciless pursuit of you.

When the train's brakes hissed and screeched, sending a whistle into the air, Esiha straightened her back and turned to look out the window, as she had said she would. Her heart stopped for a moment, and it was as if the air had been sucked from her lungs. Nkwa-daa stood at the other side of the tracks. Her kinky hair had been piled in a high bun on top of her head and fastened with a scarf, highlighting her broad forehead and sharp cheeks bones, which were quivering and keeping her face from bursting with heavy emotion. The wind pressed her loose dress against her body, revealing her lean frame, her flat breasts. Standing there, she looked so malnourished, so fragile, so old.

It was not the earrings or the sweetness of the child. Nkwa-daa owed that woman nothing. It was a dread far greater than getting caught. To live life the way she had, racked by grief, utterly shattered from a separation that should never be, to lose her senses every once in a while, to keep walking away from every river that called her to throw herself into it—was a terror she would never wish on anyone, no, not on a mother. It was beyond any madness she could think of, and her hands could not dare kindle the same fire that even now continued to burn her.

And so there she stood, watching her friend frozen on her seat in the train, her hand raised to her chest in shock, her lips parted as if to say something but there was no sound. Nkwa-daa shook her head, the tears already free from their hold. She heard the train horn blare and when she looked up, Esiha had turned her face from her, her flaring eyes fixed right ahead. Her rigid neck carried its bounding pulse, her pursed lips, her small poise of what dignity she had left. The train started to move. Nkwa-daa looked on, every part of her body shook, threatening to collapse. Something took hold of her then, crippling her legs, but she did not give in. Not now. She will not look at me, she thought while praying against it. There was an ache spreading through her heart, a throb swelling inside her belly, pushing itself up her throat as the train rapidly faded from view. The friend of my heart will not turn for me, she thought.

And she was right.

Bridling

Nadia Davids

Originally published in *The Georgia Review* (2023)

He doesn't lock the mask every rehearsal. There are some days I say, *I can't, not today, not for all those hours.* Attached to the mask is a rope that sways down my back and dangling from the rope is a bell that the stage manager (the "SM," we call her) will ring every ten minutes during the performance. It gives a little chime and I give a little jerk and there are moments when I'm mid-twitch that I wonder if there was any class in drama school that could have prepared me for this role.

I'm playing a seventeenth-century bad woman, or, more accurately, I'm re-enacting a drawing of a seventeenth-century woman who's been punished for "gossiping, or nagging or snapping," or just talking, I guess. I'm in full costume—stays, scratchy dress, bare feet, dirty fingernails, doleful vibe, topped off with this mask—a "scold's-bridle," it's called. It's as weird and unsettling as it sounds; all leather and steel with a wooden bit—the kind for a horse—placed in my mouth to stop my tongue and make me drool.

We haven't decided yet how my character ended up like this (it's a *process*, we agree, an *unearthing*); a sentence from a magistrate maybe, handed down after a complaint from her husband, but just as likely from a butcher or baker or candlestick-maker or a random farm boy with a grudge, or whatever a seventeenth-century incel was back then. So, when I say, *not today*, the director says he understands. He's good that way—can show how much he understands, how much he *feels* for me, for all of us, with just a tilt of his head, a hand resting lightly on the shoulder.

We've been hard at work for months now and in a week, we'll open. He's been giving interviews all morning, sitting with journalists beneath the theater's digital billboard on which the show's title, *Now Is the Time*, gleams. Beneath it, in smaller font: "Women in Works of Art through the Ages." I hear him tell each of them that our fast-selling show with a running time of five hours (*durational*, he calls it) places intensive demands on both audience and performer.

The main idea is this: we, a company of women performers, will stage various artworks by men (and men only) depicting women. We'll create facsimile tableaus of the works, remaining absolutely still while audiences walk around the staging area viewing us as though we are an exhibition.

"We are *literally* Live Art," an actor we all call Medusa said earlier during her costume fitting. The director responded that the work is, in fact, "intersectional," which Medusa translated when he was out of earshot as "A bit of theater. A bit of museum. A bit of discomfit for everyone involved."

She's being glib. And that's okay—because it's a difficult piece, almost impossible, I think some days. Most days.

But he's held the space—and us—with deep care from the first warm-up. On day one of rehearsals, he'd welcomed us and then asked that we remember, always, that the ground we're on is unceded territory. He made a visible effort to correctly pronounce the resisting group's name and nodded deeply at an actor who looked as though she might be descended from them. She didn't nod back. "We're making immersive theater," he went on. "I like to think of it as the missing link between museumology and performance, a co-creation of meaning between actor and audience, a collapsing of boundaries while strictly enforcing them. A place where everything that so desperately needs to be said hinges on your absolute silence."

Someone said that sounded contradictory, and he agreed, "Abso*lutely*, absolutely," before explaining that this was less about "putting on a show" than it was about "showing up," "calling in while facing out," and that if that sounded contradictory too, it was because multiplicity was always complex, and that this work was nothing if not that: it was exhibition, drama, history all in one. He spoke about how the audience would become part of the performance, how they'd thread their way through the space, and that though they'd likely come in groups—in tens, even hundreds!—the real intimacy would occur between a single audience member and a single performer—the locking of eyes, the meeting of bodies in time and space, that flare of recognition, solidarity even—a flame against the darkness. This was, he insisted—by this point almost to himself—the only effective means by which to return that millennia-old gaze, the survey of women by men, the endless contemplation. The looking.

He paused as though struggling to find the words, his boyish face open, earnest, then said that in truth, we'd be embarking on so much more than a performance—this would be an *excavation* of historical agency, a Morse code to ghost-women, and that the end-product was nothing compared to the process, because this was, at its core, a way for us—the women in the cast—to time travel safely, to thin the mists, to listen to all those restless spirits, and that though the doing may shift in the course of the making, the animating force—the *mission* of the work, he promised—would stay the same.

I thought then, *I could listen to you for hours.*

And I would. We all would.

These are the final days of rehearsal before we move into the performance space. We'll be in the building's main theater, an old-fashioned proscenium arch with red velvet curtains and a thousand comfortable seats. Except, as I never tire of explaining to anyone who'll listen, the seats won't be used, because the audience is going to come up onto the stage, wander around, look right at us.

For now, though, we're still in that place of deep discovery before the tech sessions begin: rigging and plotting lights, mapping soundscapes, patiently working through cue to cue, scrambling to hold on to what we've found in rehearsal. Still in the safe space where we *created the work / manifested it / brought it into being / coaxed it into the world / invited it into becoming. It's helped that this rehearsal room is so beautiful.* Rafters criss-cross beneath the roof and every morning at least one pigeon swoops through, startling us—and itself—as it flies back and forth searching for an exit. The floor is sprung wood and the tall, wide windows open by sliding one half past the other. There are no curtains, so we track first the summer's light and then its shadows from the start of the day to the end.

The SM told me that she showed him seventeen rehearsal spaces (seven*teen*, she repeats), before he chose this one and that he'd dismissed all the others as having "poor bones."

"He's exacting," she said. "That's why he's so good."

We were told not to prepare anything for the audition—no monologue, no song or dance—just to dress as plainly and as comfortably as possible, that we'd be asked to do things and those things would be very specific to him and his methods. There were hundreds of us in the waiting area. I asked the SM how many would be cast and when she answered *Twelve*, a girl close by me laughed, "Twelve? I see his Messiah complex is still in full swing," and then, preening, "But do I *want* to be a disciple?"

The SM didn't say anything, just cocked her head, and I noticed later that the girl, who'd announced to all of us that she'd "nailed" the audition, didn't even make the first cut.

A few of the others had worked with him before, but none of us knew what this new project was about. Weeks later he'd tell me that secrecy is the great unsung power of creativity, that in an era of constant disclosure there is something magical about silence.

The corridor outside the audition room was three-girls-thick. We stood straight or slouched against the wall, sat legs splayed, ear pods in, phones out, bottles of water at the ready. We laughed, fidgeted, were anxious beyond measure, confident beyond reason, insecure beyond coaching—all for just a handful of minutes in the room with him.

The SM called us in six at a time.

We entered single file, standing tight together, waiting for him to make the first move. He stayed at his desk, head down, his pale hair falling in skeins about his face, arranging then rearranging papers and pencils. He was larger than I thought he'd be, with a stomach that rolled a little over his jeans and the sleeves to his track jacket pushed up his thick forearms, revealing tattoos that crawled from wrist to shoulder.

He called the SM toward him and softly gave her instructions. She clapped her hands and announced, "Okay! You all remember that statues game you played as kids? This is that with a twist. Get ready." She put on clanging music and told us to move as wildly ("intuitively," he corrected without looking up) as we could. "When I stop the music," she continued, "the director's going to shout a word. Create a shape-response to the word and freeze. Got it?"

Got it.

On and off went the music and from the desk the words, "Flounce!" "Scream!" "Sugar!"

We flounced, screamed, sugared.

He watched, said nothing, then, "Silk!" "Find!" "Idol!"

When the music went off for the last time, he took the sheaf of papers before him and held it up above his head. The SM said to take a "beat," fetched the papers and handed them out to us. They were color photocopies of paintings: some new, some very old, some so famous even I knew them, others I guessed were important but I'd never clapped eyes on before. All of women.

He rose from the desk and ambled toward us, smiling warmly and speaking to us directly for the first time: "Look closely at your images." And then, "You're seven / you're twenty / you're aged beyond your years. You're free / you're enslaved / you're betrothed / you're a maid /a muse / a goddess / hunted. Take a minute," he encouraged. "Really, really look."

I made a long study of my handout and asked the others if I could see theirs.

"What did you notice?"

I jumped—just a little—when I realized he was standing behind me.

His voice was low. "When you looked at the others' paintings, what did they have in common?"

I hesitated, convinced the wrong answer would be the end of me.

"Go on," he soothed. "Don't be afraid. I could tell you noticed something."

Slow at first, as though I was only just learning to speak, I said, "Well, they're different from each other—each woman, each girl," and then in a rush, "but what makes them the same is that not one of them is smiling."

He beamed then as though I'd just cracked a nuclear code. He placed his hands on my shoulders, turned me around and told me to repeat what I'd just said to everyone.

I stood a little straighter, thought *this is what being golden feels like* and I didn't care when I caught two of the other women exchanging smirks.

Next, he tasked us with what felt like the impossible: "Now. Give me the same face you see in your painting but convey three things at once: one, what the subject was feeling; two, what the artist wanted her to feel; and three, just behind those two states, an empty space within yourself, a spot on your interior canvas, so to speak"—(a chuckle at that, first from him, then quickly followed by us)—"where the person looking at you can find their own feeling."

It was a quest. Or a riddle:

Take this straw and weave it into gold.
What slew none and yet slew twelve?

I tried but couldn't manage one of those things, never mind all three. I mentally began picking up my belongings, thanking him for the opportunity, heading for the door, preparing to tell my friends how I hadn't been able to spin the straw to gold or slay the twelve, that the best I could do was to appear blank.

And that's when he said that what I was doing was "perfect."

I'd achieved, he announced with finality, the three states at once.

I knew then, before the names were called out, that I'd been cast.

And at the very first rehearsal, there we were, a dozen women, the promised twelve—mostly in our twenties, just two of us in our fifties or sixties (I was careful not to ask), tall, short, gaunt, round, heads shaven, hair streaming down our backs, ordinary, other-world pretty, breasts flat or full, limbs long or squat, constant smiles, constant frowns, skin from pale pink to fawn to obsidian. We formed, without being instructed, a semicircle around him with some moving forward very slightly, breaking ranks to be closer to him.

He looked around the circle smiling, tilting his hands toward us in prayerful thanks, stopping just once to tell one of the older women she had one of the most magnificent faces he had ever seen: lined, unapologetic, and, even when it was resting, full of fury. We younger ones laughed a little, showing him—and ourselves—that we were not angry. That magnificently furious face broke into a smile when he said that and then she reached up, tugged at her hairband to shake loose her hair. Released, it fanned out in a halo of black and gray curls round her head. He smiled and said, "Ah, *there* she is. Welcome, Medusa."

He'd call her Medusa from then on, and within a few days so did the rest of us.

He took a careful breath and announced (or "shared," as he described it) the piece's title.

"Now," he said, rapping his knuckles on his table, "*now* is the time. Let's upend all those stories. Let's take a deep dive into those archives. Let's retrieve, disrupt, explore."

We began each day with a long warm-up; mashups of meditation and Eastern battle-dances. We traced the outline of someone else's body with our own, we mirrored a partner's every move from eye-blink to leg-twist, we clapped in unison to provide a backbeat while one of us told a story. Once, he asked us to imagine the waters of a cold ocean in our right legs and the burning fires of a volcano in our left, that if we really focused, we'd feel the alternating *hot/cold/hot/cold*. But Medusa, who took the lead on most of the other exercises, said that she'd sit that one out, that she already, without thinking, did that several times a day and that anyone else going through menopause would say the same. We all laughed—including him—which I thought showed how open he could be.

He'd shift between long stretches at his desk and being with us on the floor. Every once in a while, he'd unfurl his large body from a draped hunch, get up, walk over to one of us to stand close and quiet.

"It's weird but not, like, *invasive?*" I told a friend over dinner the night it first happened. "I can't explain it. It's like he's looking not just at me, but through me and around me, placing me next to others I can't see, in contexts I don't know. I think he's a genius. G.O.A.T. level."

My friend, who's a junior in the HR department at an accounting firm, just gave her usual disbelieving laugh, saying, "I don't know how you do it."

In the second week, a new exercise. He stood on top of the desk, did a little Puck-like jig and tossed into the air strips of paper that quickly floated down past his head to the ground (*into the air, into the air, into the air,* he sang as the papers swooped). Then he said, "Quick! Grab the first few you can. A fistful. Aaaand . . . *Go!*"

Did he know we'd scramble for them, scuffle even? I don't think that's what he meant to happen. But we did. I snatched mine from another woman's fingers, she grabbed hers from the woman next to her. One of the newest actors, younger even than me, her first job (*green green green*) hung back, on the edge, eyes wide.

He stood on the desk, legs apart, smiling but quiet. When we each had our fistful, he raised a hand and said, "Good," and jumped down.

On those papers were short descriptions. We stood, as we were told, in a circle and read the text out on a loop.

A likely girl

A strong mother

Betrothed

A reliable seamstress

Letter-writer

The prophetess no-one believes

Old. Still useful

Weaves like a dream/dream-weaver

Veil drawn tight

Full battle-dress—sword drawn, shield up

Pregnant. Doesn't want to be

An unlikely girl

Crone in the woods

Clever/Pinched

Armless Girl

Tongueless Girl

Vengeful Girl

Seduced by a swan—gold between the thighs

Scold's-bridle

Woman in the Wall

Naked—before a mirror

Naked—eats an apple

Naked—lies in bed

Naked—nurses baby

Naked—stands in pond

Naked—on a conch shell

Naked—holds a sword

Naked—back turned, servant hovers

Three Graces

I got these:

Scold's-bridle
Naked—before a mirror
Vengeful Girl
Three Graces

Our recitation was gaining a rhythm of its own when he clapped to indicate that we should stop. Then, his hands still holding the clap like a prayer, he said, "These are the artworks you will each enact. Some are solo, some are in groups. They're different in time and place but we all know the thread that binds them together. Thank you. Thank you."

At the end of that day as we packed up, I noticed an image left behind on the table—a woman alone on a beach at night. In a man's patched blazer and a long, comfortable patterned skirt she sat, knees tucked up, hands clasping legs, holding herself close, bare feet on the sand, face soft and strong and beautiful, chin turned up to a deep and starry sky, eyes on the planets above with a restfulness that lived, I could tell, deep in her bones. In the distance, the ocean, and if I leaned in closely enough, I could hear its faint roar and her steady breathing. There must have been a moon somewhere, shedding its light, because I could see her and she could see herself. Her toes, splayed and unlovely, squelched into the give of the cold, wet, grainy sand. I knew, immediately, how I'd make this tableau; knew the skirt I'd bring from my mother's closet, the blazer from my father's, the beach where I'd collect sand, and a memory of a night I'd tracked a moonrise that I'd draw on. I traced my fingers over the woman and was about to place her with my other picks when the SM plucked her out of my hands.

"Sorry," she said, setting her back on the table, "that one made it in by mistake. It's by a woman artist. That's not what we're working on here. We're focused on, like, returning the male gaze by *becoming* it?"

As she turned away, I made a quick decision: I took the print, hid it in my jacket, spirited her off. At home, I propped her up on my bedside table and set an offering of wildflowers before her.

It was during an afternoon enacting the "Three Graces," a painting of soft pastels and shimmering golds, of diaphanous material and soft, dimpling flesh, that I earned my name from him.

Three of us had been holding a single pose for thirty minutes, our heads tilted, my left arm raised to twine my fingers with Grace Two, my right arm lowered to touch fingers with Grace Three, one foot crossed behind the other as if at the beginning of a curtsey. It was endurance work and he'd kept faith with us through it all, through the breakout sweats and the feelings of shame at our state of undress. As we broke the pose, Grace Two gave an exaggerated little whimper of pain and Grace Three made such a show of massaging her own shoulder that he remarked consolingly that it just never stopped astonishing him how something so beautiful could be predicated on such hurt, but that perhaps these kinds of re-enactments brought us closer to our ancestresses, and surely our bodies held those long-ago memories, and maybe, just maybe each image was a way back to them and that this, this was the work. "Don't you agree, Grace?" he said to me.

Of the three of us, I am the only one he gifts with that name.

That night as I lay in bed, I looked up and saw that the tree outside my window was casting a shadow in the exact shape of one of my other characters, Vengeful Girl. Just before I fell asleep, my jaw seized up as if something were binding it. *Oh*, I remember thinking, *it's starting*. When I woke the next morning, my legs and arms were in my Three Graces pose and I wondered at what point in my sleep they'd arranged me so.

The next week, there was a crack in the cast.

We were sculpting an image, mythical in origin, neoclassical in style, all triangles and power, about the rape of the cherished daughter of a goddess-queen. He started the session by explaining that the painting had been taught for the longest time as though it was just an abduction, but that really, all you had to do was look, really *look* at the daughter being wrenched from her chariot, her face wretched, the god's ruthless triumph—to know what was going on. And that all those details—the cloth dragged to reveal her nipple, the rippling power of the horse's body, the darkly sensuous earth-browns and gold, told us exactly what the painter felt about it all.

We were nearly there—it took all twelve of us to be daughter, god, horse, trees wild with wind, when the young actor— *green-green-green*—closer to girl than woman, broke away from being the horse's hindlegs. With her hand still holding a length of rope for the animal's tail, she said, "Fuck this. *No*," and walked out of the image and spat first on the floor, then at him before she left the room.

To his credit, he didn't flinch: he just told us to take five. He was about to go after her when Medusa stopped him, saying, "No. Not you. I'll go." Medusa's hair seemed to grow round her face, and for a moment, though she's a full head shorter, she towered over him.

I blinked and he'd grown his height again and was walking back to his desk.

From behind the door, we heard the girl shouting, "I'm done! I can't anymore," and Medusa's voice, low, reassuring.

We stood about waiting and all the while the conversation outside was getting louder: "It's just bullshit. I'm not giving *blood*. I'm just not." And then it stopped. The door swung open. Medusa was alone. "She's left. Not coming back." Medusa seemed almost pleased about it.

He asked us to come together, to give thanks for the girl's contribution, and repeated what he said the first day, that the journey would be rigorous, exacting, not for everyone. His brow furrowed. "Art is not supposed to be comfortable. When you're uncomfortable, *that's* when the work begins. To make great art, we must all always be a little on edge. There are no small parts in this work. We are the sum of each other. The hindlegs belonged to the horse, and the horse was what the god uses to kidnap the daughter: no horse, no kidnapping; no hindlegs, no horse. The hindlegs are everything."

He promised to continue to check in and make sure that we were "okay"; our "okayness" was central. And he did just that. He was good that way. Attentive.

That evening I was visiting a friend, and so Medusa and I waited for the same bus; it was a long, hazy dusk of a day's end and a drizzle kept us half in, half out of the awning. Medusa smoked one of her rollies, her hair bound in a bright twisted scarf, the small gold hoops in her ears dulled by the fading light.

"Just because they *ask* for blood doesn't mean you have to give it." She kept staring ahead. "You've got to learn how to let them think you're all in but make sure you keep something of yourself back. That's the part you go home to. You know how they all talk about the 'process'?"

I nodded.

"It's a process where you get better at telling them one thing and yourself another and they don't know the difference. That kid who left today? She's still working it out. She'll get there. If she wants to keep doing this, she'll have to. Running off shouting how she'll make *him* see . . . What's she going to do? TikTok her outrage? She's got to learn. Got to. Sometimes it's different and those are the times that take you through. *Hindlegs? Fucksake.*"

The bus arrived and though we sat next to each other, Medusa didn't seem to want to say more. She leaned her head against the window.

For the first two weeks of rehearsal, while the mask was being made for "Scold's-Bridle," I wore a soft woollen balaclava—the kind pulled on cartoon thieves or members of an anarchist group. Though we worked endlessly on locating the *feeling* of the actual thing, it wasn't until I put it on that I understood what we were really doing.

The director came over to help me fit it, easing it gently over my head, saying quietly he was going to have a go at locking it.

That's when I jolted.

I thought I was prepared. Thought I knew. I'd been dreaming about her, waking up to her whispering in my ear about the sickly sweet smell of the oiled leather, the terror of the lock rusting, the never-healing sores on her cheek.

But still, a jolt, a flinch that started in my pelvis, lurched up through my stomach and stiffened my neck.

The mask closed over my face and my skull felt as though it was closing in on my brain. The bridle locked at the base of my ear, dug at my chin. I shook my head, *No*.

"Grace? Are you okay? I can't even imagine. You must be channelling so much right now. If you're not comfortable, we can stop."

I'll be fine, I assured him. *I'll manage.*

If I could, I would smile. Beam even.

Only five of us actors remain. The girl who refused to be the hindlegs triggered a little rebellion with others leaving in various ways: tearful, attention-grabbing, others claiming they were sick or pulling out after a "quiet word" with him. One said in front of everyone that it was taking a toll on her "mental health." As always, he was forgiving, saying that not everyone could stay in the grip of the monster, stare it down, beat the path back for the ones who would come after. I don't know why that girl gave him such a hateful look—he was only saying, *I see you. It's okay.* Another actor asked if it was possible for her solo image (a woman writing a letter) to have a monologue. "I just feel that if she's writing she's got something to say?"

He reminded her that one of the core strengths of this piece was silence, hers individually, ours collectively, and (with a glance around the room) that "each one of you has something to say, not just the woman with a pen in her hand."

So, only we five are capable of manifesting his vision, making material his dreams. He tells us he will not replace the ones who have left, that this work has an energy of its own and that he is obedient to that force—that five we are and five we shall remain. He is mostly full of praise for what we do but sometimes will announce in a rage that obedience is not enough, not *satisfactory*, and that in doing precisely as we're told we are ceding "personal authority."

We all agree to work harder.

But there is one session where even we five are left wondering if we can pull this off. We're getting stronger, can stand stiller for longer, remain resolutely in character (though Medusa tells us all backstage, to consider zoning out occasionally—that he'd never know anyway beneath all the makeup). But we're all suddenly worried about the audience. About them being so close, about how to handle them if they get too much in their feels and start touching us or making contact. Because they're free to walk right up to us, stand, circle, stalk, hover, look, look, lash out, and we can't move, can't do anything in response. They may laugh or weep or try to talk to us, console us, hurl abuse at us, be overcome, be indifferent, and our only task is to remain still, absolutely still, silent, absolutely silent. At most, we can make eye contact if their gaze is level with ours, but he's asked that we try not to do this, because the stiller and quieter we are, the better the audience will be able to see our torment.

We suggest to him that we do a practice run—ask him to invite colleagues in to play audience, *let them do their worst*, that this will help us prepare, develop resilience. He's amused and says this is the most "meta" thing anyone has ever suggested to him. Then he shakes his head, very serious now, and explains that this isn't the military, that we don't stage assaults to withstand them. As artists we need to remain alive, open, receptive, always. Mock-stagings would short circuit that. That's not what we're about, not at all.

Medusa starts to really chafe after that, saying that sometimes he just goes too far, that he's pushing us, that he won't *listen*, but that life has a way of making you listen whether you want to hear it or not. I wonder then if she, like me, has been hosting the women from the artworks in her home, has noticed how they're growing bolder, each one trailing the actor who plays her. I want to ask her if she's seen them standing in the wings and behind the dressing-room door, seen how they float into our costumes as we dress, drape onto us as we assume our positions, even circle him sometimes, ready to raise hell if he asks for one more thing—not that he'd notice.

Better not to mention it, I think. Better not to risk sounding crazy.

But they're busy, the women from the artworks, busy-busy, all over the theater. The only one who remains in her own world, minding her own business, is the woman on the beach. When the final costumes are approved, I bring her back to work, and in secret, tape her to the inside of my stays.

Opening night in the dressing room: each one of us has an individual table with a mirror rimmed with bare bulbs and a built-in ashtray.

"Chorus girls' dressing room," says Medusa, who knows everything, as she points at the ashtrays. "Remnants from a different time. Boozy, bawdy bitches every one of them."

She's got a wildness to her tonight.

I've gone quieter, she's fizzing.

Our tables are covered with little pots of thick makeup, brushes, kohl, wigs on white Styrofoam heads. Our costumes hang on the rails behind us.

I think about the last twenty-four hours: I'd woken up this morning to find one of the Graces pressed up against my bedroom window, her breath hot on the pane, while another Grace had transformed herself into a stream of cool air that strayed around my ankles that I can feel even now. Last night, as I fell asleep, Vengeful Girl slid into bed next to me, asking, *Will you place the coins on my eyes? Will you cross the river with me?* When I made breakfast, the bridled woman, the scold, stood close, *Let me tell you how I've brewed poison for my husband, casting spells into the rabbit stew, calling on every wraith in the nearby mountain to send him terrifying visions during the day and madness by night.* As I brushed my hair, Grace appeared again, this time to show off her arms, which bulged and grew muscles before my eyes. *When the theater is dark*, she told me with a wink, *my sisters and I break into a wild run and race into the forest.* She claimed their bodies grew stronger, more luminous with every step and that fruit and flowers sprang up in their wake. When I took a morning bath, the naked girl on the couch climbed in with me, lifting her sad eyes to say that nightly she is spied on by an old neighbor: *It's his ritual*, she told me; *I'm his pastime.* At this, on cue, Vengeful Girl burst into the room, laughing, announcing that *her* ritual—her *pleasure* (guffawing now)—is to take her sword night after night and gouge out the peeper's eyes.

"What do you think?"

It's Medusa next to me, hair coiled upwards, each ending flicked with a red tongue to suggest an eruption of snakes. Her brows are drawn toward each other and a line of jagged blood circles her neck. She grins and says to me via her reflection, "May this be the last face he sees at night and the first one he sees in the morning."

He comes backstage for a pep talk, thanks us for giving "heft" to work forged in a "cauldron of rage and possibility," and says that in the final analysis, the process, the *meanings* we'd made in the rehearsal room, were everything, and the final product—indeed, this *night*—is just another step, nothing more, in the work's development. He seems very happy with this little speech. The SM walks in, announcing that all invited reviewers are in attendance, and he pales a little, saying he'll see us in the foyer after.

Final call.

We're laser focused as we walk onto the stage, ready to take our places, assume our poses.

The stage is divided into three different sets, each exactly replicating the background of the painting we're performing. Upstage, I stand in a cottage doorway, breathing in short gasps through my stays, my head closed in by the bridle, the rope with the bell looped around my waist. Creeping up the cottage walls behind me is pretty honeysuckle, and around my neck is a wooden placard with the word *Scold* carved into it. Every detail is true except for one small rebellion—I've not placed the bit in my mouth.

Downstage, draped over a chaise longue, entirely naked, a gorgeous bolt of blue silk dripping from one hand, a mirror in the other, lies one of the other Graces. She's surrounded by a huge gilt frame and though she cannot see herself (the mirror is angled away from her) the plaque next to her bears the title *Exhibit: Vanity*. Stage left is Medusa, a wall built up in front of her with a hole in it, just her head poking through, the snake hair, eyes rolled up, bloody neckline, all form a nightmare version of old-fashioned seaside photos.

In an hour we'll close this scene, the next two actors will come out while we change costume, and so on, until five hours have passed, and thirteen paintings have been re-enacted.

I'm still, so still, in that knowing hush between house lights down and spotlight on, the beam trained slow and bright and true onto me, the warm orange of it all spooling out onto the floor. Just behind me, carefully plotted shafts of light are alive with twirling dust and my face is hot—burning even—beneath the claggy makeup. *Here they come, here they come.* My eyes are wet and blinking as the audience moves toward us. There are so many of them, in groups, alone, old, young, she, he, they, them, clutching programs, leaning in to read the plaques, standing just at the edge of the rope that cordons them off, some tilting ever so slightly over it to get a better look.

A group of young men hover at "Vanity," laughing, circling close, offering the girl-actor all sorts of things, taunting her.

She does not reply. An older woman, an audience member, puts herself between them.

A man stands before me and tells his teenage son, correcting the information in his program, that I'm based on a *charcoal* not a pencil sketch, while the boy looks at me, his hand moving to touch his own face, as if to assure himself that he remains unmasked.

An hour of this and just as the director predicted, some attendees begin to cry, some giggle, some recoil, some lean in too close, others turn away; some won't leave and become very angry. The women, especially, do one of two things: walk out in protest or stay in solidarity.

Every once in a while, Medusa lets her tongue loll out and her eyes drop down. I'll know when this happens because someone will give a small cry of surprise or a laugh of relief. It's rule-breaking and Medusa knows it—it makes her tableau look more seaside-wall than ever, but it helps everyone to become human again.

I find myself drifting in and out, my body either floating up toward the lighting rig or traveling toward the Exit sign. I'm rarely where I am, but then an odd noise brings me back to the stage—a growl, a groan, a stuttering. Then nothing.

No, there it is again, a cough, maybe a gathering of phlegm, and a woman, saying urgently, "Do you think she needs some water?" It's Medusa. The noise switches into another sound, song-like, then a hiss, now a rattling, and a man says, "Look, this one is actually baring her teeth. I thought they were supposed to be totally still."

What is she *doing?* Don't break focus, I tell myself. Find the still-point. Find it. If I'm disciplined enough, that control will radiate over to Medusa, help her get ahold of herself, rein herself in. Look, *look*, I shout my thoughts to her, a new group is coming toward us. Teenage schoolgirls, uniformed, giddy, accompanied by a young teacher whose boots and bangles and artfully messy bun put just a decade between her and them. She ushers the girls from tableau to tableau. Shoal-like, they come toward me, so many eyes trained at once, blinking, blinking. The longer they look, the longer I stare back, the tighter the mask feels, the stronger the lock seems to grow, the sharper my flail when the bell is rung, and the girls, the girls, the longer they stay, the longer they stare, the more something seems to settle—squat even—on their shoulders so that they droop just a little, even that one, on the right, who walked in beautiful, cocky, strutting.

Now, Medusa is *barking*, literally barking, snapping if anyone comes too close, and a small crowd is gathering round her.

I shift so slightly that no one notices. I imagine the woman on the beach pressed against my breast. I summon the moon she sits beneath, remember the cold sand between her toes, feel the warmth of the blazer, the drape of her skirt, the night of stars and stillness that lie ahead for her. This is enough, I tell myself, enough. No need to growl. No need to do anything just because Medusa is. No sense in giving in to the sway and push of the art women, their clamoring and chattering.

But then, something strange; I feel my head growing larger and larger, fit to burst the leather seam, bust open the iron lock. I feel a laugh roiling up inside, and I have to clamp down my left arm to stop it from flinging back and shoving over the painted cardboard cottage-set behind me.

My shoulder blades push out and back and from them— *impossible, impossible*—I begin to grow fins, sharp wings, that slice through my costume. In my hand, in Vengeful Girl's hand, the heavy weight of a weapon is taking shape—I dare to look down, make it out, and just as I do, it catches the light—a sword's hilt, glittering, gleaming, waiting. My perfect pose broken, I'm able to see the flowers that are growing madly, unbidden, all around my feet and notice that even though the bell is being rung and rung and the rope jerked and jerked—out of the corner of my eye I see the SM, frantically pulling and pulling—but I am unmoveable. Ahead of me the girls stare and stare at the fins and flowers, at the weapon and my ever-expanding head, and as one their mouths open to sing in wonder, in wonder!

And my tongue, resting so heavily behind a clamped mouth, becomes light, so light that it starts to writhe and dart like a small fish, forming even in the silence, the testimony of the art women—their spells and flowers, their mirrors and swords, their poisonous recipes, their words ready to be spoken, turned loose, raining down hell, now vomited up, *here's your Morse code, take your thinning mists, your time travel, your deep dive, your holding space.* I'll set the record *straight*, nothing to stop me, nothing to stop them, they're all gathered now, all present, just here, in my mouth, Medusa's generous growl in the background reaching a crescendo, the once-shrinking now-singing girls swaying as one. The light is moving from spot to general, just a few moment before the dark, on the edge of being said.

Adjustment of Status

Samuel Kolawole

Originally published in *New England Review* (2023)

Folahan slouched on the shady bench of the roadside paraga bar five minutes away from the apartment he shared with a bus driver who was never home. He checked his pocket for his phone after hearing a ping and discovered that it was from his wife. He sighed and put it back without even glancing at her message. He was exhausted from walking in the scorching sun and needed to get his mind off his problems.

Mama Nkechi, the owner, poured him a plastic cup without asking. He took the cup with a smile and drank as he watched vehicles and passersby. His head filled with warmth. His eyes watered. Alerted by another ding, he dug into his pocket for his phone and saw that message from his wife again, and again he returned it to his pocket unread.

A wispy fellow waved as he walked past the canopied bench and called out to him: "Londoner!"

Folahan had never been to London. He could not quite recall when he acquired that nickname—it must have been during one of his drunken roadside rants about America. He must have informed his drinking companions in his *gonna-wanna* accent that in his two years of living in America, he had never experienced a power outage. He must have told them about Tyler Perry Studios, Coca-Cola, and the place where Martin Luther King Jr. once lived. He must have told them about massage parlors where "anything goes"—nondescript buildings in neighborhood strip malls—and even sounded a little emotional about it. He must have tried to explain who Martin Luther King Jr. was, even though one or two of them must have wanted to tell him they already knew. He must have peppered his speeches with *fuck* and *shit*.

One of them probably called him a Londoner as an insult: "Because you are a Londoner, you think you are better than us, abi?" Maybe the person who first called him Londoner didn't care where he'd traveled as long as it was overseas. The nickname apparently stuck, but Folahan didn't care what they called him as long as he didn't have to offer his real name. Yes, he frequented the joint and had conversations with them over shots of cheap, locally brewed rum, till the church bells nearby rang for the umpteenth time, but that didn't mean he should tell his business to strangers. Folahan was well aware that they regarded him as a "been-to," someone who had traveled abroad and was now living large at home. Only he had been back in Nigeria for three months without informing his wife or children. Only he had lost his dignity and returned home almost penniless.

Folahan waved back at the fellow and wiped the sweat from his brow. He was sober now. Not for long.

Earlier that day, he had heard about the explosion in Lagos but was too preoccupied to care. He had seen an okada man shuffle over to a young girl sitting in a kiosk with a transistor radio pressed close to her ear. The fellow had pinched her cheeks playfully, and while the girl with a serious-looking face tried to fend him off, the announcement had spilled in from the radio. The girl screamed with shock before repeating the news aloud: "A bomb blast in Lagos."

"Bomb blast? Where? How did it happen? Was it a gas explosion?" the fellow demanded with urgency in his voice.

"Shhh. I am trying to hear the rest . . ." the girl said. Other people brought out their portable radios. A nearby store owner switched on his TV. There was a flurry of words from the newscasters.

Folahan moved from shock to disbelief to empathy to helpless acceptance in seconds. This was how people constantly dealt with the waves of misfortune in this country. They gasped with shock, sorry for the victims for a few moments, and then forged ahead, hoping the next calamity wouldn't come near them or their loved ones. His family lived far away from Ikeja, the site of the blast. He wondered if his wife had even heard about it.

Another hour had passed when the church bell tolled again. Folahan sipped his drink and heard the distant sound of a band playing, the drums rolling and a trumpet blaring mournful music. The sound grew louder, and a slow-moving convoy of vehicles led by a station wagon emerged from around the bend. Traders stepped out of their stalls. Children gawked.

"Eeyah, so sad," said Mama Nkechi as she served a customer who had just arrived. Folahan caught her looking at the convoy only once. She carried on with business. He reckoned she must have witnessed many funeral processions.

The convoy came to a halt in front of the chapel, about two hundred meters from Folahan. A man dressed in a priestly robe stepped out of the station wagon with a woman and two children. Clad in black, the family huddled together, clutching handkerchiefs. Maybe the deceased was the head of the household. More people streamed out of the other vehicles with somber faces. Mama Nkechi filled his cup again, and he emptied its contents in one gulp. The station wagon's back door opened, and the pallbearers, young men in black suits, dark glasses, and dirty white gloves, sprang out like rats from their nest. They dragged the coffin out, hoisting it to their shoulders. The mourners moved single file: the priest, the band, and the pallbearers leading the way. The band blared out a new tune, and though there was no singing, Folahan knew the words:

> When peace like a river attendeth my way,
> When sorrows like sea billows roll,
> Whatever my lot, thou hast taught me to say,
> It is well, it is well with my soul.

Yes, he knew the song all too well. He took another swig from the cup, looking at the drawn faces and the crying family as they filed down to the cemetery next to the chapel. Clumps of elephant grass and small trees dotted the burial grounds, and gravestones poked out of bushes, white and gray, caked in mud. The band stopped at the cemetery gate, and the mourners walked on, meandering through the graves until they reached the place marked for the interment. He'd seen processions like that many times in Georgia; the family of the deceased would sometimes request that the funeral director be present for the ceremony, and he'd accompany Bill. Folahan wondered who was in the coffin. He wondered who had prepared the corpse for burial, and how. Was it anything like he'd done all those months abroad? Within moments, the roadside watchers dispersed and went about their business. The bustle returned. Life went on. Folahan asked Mama Nkechi to pour him another drink.

***

Folahan's job as a washer of the dead had no official designation, and its legitimacy was questionable. He had come to America on a visitor's visa and refused to return even after his time had run out. His objective was to overstay his visa, and his plan was straightforward: file for a green card using the procedure known as adjustment of status, based on immediate relative relationship with a US citizen. He had heard about American citizens who would get married to an undocumented migrant for a stipulated period for a fee, and since there was no record of his marriage in the US, this wouldn't be a problem. All he had to do was make enough money to get one of these spouses for hire and avoid getting picked up by the immigration authorities until the day he submitted his application for adjustment of status. A year or so after getting a green card he would leave his contractual marriage and send for his real family.

As part of the under-the-table arrangement with the funeral director, he had lodging, enough food, and other necessities. Folahan's free housing was a small room in the basement next to the refrigeration unit at the back of the funeral home. He had no social security number, which meant he couldn't do what other people did without attracting attention and subsequently being in danger of being deported. Therefore, no hospitals if he got sick, just home remedies; no driver's license; no apartments; no bank accounts, only cash. If he were arrested or even talked with law enforcement, that was it—he was gone. Whenever he went out, he was sure to make himself inconspicuous. Bill was particular about Folahan laying low because whatever he did impacted him too.

Bill had once traveled to the Congo on a one-week trip when he was young and turned expert in all things Africa, at least in the eyes of the members of Community Saints Church in Lawrenceville, Georgia. He was an influential elder in the Church.

"Thank you for what you are doing for the Lord. I am sure this young man will be in good hands," said Margarete, one of the nosy white church ladies, after a service. Bill told the church folks that Folahan lived with him and was in the United States to attain the American dream. He did not say what that meant. When Folahan first got to the United States, he stayed with Gbadebo, his friend who was a graduate student at Emory, in Atlanta. Folahan quickly concluded that his plans for supporting himself in America and making enough money to get a green card and bring his family to the country were unrealistic. Soon it became clear that Folahan's reliance on Gbadebo was an inconvenience, so when Bill, whom he met at church, offered him a job and housing, he saw it as a sign of God's blessings.

Did Folahan conceive a situation where he would be washing corpses in America? He had left his job as a manager of a cement factory in Nigeria. He left a wife and three children, Junior, Oluwadara, and Semilore. But he, and many others just like him, had been drawn by the allure of the West, convinced that life there was better and that nothing could be worse than the conditions they lived in, so they left, abandoning what was left of their dreams. Once they discovered otherwise, it was too late. So, they clung to hope, worked hard, and wished for good fortune. Folahan had sold off his cars to afford the flight and rent for the first two months. Maybe he did not imagine himself in such a dire situation, but that was what attaining the American dream meant—rising from the dust of wretchedness to an enviable status in a strange land. However, some days he wondered if it was worth it—if he'd made the right choice.

Margarete had turned to Folahan and spoke about never being to Africa. She asked what Africa was like. Did they have paved roads? Modern buildings? Folahan wanted to say, yes, we do, just like you have here. But Bill spoke before he opened his mouth. "He is from Nigeria, Margarete, one of Africa's richest countries," he said with a smile. Folahan couldn't decide which was worse, Margarete's question or Bill's comment.

Margarete gave a surprised look and mumbled something about her daughter spending time in South Africa as a study-abroad student. She said something about the safari, wished Folahan well, and shambled on to speak to the next church member.

***

Folahan worked mainly night shifts at the morgue, down in the basement. That was the only way he could work without drawing attention, and the arrangement worked for Bill. A family could bring their dead one day, and the corpse would be prepared for burial the following morning. It took about forty minutes to prepare a corpse plus the time required for embalmment. Folahan only assisted in the embalmment process if needed.

Folahan would open the body bag slowly from the head down, armed with a disinfectant spray. Then he would transfer the deceased to a stainless-steel slab with slats for the water to run through. The head reveals the fact of death—vacant eyes, gaping mouth, the vomit-inducing smell that rises out of orifices. Sometimes fluid gushed out of the ears and nose.

Folahan's first time opening a body bag sent him heaving into the toilet of the prep room, but he got used to it. Thinking helped him work and gave him fortitude. He thought about his family. Junior, a pre-adolescent, was growing tall when he left. He wondered how tall he was now. He remembered his children's smiles, longing tears, and questions about when he would bring them to America when he was about to leave.

He sometimes imagined following the traditional trade of *mghassilchi*, something he had read somewhere months ago. *Mghassilchi* washed and shrouded the bodies of the dead for religious burial. It was an honorable profession, he learned, and God bountifully rewarded those who did it. He imagined purifying the body for burial after the soul rose to the sky, leaving the shell on earth, back to the dust from whence it came.

Folahan sometimes imagined Bill as a *mghassilchi* too. Bill insisted on showing respect to the bodies no matter their condition. They lost their lives; they shouldn't lose their dignity, he would say. Bill provided cloth to cover their private parts and taught Folahan how to wash them gently with warm water splashing out of a long hose hanging from a single faucet. Folahan learned to sponge them with soap from head to toe and towel them off without chipping their delicate skin. He learned to close their eyes and mouth, positioning them with their hands crossed over the abdomen, as in a casket. He learned to wash the hair. To oil and comb it. If the corpse needed to be embalmed, the body was wheeled to another room, where Bill got to work under the glare of UV lights. Folahan hardly participated in that process, which involved making a small incision in the neck to allow the blood to drain, injecting embalming solution into the carotid artery through a small tube connected to a machine. He waited on Bill, handing him tools and helping him hold them. Bill injected a solution to plump facial features if the body was emaciated. If trauma or disease had altered the appearance of the deceased, he enhanced it using wax, adhesive, and plaster. He took proper care, like a sculptor remodeling a stone or an artist touching up a painting.

In the end the deceased could be viewed in the casket, dressed, cosmetics applied. The body would be beautiful again.

***

Another loud ding. He checked his phone. Another message from his wife. He had sent her a Blackberry he bought with installment payments he made in America for ease of communication. Transatlantic calls were too expensive, they had agreed, so they stuck to "pinging," which worked out for him still, even after he had returned to a neighboring state in Nigeria three months ago without her knowing. When she requested him to send her images of America, he said he was too busy. When she asked for pictures of him working, he mumbled something about not being allowed to photograph the bodies. Folahan heaved a sigh and scrolled through his messages until one caught his attention.

Baba Junior,
Did you hear about the bomb blast? Junior went to Ikeja with his friends this morning, and he has not been back. I am driving there now to look for him. Call us as soon as you receive this. Find a way.
Omowunmi

He felt shock, then cautioned himself. She was probably overreacting. He looked at his cup and wished it wasn't empty. Mama Nkechi took a hint, pouring him more. Dizziness set in. He gulped the liquor. Now he tasted nothing, but he felt a burning in his throat. She asked if he was okay. Folahan fumbled through his wallet, gave her cash without counting, and lurched off the bench.

"Is everything okay?" said Mama Nkechi again as he reeled and swayed, drifting onward. He was her customer, nothing more, so he did not owe her any answer. She knew nothing about what he had been through, the shame he had to endure.

She knew nothing about the pain of his dashed dreams. Better to walk away without saying a word. He kept walking, and when the ground began shifting beneath his feet, he stopped to gather himself. He leaned against a utility pole and drew deep breaths. He tried to will himself to be still. Stay still. Still . . . still . . . still . . .

***

Work was sometimes hard, and his small, formaldehyde-smelling room suffocating. The silence, pierced only by the distant rumbling of trains, was tolerable for the first few weeks. But weeks turned into months, and the dense silence seemed to animate the concrete walls. There was the loneliness of being an outsider in a strange country—the cold smiles from strangers, the prying eyes of busybodies, the insensitivity, and the insularity of well-meaning folks like Margarete. To keep sane and tend to his needs, he touched himself, conjuring images of his wife's beautiful body. He stirred up memories of her warmth and moisture. He recalled how they would lie close, and her naked flesh would quiver under his hands, her breath hot against his sparse chest hair. But again, the walls and the silence closed in, fogging his brain. Soon, even the memory of his wife began to fade. Not her essence but her smell, how her skin felt, the contours of her body.

One afternoon, after sleeping off the exhaustion of the previous night's work, Folahan typed "porn" into the Google search on his phone. Two links, Pornhub.com and XXNX.com, caught his eye, and he went for the latter. Captioned videos of naked bodies engaging in intercourse appeared. He moved his cursor down the horizontal links as he felt his body stir. *Riding homemade. Female amateur swinger.* He hovered his cursor around the *Female ejaculation* tab for some seconds and changed his mind, clicking the webpage shut. He wiped light perspiration from his brow and adjusted the bulge in his trousers, shame coursing through him.

Three days later, he went back to the site, this time stroking himself until a sweet spasm went through him. After a while, even porn-enhanced orgasm could cure neither his loneliness nor his desires. That was, however, what he had. He made do. One night, he stumbled on the "massage" porn of XXNX.com. He had heard of massage parlors that provided "happy endings" but never thought it was real. Porn actors mostly roleplayed the massage videos, but some seemed more candid, taken from cameras that were hidden, the shots dark and unsteady. His search led him down the rabbit hole of review boards, forums, and blogs about happy endings, code words like "rub-n-tug" and "full-service." He found a community of men online who frequented erotic massage parlors and referred to themselves as *mongers*. It was not long before Folahan realized massage parlors weren't just scenes from porn videos. He learned, to his astonishment, that there were such parlors as close as two miles away from him. He could visit one, if he wanted to. Part of him felt guilt. He was also angry. Angry at himself for being vulnerable. Angry about how hard everything was, and how he couldn't do anything about the desire gnawing inside him.

Bill brought in more work. Hours of washing corpses made Folahan's muscles ache and plagued his mind with desperate thoughts. His craving for living human contact made him look forward to services at Community Saints Church, even if it meant he had to put up with Margarete. Her daughter, Heather, was visiting from Colorado Springs, and he spoke with her after church service one Sunday. She wore a flower-patterned gown and smelled of lavender. Her blond hair was straight and lustrous. Folahan reckoned she had to be in her thirties, some years younger than him at least.

"Do you have a family? Are they here with you?" she asked him outside on the church lawn. He considered lying about having a family, but what if she found out the truth from Bill?

"Yes, my wife and kids are in Nigeria."

"It must be hard to be so far away from them."

"Yes, very hard."

"I am very sorry about that."

"Thank you."

They took the back door and strode down the street from the chapel for ice cream. Folahan got two scoops, vanilla and strawberry, and Heather got one scoop of chocolate. She loaded up some with her wooden spoon for him to try.

"No, thank you," he said with an impish smile, and after an awkward silence Heather muttered something of an apology for offering. He told her not to worry then asked her about South Africa. They talked for a time before falling silent again. Folahan was searching his thoughts for something to say, anything to fill the silence as they walked back to the church building. She extended her hand as they approached the church doors, and he hesitated for a second. He saw the smile on her face and took her hand. Her palm felt warm.

In his room later that day he felt the need to scratch the stifling itch in his sex. He sniffed the lavender on his hands where she had touched him and opened his fly.

***

Folahan stepped up and pressed the buzzer. His hands bathed in a cold sweat, he promptly rubbed them against his trousers, looking nervously over his shoulder across the large parking lot. The box-shaped building that housed the massage parlor stood at the end of a strip mall that looked like it hadn't received a touch of paint in years. Lace curtains covered the windows of the storefront. Neon-red inscriptions of "Body Massage" and "Open Massage" flashed in the midday sun from signs above the door.

A white woman Folahan assumed was the manager opened the door and gave him a once-over before smiling. She could have been in her fifties or sixties. He stepped into the waiting area, a vestibule with a gray couch and decorative plants, trying to calm his nerves. She asked him if it was his first time, and he said yes. She said "welcome" again and opened a logbook from a stool beside the gray couch. She asked for a name and an address. He hesitated, then gave her a made-up name and the address of the church. Maybe she didn't care. She explained the tariffs, Folahan produced the cash, and they went through a beaded curtain.

The manager slipped past him in the dim hallway beckoning for him to follow, then pointed at a door. There were other doors. He could hear voices from them.

"Private rooms are at the end of the hallway."

A massage table stood in the middle of the red-lit room they entered. Bottles of oil, talcum powder, tissues, and clean towels occupied a bench at one end. Small crystals were arranged in a line on a table in the room's corner. Zen-like music played softly over the speaker system. The masseuse walked in moments later. What Folahan first noticed was her beautiful smile. Her age showed in the laugh lines around her dark eyes, but her body looked lithe in her strappy, knee-length zebra-print dress. She had small breasts.

She instructed him to disrobe, don a towel, and lie on the table. Folahan waited for her to leave before removing his shirt and sitting on the edge of the massage table, looking around. Fear lodged in his chest; it was laced with anticipation. The masseuse's instruction did not register properly, or perhaps he was careful not to do anything wrong, so he kept his trousers on. He did not know what to expect.

She walked in moments later, a look of surprise on her face. She grabbed a towel from the neat pile on the bench and handed it to him.

"Take off trousers." Her voice was hard and authoritative. Once again, she vanished. Folahan shucked all but his boxers and wrapped the towel around his waist. He roamed around the room, picking up the crystals and setting them back down, when he heard her approaching footsteps.

He lay down on the massage table and planted his face through the hole at the end. She began by standing above his head and kneading his temples. She smelled of talcum powder.

Ripples of pleasure went through him. She moved to the other end of the table, covered his boxer shorts with a towel, and sat on his buttocks. She squirted oil on her palms and pressed deeply into his shoulder blades. He felt her hands slick and warm on the knots on his shoulders, and she slowly wound her way downwards. She plowed her thumbs into the grooves of his tailbones, nudging at the edges of the towel around his waist, drawing moisture from his skin. For a moment, he felt her hands drawing his boxers down, cold air moving in against his bare buttocks, but she stopped without removing them completely and proceeded to work on his calves and thighs.

Was she going to tell him to roll onto his back and take away his towel? That would surely make him feel even more awkward. Would her nails brush slowly, teasingly against his chest? Would she seek consent before pulling down his boxers the rest of the way, or did he have to ask her first, as some of the internet forums instructed? He had never felt this vulnerable before.

Without thinking, he reached out for her breasts when he was told to lie face up. The masseuse objected with her eyes and then asked for a tip. Folahan was about to agree to her request when he heard a door slam somewhere down the hall and the shouts of "Police! Police!" from the other women. He pushed her off and rushed wildly to recover his clothes.

Dressed and in the vestibule crowded with masseuses and their customers, he told the police, between short, quick breaths, that it was his first time and that he had come for a professional massage. They told him there was no cause for alarm, questioned him a bit, asked for his name and address. This time he felt he had to give them his real details. They let him go soon afterwards.

Two days later, the funeral home was visited by ICE officers in tactical gear. The next two weeks were a blur—with more questioning, and with Bill denying his knowledge of Folahan's undocumented status then demanding to talk to his lawyer at the ICE office, Folahan being transported from detention center to detention center, more questioning, and paperwork. Finally, Folahan was transported to an airplane that flew him back to Nigeria.

Failure was what he feared the most. The story of his fall from grace would be whispered in village verandahs and the corners of households. No one traveled abroad and returned empty-handed, not if they had nothing to fall back on. He could not return to the job at the cement mill, which would have been filled by now. Even worse, to him, was the fact that he lost everything as a result of his sex-solicitation. He could conceal that to others, but he would forever have to live with the consequences. At first, he thought he would tell his family he had been deported after a few days, but as time went on, he had more time to reflect on the catastrophe that was his life. He had ruined his life for what again?

***

Ding! Another message rolled in. Junior is in the hospital! A wave of fear tore through him, much like he felt when the police barged in on the massage parlor. With trembling hands, he typed a message: What? What happened? Which hospital?

One minute felt like an eternity. He told himself there was no reason to be alarmed. Maybe it wasn't anything too serious. Stay still. *Still . . . still . . . still . . .*

Another ding. *He was in Ikeja where the bomb blast happened.*

He responded too quickly. *What you mean?*

One minute passed, then two, and he could not wait any longer. He stumbled away from the utility pole on which he was leaning, his legs unsteady. He noticed people glancing at him from the corner of their eyes. He searched around for a GSM stand or a kiosk where he could make a call. When he found one farther down the road, someone was using the only cell phone available, and another person was in line. He went up to him, beseeching him. "My son is in the hospital. I don't know what happened to him. Please let me make a call next," he said with tears in his eyes. Passersby stared. One of them said, "Your son will be healed in the mighty name of Jesus," and a chorus of amens followed.

"Take my phone and call your wife," said the kiosk manager. Folahan thanked him and walked away from the kiosk to make his call.

"It's me."

"You are in Nigeria?"

"I just landed. I wanted to surprise you. How is Junior? What's the doctor saying . . ."

She was silent for too long. Then, "What do you mean you wanted to surprise? When were you going to call to let me know you were in Nigeria?"

"I was—"

"Folahan, what is going on? Were you deported? Are you with another woman?"

Folahan was taken aback by her onslaught of suspicious questions. He quickly attributed it to raw emotions.

"Is my son, okay? That's all I want to know right now."

"You have been drinking. I can tell. What is really going on? So, you've been in Nigeria all along?"

Folahan had no response to her question; there was no point in attempting to deny the situation.

"This is not the time and the place, please, is my son okay, I need to know?"

He could hear her quiet sobs on the other end of the line. Folahan choked back tears, tried to compose himself.

"Will Junior be okay?" he asked again.

She finally caught her breath, then was silent again for a long time.

"He has been admitted, but he will be fine," she said.

"Thank God."

"Please come home."

"I am on my way, my dear. I am on my way."

Animals

Uche Okonkwo

Originally published in *ZYZZYVA* (2024)

Nedu named the chicken Otuanya because it was missing an eye, a film of pink tissue sealing the space where the organ should have been. He summoned his father, older sister, Cherish, and unsmiling mother to the backyard for a naming ceremony, where he served peanuts and Fanta and solemnly announced the chicken's name to polite applause from his father and an eye roll from his sister. After his family dispersed, Nedu lingered in the backyard. He fed Otuanya leftover grains of rice and tickled the fleshy red wattles that dangled under the chicken's beak.

The chicken had come into their lives two evenings ago, crouched on the floor in the back of his mother's car. Nedu and his sister watched her open the rear door of the car as wide as it would go. She bent toward the chicken. It gave a warning cluck and she straightened up, wiping her palms on the front of her skirt. Nedu frowned. He'd never seen his mother afraid of anything. Not too long ago, she'd gotten their whole family dragged to the police station after she called an officer and his future generations useless and unfortunate. In the days following that incident, Nedu had hoped someone would bring it up—maybe his dad would make a joke to open the conversation, or his mother would cite yet another news story about the police. Maybe then, inside the nest of their words, he could confess that since that day, each time he saw the impenetrable black of a police uniform, his heart threw itself against the walls of his chest. Was it just him? That afternoon at the station, his eyes had fixated on one officer's weapon: a dull AK-47 with a rash of rust creeping across the barrel like an infection. He'd seen police guns before, but never that close. The way the gun hung by a dirty strap from the officer's shoulder, with the ease and innocence of an old backpack. The light-headed dread that had him blindly groping for Cherish, to hide his shaking hand in hers.

"Mum, should I google how to carry a chicken?" Cherish asked, a hint of amusement in her voice, her phone materializing.

Their mother, Uzoma, waved a dismissive hand. She ducked again into the back of the car and reemerged clutching the squawking chicken by the wings. The chicken's legs were bound with a length of string, claws scratching at air. Uzoma hurried around the side of the house to the backyard. Nedu and Cherish followed, Cherish brandishing her phone, camera ready, in the hopes of capturing some social-media-worthy shenanigan. In the backyard, their mother undid the string binding the chicken's legs together and tied one leg to a clothesline pole. Nedu stared at the chicken in the fading evening light. That was when he first noticed the missing eye. Nedu had once had a boil on his left eyelid so big that he couldn't open it for days. His heart went out to the bird.

When their father returned from work that evening, Cherish told him about the chicken in the backyard. He seemed pleased. "You can always taste the difference between the frozen kind and the ones that are cooked fresh," he said. Then, to his wife, "But, Uzoma, I didn't know you could kill a chicken o." He smirked at Nedu and Cherish. "You see this my wife of secret talents?"

"Lol," Cherish said. "Mummy the chicken slayer."

Nedu knew, of course, that his mother hadn't bought the chicken as a pet. His parents had made their no-pets policy clear the day he cried himself sick begging to adopt a puppy from his friend's dog's litter. Besides, nobody kept chickens as pets. But he lay in bed that night thinking about the chicken, alone in the backyard. He wondered if having one eye made it easier to fall asleep. He crept out of bed to watch the bird from his window, a dark shape barely visible under the blanket of night. That was when the idea for the naming ceremony came to him. It made

sense: if you gave a thing a name, you couldn't turn around
and eat it as food. And so after Nedu performed the ceremony,
and the third and fourth and fifth days of Otuanya's life passed
uninterrupted, he let his heart settle.

The chicken became the best part of Nedu's days. When he
woke up, he would race from his room, down the stairs, and
out to the backyard. He hung up his mother's old banana-print
wrapper, tying its four corners to the clotheslines and creating
a small canopy to protect Otuanya from the sun. He extended
the tether that tied Otuanya's leg to the clothesline pole by using
strips of cloth cut from an old dish towel. He took some of his
toys out to the backyard and was disappointed when he couldn't
get Otuanya to perch on his remote-controlled monster truck
for a ride. Every time Nedu had to leave Otuanya—to make his
bed, or for his mandatory study period supervised by Cherish,
or to watch reruns of Ben 10 in the cool of the air-conditioned
living room—he felt guilty, worried that Otuanya would be
lonely without him. The thought was almost enough to bring
him to tears.

***

At first, Uzoma was amused by her son's fondness for the
chicken and allowed him responsibility for its care. With school
on break, she figured, the bird would keep the seven-year-old
occupied. But, as the days passed, Uzoma became wary of her
son's growing attachment to the animal. She began reminding
him of Otuanya's ultimate destiny. Pulling her earlobes and
adopting a singsong voice, she'd say, "Remember, remember,
all roads lead to my pepper soup pot."

But it was now two weeks since she'd brought the chicken
home, and even as Uzoma sung her reminders to Nedu, she was
losing confidence in her ability to usher the bird to its savory
fate. Ebube, her husband, had sounded so impressed that she'd
bought a live chicken, and with each day that passed, it became
harder to admit to him that she hadn't given prior thought

to the logistics of the killing. The first week they'd had it, her husband had returned from work each evening sniffing his way to the kitchen, wide-eyed and hopeful. She'd made excuses all that week, her tone getting sharper each day, and was relieved when he stopped asking. But her relief soon turned to shame. This past week, she'd imagined the chicken taunting her each time she went to the backyard to set out the trash or bring in laundry from the clothesline. She considered returning to the market for precut chicken parts to make her soup with, but then her husband would know she was avoiding having to kill the chicken she'd bought on impulse.

She still wasn't sure why she'd bought a live chicken in the first place—she'd never killed one before. Maybe this was a new iteration of the strange unrest she'd been feeling for weeks, ever since that thing with the policeman. Or perhaps it was simply the curl of the chicken seller's lip when Uzoma had asked for the price on a whim. The woman had gestured toward her freezer full of chicken parts instead. "Fine madam like you," she said, "you go fit kill chicken?"

She would do it today, she decided, while it was still the weekend. She'd spent all of Saturday watching video after video on the internet showing how to kill a chicken at home. She'd learned that a sharp knife, a firm hand, would minimize the chicken's pain and prevent it from running around the backyard with blood spouting and a partially severed head flopping about.

She stepped out to the backyard with a stainless-steel bowl and her sharpest knife, which she sharpened further against the concrete step that led down from the kitchen. She held the knife in front of her face. She was pleased at the glint of the blade, the way it grazed the skin of her palm with the threat of blood.

As Uzoma approached the chicken, she could feel Nedu gazing at her from his upstairs bedroom window. Sometimes she worried she was failing her children, raising them too soft. There Nedu was, acting like a great tragedy was about to befall him. The other day, he'd untied the chicken's tether and snuck the bird into the house. He'd almost reached the second floor before Uzoma caught him. He stared back at her with wet eyes, mouth gaping open like his lips were made of melting wax. When she asked what Nedu was doing, he said he wanted to give the chicken a shower. It was almost funny. She made Nedu return the chicken to the backyard and watched as he retied the tether. "All roads lead to where?" she'd said. "To your pepper soup pot," Nedu responded, with an incongruous gravity, as if he wouldn't lick clean the bowl of pepper soup she'd place before him when all of this was over and the smell of uziza and scent leaf filled the house. And now here Cherish was, fluttering around Uzoma with her phone's camera recording. She wanted to point out to her daughter that at age fourteen she herself had been attending school *and* working part-time at a big supermarket in Awka. And yet Cherish sat around all day, pressing phone like it was paid work.

Uzoma untied and retied her wrapper around her waist. The chicken was staring her down with its single eye. Her pot of water, to dunk the body in after the deed was done, was simmering on the stove. Her knife was sharp enough to cut breeze. She took a breath. It was time.

Uzoma placed the knife on the ground and returned to the house, ignoring Cherish's "Where are you going?" She went to find her husband in the study. When she opened the door, he snapped his laptop shut.

"Husby, sorry o . . . are you busy?"

He was probably watching porn. She didn't care about his occasional indulgence, but she would never tell him this. She thought it potentially useful to make a man feel like he had more to be guilty about than he really did. And her husband, he was see-through, with his guileless face, his lack of ego—a thing she at once loved and despised about him. It was this lack of ego that had freed him to pursue her without shame, his besotted heart adorning his sleeve for the world to see. It was what made him the children's preferred parent. Not that they'd

ever said as much to her; they wouldn't dare. But it was clear
from the way they gravitated toward him, offering him jokes
and jabs they would never send her way. He was particularly
good with Cherish, who seemed to grow further away from
her mother as her young body filled out. Wasn't it only a year
or so ago that she and Cherish would spend Sunday afternoons
watching movies on Africa Magic and taking turns scratching
dandruff from each other's scalps? Now, Cherish preferred to
sit for hours with her father while they each scrolled through
their individual social media pages; every once in a while,
one of them would thrust their phone in the other's face and
they'd laugh in sync, their heads colliding. And Nedu. How her
husband indulged him, rallying her and Cherish to attend that
silly naming ceremony for the chicken, breaking the peanuts
Nedu had offered as if they were the kola nuts one would serve
at a child's naming.

Uzoma told herself there were advantages to having parents
with different styles, one with a gentle touch, one to lay down
the law. But sometimes she would hear the echoes of laughter
in the house and feel her heart sink, knowing from experience
that if she tried to join in, the laughter would sputter into
silence. She'd learned to comfort herself with her practicality,
her sheer usefulness. She was the one the kids came to when
they suddenly remembered on a Sunday night that they needed
sheets of cardboard paper for school on Monday. She was the
one who could tell, before Cherish could, that the pain pulsing
in her daughter's abdomen, the fist clenching and unclenching,
was heralding her first period. She was the one who'd hunted
down Panadol Extra and soda water after midnight while her
husband slept.

As Uzoma watched her husband watch her, she decided that
he, too, had grown to over-rely on her. Why else would he
assume that she would be the one to kill the chicken? Why
should she have to kill an entire animal when she had an entire
man in the house? She could picture him telling her, without
shame, sorry, he had never killed a chicken before and he didn't

feel like starting today. Just like he'd been without shame that day—what was it, two months ago?—when that lousy police-man had taken their family to the police station and made Ebube lie flat on the ground and beg before they were allowed to leave. She remembered how the officer had stopped their car that afternoon at the checkpoint, how his belly strained against the black police-issue belt, how unbothered he'd seemed by her threats to call her friend, the wife of the police commissioner, to report his demand for "weekend allowance." No such friend existed, but the officer had no way of knowing this. Still, he stood very calm as she plucked her phone from her handbag and waved it at him through the car window that she'd refused to roll down beyond a crack. He regarded her with eyes that looked half-open, as though he couldn't be bothered to give her his full attention. "Madam," he said, his voice unhurried, even playful. "You can return that phone to your bag. You have phone and mouth, I have gun and bullet." And then, to her utmost horror, he'd winked at her! Or she'd imagined him winking at her? She would never be sure. The toothpick in the corner of the officer's mouth bobbed, and a pink slice of tongue slipped out to moisten his bottom lip. She looked away, let the phone fall back into her bag. It was at this point that the officer got into the back of their car—Cherish and Nedu squished themselves in a corner and left a wide space between their bodies and the officer's—and ordered her husband to drive, giving him directions to a police station at Onipanu.

Uzoma and her husband hadn't had sex since then. At first, it was because he was angry at her—he didn't speak to her for the rest of that day! But even after his anger faded, after he started reaching for her again, her body would curl into itself like a disturbed millipede. Each time his hands grazed the insides of her thighs, she would think of those same hands flat on the ground outside the police station, those hands that had come away darkened with dirt after he'd prostrated before the policeman, so low that sand kissed his forehead, and her thighs would clench closed. She'd imagine him thrusting on top of her and cringe at how similar that motion was to him pushing off the ground when the policeman finally gave him permission to stand. He'd even managed to smile with Officer Toothpick after the whole thing, after the policeman had warned him to control his wife or she would get him in trouble one day. "Officer, I don already dey the trouble," her husband had said, his laughter loud like fireworks as the policeman slapped him on the back. You'd think they were old friends.

It was bad enough, this new aversion to her husband's touch, for no reason that made sense. But, to compound her frustrations and further unseat her sense of self, her wayward brain chose to entertain thoughts of that horrible police officer while she lathered herself in the shower, or as she stirred pancake batter, or in those formless moments just before sleep claimed her. She imagined him putting her in handcuffs, making her kneel, prodding that saliva-moistened toothpick with his tongue, grabbing her by the back of the head, telling her to put that foul mouth of hers to good use. By the time she caught herself, there'd be a creeping wetness between her legs. Yet, for her own husband she was dry like dead skin.

Uzoma looked away from her husband, who was now leaning forward in his chair. She imagined he could suddenly see into her depraved depths, see that there was something very wrong with her. She imagined his insides filling with disgust.

***

Ebube felt a lot of things in the moments after his wife appeared before him, but disgust was not one of them. First, Ebube felt surprised—Uzoma usually knocked, but there she was standing inside the study door in her T-shirt and her wrapper snug around her hips. Then there was a twinge of shame. Before his wife showed up, he'd been festering in a cloud of self-pity, troubling Google with queries: Wife sex drive vanished. How to turn wife on. Why won't wife have sex with me? His search history wouldn't spark any fires in his wife's loins, that was for sure. And then came annoyance, at Uzoma and the new agility with which she shrank from his touch.

But his annoyance was short-lived. Something in his wife's stance, in her voice as she said, "Husby," was causing him to melt.

He made his voice soft. "I'm not busy. Do you need something?" She took a step into the room, said not to worry, it was nothing. Then she was gone.

Ebube stared at his closed laptop. He tried to remember the exact time they'd last had sex, but he couldn't pin it down. They definitely hadn't had sex since the day of Tosin's wedding, which they'd ended up missing because his darling wife wouldn't keep her mouth shut and let him grease that officer's waiting palm, like most Lagosians, most Nigerians, did literally every day. Was she still angry at him for humoring the chubby policeman when he'd made that joke about putting a leash on her? See, that was her problem, she'd never understood the little things normal people did to defuse situations, to oil the wheels of ordinary interaction. It was why she had so few friends, why his mother had never quite warmed to her, pleading with him up until a week before their wedding to reconsider. "You are too soft for that woman," his mother had warned.

His mother was wrong. His wife's self-reliance, which his mother read as hardness, didn't bother him; it drew him to her like a spell. And over the years, even as the excitement of their union mellowed and settled into normalcy, the dexterity with which she managed their lives continued to amaze him. But some days he understood his mother's reservations. He could imagine Uzoma getting suddenly bored with him and marching out of his life. She'd demonstrated many times that she didn't need him. She hadn't needed him when she'd started her accounting business. Or when she'd gone into early labor with Nedu and driven herself to the hospital while he was trapped in Third Mainland Bridge after-work traffic. And now she'd shown it again. Whatever she'd needed, whatever had made her stand before him for those few seconds, she would go take charge of it, as though the sight of him sitting flaccid in his chair had fed new resolve into her bones.

***

That evening, Ebube, Nedu, and Cherish congregated around the dinner table.

"What are we having?" Ebube asked.

"Rice," Nedu said.

"With chicken stew?" Ebube asked hopefully.

"Mum couldn't kill the chicken," Cherish said. "Lol."

"Cherish, you know you're allowed to just laugh," Ebube said, tucking the nugget of information about the still-alive chicken in a corner of his mind.

"Ha ha ha," Cherish said. Ebube shook his head in mock disapproval.

"Dad, Mum couldn't kill Otuanya because he's now part of the family," Nedu said. "His name is Otuanya Isichie."

"I know," Ebube said. "I was at the naming."

"The next time we take a family portrait," Cherish said, "Otuanya can sit on Nedu's head; it's kuku shaped like a nest." Uzoma walked in from the kitchen holding a serving bowl filled with stew, in time to catch the laughter from Ebube and Cherish. "What's the joke?" she asked merrily.

"Nothing," Cherish said.

Cherish noticed her mother lower her eyes to the floor, the subtle pucker of her mouth. She felt a pinch of remorse. But if Cherish told the joke, her mother would think she was the butt of it, that her family was mocking her for Otuanya's continued state of aliveness. Instead of playing along, she might point out the impracticalities of preparing a chicken to pose for a family photograph, the same way she sucked the fun, like marrow out of bone, from every meme or viral video Cherish dared to share with her. It wasn't Cherish's fault that her mother's sense of humor was fixated on the likes of Aki and Pawpaw and their fellow Nollywood pranksters.

Cherish couldn't believe she used to sit through those silly movies with her mother. The woman became an entirely different person once the opening credits began, with her honking laugh and running commentary. "These boys will soon tackle the old man to the ground . . . Cherish, lekwa, lekwa . . ." Cherish would groan, "Mummy, I'm seeingggg." Still, she'd enjoyed those afternoons, not for the movies themselves but because of her mother's childlike engagement with them, her overreactions to plot twists even when they watched reruns.

If only her mother could be that person all the time. Easy. Maybe then Cherish could tell her about Afolabi, the boy she liked; ask her why, whenever he came close, it suddenly felt like her limbs belonged to someone else. And also, maybe that thing with the police officer would never have happened. She'd held Nedu's hand that afternoon and looked away from the spectacle of her dad lying on the ground begging the officer while her mother stood aside, defiant and arms folded. On the drive home she'd felt the force of her father's anger, so rare, so alien, that it sat on him like a costume that kept slipping off to reveal glimpses of the familiar person hidden inside it. The way he'd slammed on the brakes, the curses he threw at the other drivers who were too slow or too stupid and needed to park their cars at home before they killed someone. Cherish hadn't forgiven her mother for that day. Not that Uzoma would ever ask.

Uzoma placed the bowl of stew on the table with a little more force than Cherish thought was necessary and headed back into the kitchen, calling over her shoulder, "You people can keep laughing, or you can help set the table. Whichever you think is best."

***

Of the many possible reasons offered by the internet know-it-alls for his wife's recent coldness in the bedroom, one listicle item from an obscure Christian website worried Ebube's mind like a flickering neon sign: She's lost respect for you.

Are you a poor decision-maker? A bad father? Riddled with vices?

Ebube was none of those things. Yes, Uzoma made most of the household decisions, but she liked it that way. It was easier for everyone. And he was a great father; the kids adored him! Even Cherish, who was in her so-called difficult teen years. He did worry about Nedu sometimes: What kind of child got teary-eyed at the pretend naming ceremony for a chicken? And vices . . . well, if you wanted to call them that, sure. But "riddled with" wasn't the way he'd describe his relationship to them.

Cowardly?

His behavior with the police officer was not a show of cowardice. That was him doing what was needed to get his family out of an unnecessary altercation. But he could see how someone—someone like Uzoma, perhaps—might read it as cowardly.

The judgy listicle had called for self-reflection. Perhaps there was something Ebube could do to arouse some respect from Uzoma. A plan began to form in his mind, one that wasn't entirely selfish. First, he'd do some research on chicken slaughter. He'd pick a time when his wife was busy in the kitchen. He would stroll to the backyard and be nonchalant. At the tail end of a yawn and a stretch, he would offer to kill the chicken for her. Casually. Like it was an afterthought.

He practiced in front of the bedroom mirror.

Yawn, stretch. "Ah, Uzoma, Otuanya still hasn't entered your soup pot?" No, too playful. She could interpret this as mockery.

Yawn, stretch. "Uzoma, you know, I can help you kill the chicken." Too direct. She might take it as a challenge.

Yawn, stretch. "Uzoma, ngwa, bring a knife and let me kill this chicken." No, too authoritative. He'd never pull that off.

How about no yawn, no stretch: "Uzoma, I think you're having a hard time killing the chicken. I say this because you've been bent on making chicken pepper soup for weeks. Would you like me to handle it? You don't have to do everything all the time. You'd still be a wonder to me."

He discarded the idea. Uzoma would hate that.

He would just go into the kitchen and begin sharpening a knife, ask his wife to put a large pot of water on the fire. She would get it. Her eyes would tear up with gratitude. And so, after fortifying himself with chicken-killing knowledge, he went into the kitchen, began sharpening a knife, asked his wife to put a large pot of water on the fire. Her eyes did not tear up.

"Have you killed a chicken before?" she asked.

"Have you?"

She regarded him in silence for a moment. "Thank you," she said.

She was welcome. She didn't need to know how many videos he'd watched in preparation, or that his goals went beyond helping to manifest Otuanya's destiny.

"But not now," his wife said. "It's too hot outside." He agreed. "We'll do it in the evening."

"Do what?" Nedu asked as he walked into the kitchen.

Ebube hesitated. If Nedu were a different kind of boy, this might be a chance to teach him something; something about doing difficult things, maybe? It wasn't entirely clear to Ebube how to frame the death of a chicken as a teachable moment. "I'm going to kill the chicken."

Nedu's face looked stricken. "You're still killing Otuanya?" Ebube tried to be gentle. "Nedu, your mother has been talking about making chicken pepper soup for weeks; which chicken did you think was going to feature in the soup?"

"But . . . he's one of us now," Nedu said. "All of you came to his naming!"

Cherish appeared in the kitchen doorway. "Nedu," she said. "It's not a 'he,' it's an 'it,' and it is a chicken."

As Nedu turned and ran toward the stairs, Uzoma saw an opportunity for a joke. She called after her son, "Nedu, the chicken will fully become one with our family when he dwells inside our tummies!" She laughed too loud, hoping her husband and daughter would join in, but her laughter died alone.

***

As the sun started to set, Uzoma prepared the tools for Otuanya's slaughter. She hoped Nedu would stay in his room; she didn't want any drama. She briefly worried that killing the chicken might traumatize the boy, but she dismissed that thought. It was only a chicken. By the time the pepper soup was ready, Nedu would have forgotten the bird's name.

The whole family gathered in the kitchen, except for Nedu. A large pot of water bubbled on the stove. Ebube girded himself. Cherish, with her phone out, camera recording, asked, "Dad, are you ready to slay?"

"Ready," Ebube said.

Uzoma snorted with mild derision, but the laughter in her eyes warmed Ebube's heart. Uzoma grabbed the knife and they all stepped out into the backyard. But under the wrapper-canopy where the chicken should have been, there was nothing. The length of rope that had tethered the bird to the clothesline had been snipped in half. Uzoma could think of only one culprit.

"Neduuuu!"

"Shh, shh, shh," Ebube said. "Look."

He pointed, and his wife and daughter followed his finger toward the gate, where Otuanya stood, the other half of the tether trailing on the ground. The chicken was at the threshold of the pedestrian gate, which stood wide open. Otuanya was perched on one leg, the other poised to land on the ground, on the other side of the gate. The chicken turned and skewered the family with that single eye before disappearing across the threshold.

The trio chased the chicken down the street. The few people they passed gave them a wide berth, ignoring Uzoma's cries to "Catch that chicken!"

Near the end of the street, the bird launched itself over a low wall and into a compound with a white house and hibiscus hedges. Without hesitation, Uzoma banged on the gate, and when a bewildered gateman opened, she barged in. "I must cook that pepper soup today!"

They found Otuanya cowering by a banana tree behind the house, legs entangled in the tether. The family left with their prize secured in Ebube's grip.

***

That evening, the smell of Otuanya's destiny filled the house and woke Nedu from his angry nap. But when his mother called him to come down for dinner, he stayed in his bed. Nedu imagined his family, betrayers and murderers all of them, sitting down to eat his friend, not caring that there was literal blood on their hands, blood in their stomachs, and blood on their fangs. They were animals.

His mother sent Cherish up to get him.

"I'm not eating," Nedu said.

When Cherish reported Nedu's response, Uzoma felt a twinge of worry. Nedu never refused food. He ate with a fearsome appetite, meals disappearing into his skinny body like stolen evidence. She decided to be annoyed.

"Imagine Nedu releasing the chicken so we wouldn't eat it," she said. "What he deserves is a spanking, not my delicious pepper soup."

***

There had been a subtle heat in his wife's gaze all evening, but Ebube stifled his hope. He didn't want to reach for Uzoma and be rebuffed again. When it was time for bed, he got under the covers and turned his back to her, even though she was wearing that chemise he liked, the one with the red pouted lips all over it, the one whose bodice cupped her small breasts like a prayer.

He felt the sigh of the mattress as she joined him on the bed. And then her hand was on his shirtless shoulder, traveling slowly down his back. Ebube's eyes flew open.

"Bubu," she said, the mist of her breath tickling his ear. She hadn't called him that in ages. "The way you handled that chicken today ehn . . . I was very impressed."

Ebube turned toward her. "Really?"

She took his hand and guided it between her legs. "The way you took control . . ."

In one fluid motion—one that Ebube hadn't known he was still capable of—he launched himself on top of his wife and pinned her hands above her head. Uzoma yelped, the sound of her laughter bouncing off the walls.

Ebube clamped a hand over his wife's mouth. "Shhh . . . the children."

She shrugged an I-don't-care and licked the inside of his palm. Maybe she was being a little reckless, but they'd lived in that house long enough to know that the walls weren't thin. He unclamped her mouth, placed a quick kiss on her lips, and rolled off her.

She held on to his arm. "Where are you going?"

"To lock the door."

Her grip tightened. "Don't."

He laughed. "One of the kids might come in."

"They won't."

Cherish would be on her phone, and Nedu was either still sulking or had devoured the food she'd left outside his door and was now in a post-meal stupor. Either way, Uzoma was sure her children wouldn't show up at their bedroom door. Like ninety-two percent sure. There was something about that eight percent uncertainty, though, the danger it represented, that was doing things to her insides. She wanted Ebube to revel with her in the eight percent, to hold her hands above her head again and make her do every single thing he'd ever been afraid to want.

"Why risk it, though?" He pried his arm free and rolled off the bed. The lock clicked into place. "Much better. Now, where were we?"

Ebube's eyes fell on the bed, on the wall of Uzoma's back now turned against him. He lowered his body carefully beside hers. He asked if everything was okay. She said yes. If he believed her, he'd have the courage to reach for her again, to try to tease out the Uzoma who, just moments ago, was aligning her body with his, taking his hand and leading him places. A space was opening up between them, vast and treacherous. He was too tired to navigate. A soft sadness enveloped him.

"What did I do?"

Uzoma sighed. She had no words to account for her new appetites. Her blooming perversions. These thoughts of moist toothpicks and black uniforms.

"Nothing," she said. "You did nothing."

                              ***

Uzoma had been right. The children were occupied. In Cherish's room, footage of the chicken chase was being intently edited, with added music and sound effects. She kept the video's caption simple: "Epic chicken chase." Cherish watched the likes and comments pop up on her phone, each one giving a little thrill. She whispered a thank you to God or the universe for giving her the idea to cut Otuanya's tether.

Cherish saw a like from Afolabi, and then a comment: [Laughing-crying emoji] omg @CisforCherish your family is comedy goals fr!!!!

Did Afolabi mean comedy goals or comedy gold? Did it matter? All Cherish knew was that her video had made Afolabi laugh. With four exclamation points! Warmth invaded her face, her chest, spreading like fire, claiming territory. On the last day of the school term, standing in line behind him at assembly, she'd pressed her finger to the mole on the back of his neck, something she'd been wanting to do ever since she'd discovered it peeking over the horizon of his uniform collar like a dark, shy sun. He'd turned to her with a quizzical frown, and she'd mouthed sorry and looked away, her stomach quivering with shame. She was sure he'd avoid all interaction with her from that day till forever, but here he was liking her video. Cherish cradled her phone to her heart. She gazed at the ceiling. When they kissed for the first time, she would poke her tongue between the gap in his front teeth.

Meanwhile, Nedu had just woken from a second nap, a hungry nap, and he remembered that Otuanya was gone. Well, not gone gone, not exactly. He was still around, in his mother's soup pot, his final resting place. Nedu's stomach growled, reminding him that some things he couldn't escape. Like hunger. He had taken a stand without thinking, and now, as the pangs pulled at his insides, he hoped none of his family was still downstairs. He didn't want to encounter anyone when he went scrounging for food in the kitchen.

He opened his bedroom door. A tray with a plate of pounded yam and a bowl of pepper soup had been left there, on the floor beside the door, for him. The pepper soup had a light film over it. The food would be cold by now, the white ball of pounded yam slightly hard on the surface. Nedu wondered if it might be okay to still eat the food his mother had made, without actually eating any of Otuanya. He could eat around Otuanya.

Nedu lifted the tray, careful not to make a sound, and retreated into his room, closing the door quietly behind him. He placed the tray on the floor at the foot of his bed and sat before it. From the pepper soup bowl, a large piece of Otuanya confronted him, and Nedu was distressed to realize that he didn't remember which side of the chicken's head had the missing eye. He dipped a finger into the pepper soup. Yes, he would eat around Otuanya. He popped the soup-covered finger into his mouth and sucked on it. His eyes and mouth flooded with liquid as the flavors registered on his tongue, that hint of ginger his mother always added to her pepper soup.

When Nedu tells the story to his family, days later, he will say he left his body, and that by the time he came back, the pounded yam had disappeared, the pepper soup bowl was licked dry, and the chewed-up bones of Otuanya's leg were littering the tray. He will be sincere, and when his mother smiles and calls him her food warrior, when she says she knew he would forget about his chicken friend and make her proud, he will decide that the rest of the story—the part where he'd hidden in the bathroom and stuck a finger down his throat to bring Otuanya back up and into the toilet bowl—will stay with him. That part he will keep for himself.

Breastmilk

Pemi Aguda

Originally published in *One Story* (2021)

The warm, slimy creature that is my son is placed in my arms. He is crying a grating, lusty soprano. I stretch my mouth into the likeness of a smile. I don't look down at the baby. I hold him loosely: too tight and he might squirt out of my grip and ricochet off the white walls of my hospital room.

"We're going to cut the cord now, mummy," one of the nurses says, and I nod. She says *mummy* in that patronizing tone I use when I tell my cousin's children that they are so big and tall and grown now.

"Can I cut it?" Timi asks.

I don't hear what they say to him, how these efficient women tell him no. But I see him step back, his head lowered as if he's been chastised. I could have told him that this is not one of those New Age hospitals that allow men to actively participate in the birth, that the father is merely a bystander here, a witness. But I didn't. There are many things I don't say to my husband.

The baby is taken from me so he can be cleaned, so I can be cleaned too. Through the haze of twelve-hour labor pains, I watch my husband reach out to receive our baby from the nurse, now swaddled in the ewedu-colored cloth we bought. I am tired. My gritty eyes want to close against the world, and my aching body wants to gather its leaking, melting shape into itself so I can recover from all the pushing and groaning and bloody catastrophes of childbirth. But I want to watch Timi's first moments of fatherhood. His body is stiff, in the practiced hold they taught us in prenatal classes: baby's neck in the crook of your elbow, the other hand supporting the rest of the weight. He swings his head toward me—the only part of his body he releases from this wooden stance that proclaims fierce responsibility and a dash of pride—and smiles. Through mine, I see the sheen of his tears.

I turn away and settle back into the pillow.

***

In the morning, my mother shows up. She is telling me that she came as soon as she could, that my father would be proud of this feat of mine, bringing new life into the world. And am I glad? Am I relieved? Am I fine? Am I proud?

I am excused from responding to her barrage because I am a woman who just had a baby, an exhausted woman who endured earth-shifting contractions, who thrashed through a forest of clawing pain, whose pelvic region throbs as if pounded by a pestle. My mother doesn't sit; she hovers above me, tucking a braid away, stroking my cheek.

I roll my eyes. "What of the conference?"

"Bah," she says, waving fingers as if she hadn't spent the last six months putting the event together. "I have a grandchild!"

The headliner of the conference is a friend of hers, a woman who is combining her research on chemosignals at some Netherlands university with knowledge from her grandmother's traditional beliefs and claiming that with practice, we can all smell emotions. When my concern doesn't fade, my mother adds that her assistant is very capable.

A nurse comes to save me from my mother's goodwilled pawing.

"DaSilva?"

Her uniform is so white, her waist so small. She looks like a cardboard cutout, this nurse. She also looks faintly like someone I have seen on Timi's Facebook when I hit "Load More" so that the life he had before me appears in grainy frozen laughter with strangers. Why do some Nigerian hospitals insist on these silly white caps for their nurses? Her cap looks like a diamondless tiara tucked into her afro bun.

"Yes," my mother answers for me. "This is her."

There are many times I wish my mother would be present to speak for me, with her impassioned activist's voice. Like the night Timi confessed his affair, thirty-eight weeks ago. But am I not an adult?

"Your baby is scheduled to receive formula again in thirty minutes," the nurse says, "but I came to see if there are any changes. Any thick liquid? Clear? Yellow?"

As she reaches for the neck of my hospital gown, I catch her wrist. Her face rearranges itself in surprise, and I think she isn't that pretty; her eyes are too close together. "There's no change," I say.

She twists free and brushes the rescued limb against the front of her dress, as if to restore her composure. "Okay, but I still need to take a look, Mrs. Da-Silva—"

"Ms.," my mother corrects. *"Mizzz."*

What does "Mrs." really mean? is a question I grew up hearing my mother pose to people who could only stutter in response.

The nurse's frown deepens; she is unsettled by this interaction with me and my mother. "I'm sorry, *Miz* DaSilva. Your son isn't pooping as much as we'd like. He's okay, but to be safe, I'm going to have to feel around for colostrum, milk."

That's all I did last night while Timi slept in a chair beside me. I prodded and tugged and massaged, but my breasts have stayed swollen to unfamiliar Dcups, nipples stubbornly dry. They told me milk, or something like it, would come a few months into pregnancy, or around birth.

"I said there's nothing." I jerk the top of the gray sack of a gown they have put me in. I turn away from the nurse's unpretty face to my mother's, which is now contemplating me with a frown.

***

Timi holds my hand, and my mother caresses my shoulder while cradling our baby in one elbow. Another day has passed, and the doctor is asking questions before discharging us. I hang limp in Timi's clasp. His palms are always so dry. How do I trust a man whose sweat glands won't betray him? His palms were dry then too, when he stroked my arm and informed me he was going to Abuja for business, just business. But should this man trust his wife who claims she forgives his affair, who pardons his cheating so easily, a wife who says everything is forgotten and buried? A wife who kisses those dry palms the morning after his confession and says, "We're good, babe." Should he trust this woman if she doesn't believe the truth of her own forgiveness?

I wriggle free from Timi's hold and reach for the baby we have not yet named; we have two more days till the naming ceremony. My mother lowers him into my arms.

"And don't worry about lactating," the doctor is saying. "I don't want you to worry at all. Lactation happens late for some women, others not at all. Some women even say breastfeeding is oldfashioned! But everything is fine as long as baby is loving the delicious formula."

I want to ask the doctor how he knows the formula is delicious, if it is more delicious than breastmilk, if the baby can tell the difference.

When we saw the baby's penis for the first time, pointed out to us in the jumble that is an ultrasound, the nurse gave a practiced chuckle. "See how he's proud of that penis!" she said. Timi's eyes liquefied. I turned away from him and away from my son's penis, to look at the fetal growth chart on the wall. A son? My heart broke a little. A son who could grow up to become a man, a man who might hurt other people no matter how well I raise him because a man is a man, even when he is the best man—as Timi has shown me. I gathered myself and turned back to smile at the monitor.

Maybe it started there, my body's rejection of my child, visiting the sins of father on son?

I lower my head to blow air into my baby's face, my mouth a soft *o*. My smile is not forced when he wrinkles his face and blinks at me.

"If you want to see our lactation consultant," the doctor adds, "you're welcome to do so. He's not in-house, though well recommended. Give it some time, I'd say. Baby is fine, poop is fine, all is fine!" The doctor has three horizontal tribal marks on each cheek that squirm when he speaks. My baby's cheeks look extra smooth in comparison. I press my lips to that smoothness. Timi beams at this picture and asks if I'm ready to go home.

***

All our family members come out for the naming ceremony. Their voices ring loud as they celebrate me, celebrate Timi. A first child, a son! Someone has dropped a thick white envelope into my lap—for my hard work, they say. I let the insulting thing slide off.

Timi strolls around in his agbada made from the matching guinea brocade his mother bought for us, a baby-blue shade of sky we haven't seen since harmattan started. He stops to laugh at someone's joke, the cloth billowing around him, so natural, so *man*, so *Timi*. He has been cradling our baby all day, as if eager to show off how modern he is, a rare Nigerian man who "allowed" his wife to keep her mother's name, a man who will be involved in the care of his child. I want to yank the baby from him, but I do not have the right. The one bond that ties baby to mother, at least for the first year, is missing. My breasts oppress me with their emptiness.

We name him Fikayo; we call him Fi. Olufikayo. All the names I suggested were Finn, Fenton, Fran, because my love of *F* names had lingered from devouring all that angsty British literature when I was a teenager. But Timi reminded me that we are Yoruba, not English, and the name should reflect that.

Is there a Yoruba name for "this child was conceived in the throes of hurt and anger"? An Egun name for "this boy is a result of your forgiveness sex after your husband confessed his wrong"?

I acquiesced easily to his sensible argument about the names, remembering how he had quietly rebutted my reservations about becoming his girlfriend six years ago, an elevation from our casual fling. "Come on, we have the same views on the important things, Aduke!" he said. "That's what's important ni t'ori Ọlọrun. That's a foundation not many folks have."

Timi's mother's pastor calls out the names, Olufikayo Olujimi Olatunde. The people cheer and toast with glasses of wine and zobo under the canopy we rented for the day. When the robed pastor dabs anointing oil on Fikayo's head, the baby begins to cry. I jump up to snatch him.

"He's hungry," I murmur to no one in particular, and retreat into the house. I hear music pick up behind me, Sunny Ade blasting from rented speakers, my cousin's children screaming at each other, Timi's mother shouting for the caterer to start serving small chops. The woman's Christian benevolence is what prevents friction between her and my mother, between me and her, between her and Timi. "Love thy neighbor as thyself," she mutters to herself frequently, like a calming mantra, shrugging in acceptance even when she doesn't understand why her son is acting "like a woman," doing household chores and sharing the financial decision-making with me. The microphone screeches and I close the nursery door behind me, but the door is not thick enough to drown them out.

One of my aunties has tied my iro for me, insisting that the tighter the wrapper, the faster my pregnancy pouch will shrink. I release my belly now and flop down into the armchair. I shift Fi in my arms and draw the diaper bag closer with a foot. It is an awkward process; I haven't yet perfected the juggling acts of motherhood.

He quiets when the nib fills his mouth, and I am envious of a plastic bottle.

My aunt finds me dozing off while Fi feeds.

"Ahn ahn, feeding bottle kẹ?" Her gele is maroon and silver, and the light from the window reflects against the scaly material. I squint and look down at Fi. He has fallen asleep.

"Auntie," I say.

"But kilode? Why are you not breastfeeding, mgbọ?" She crosses her arms under her own breasts. "Deyemi's wife had the nerve to tell me she was not breastfeeding so her breasts won't sag. Sag! You too, Aduke? Does your mother know about this decision?"

"Auntie, auntie!" I check to make sure Fi is still sleeping and lower my voice. "There's no milk, auntie." I have begun to cry.

My aunt's face relaxes. She moves to pick Fi up, places him in his cot. She leans forward then, as if to hug me.

"I know what to do. Jumoke had this same problem, but you should see her now! The baby girl is three, and we're begging her to stop. I will send you one agbo that my sister makes in Ijebu. You will rub it like . . ." She reaches for my breasts, through the babyblue brocade, through my bra, and begins to knead. I feel myself leaving my body through a frustrated sigh, floating to the ceiling of the lilac nursery with the white silhouettes, above my own gele, above my auntie's gele, which dips forward in rhythm with her hands, above my body, above my shame.

***

Our friends visit with gifts that are not newbornbaby appropriate. Only Sandra, who writes an annoyingly wholesome mummy blog with a large readership, shows up without a hard-edged toy, but she also brings along a pious look to throw at the feeding bottle and formulas. If I were to check, I would probably find an irate blog post railing against them. When he catches the glance, Timi tells Sandra that I need to rest. The others bring laughter and warmth and kisses for Fi, but I am grateful when I walk the last person out the front door and return to the silence of our living room. Timi is sitting on the edge of an armchair, and I know he wants to speak with me. I grab a bib from the floor and head to the nursery, to my baby, to hide.

"Aduke."

I turn to look at my husband, his wide nose, the Cupid's bow that would fight Rihanna's for perfection. The first time I kissed him, I let my tongue trace that dip, recarving it with my lust.

"Are you okay?" he asks now.

"Yeah, why?"

"You've been kind of distant."

What I should say is: I don't care about your stupid ex; I care that I don't know how to be angry about her. What I say instead is: "We just had a baby, Timi. Have you read any of Sandra's articles about motherhood?" The laugh that punctuates my sentence is a weak sputter.

Timi points at me, then at himself. "We're okay?" He wants my eyes to meet his; I hear it in his question. They meet. Mine skitter away.

"We're great," I say. I look down to find my baby's bib crumpled in my fist. I straighten out the butterflies on soft white cotton, blue and orange and pink. "I'm just tired, you know?"

"But you—"

I look up, afraid he will say that I am not even breastfeeding, that he will ask me what is making me tired.

"You don't even let me help with Fikayo. You're always sleeping in the damn nursery. This wasn't our plan o, Aduke."

Of course, Timi is not insensitive. He rises right along with me when Fi cries us awake. I keep shushing him away, back to sleep, away from the nursery.

"I just feel a bit guilty about the breastmilk thing. Maybe I'm overcompensating." I push the fiction out of my lungs easily.

Back in Sunday school, where my mother used to send me before she decided religion hated women, the teacher would pipe, "To err is human; to forgive, divine," even if we kids didn't know what it meant to err. Now that Timi has shown me what it means, the homily taunts me. If to forgive is divine, why am I resisting my own divinity? I want to feel the righteousness that comes with forgiving infidelity, but all I feel is shame at my lack of backbone, my lack of indignation, and fear that if it happens again, I will just as easily forgive Timi.

My husband is good, has been good. This was a fluke, and he confessed immediately because he knew I would want to know immediately, and he was sorry, and he is sorry every day, and I could see him hurting because he knew he had hurt me, and he is so very sorry, sorry in a way that I believe?

Am I even my mother's daughter, to be thinking about forgiveness?

Now Timi is asking if I think this is postpartum depression.

"I'm not depressed. Just tired."

"Come back to bed," he begs. "I miss you."

I flinch.

"God, I'm not talking about sex. I'm not a monster!"

I raise both hands in surrender. "Yeah, we can move his cot to our room tomorrow. How about that?"

When Timi lets out a dissatisfied breath, covering his face, its beautiful features, with his hands, I flee into the nursery, closing the door that is only wood, not metal, not thick enough to protect me. But why do I need protection? Why shouldn't *he* be seeking protection from *me*? I want to be the type of woman who would have turned into a pillar of flames when Timi told me about sex with the ex in Abuja. I want to have singed the confession off his tongue until the smell of his own burning choked him, robbing him of oxygen till he was flat on his face, at my feet, melting in my fury. I want to be a woman like my mother. There are YouTube videos of my mother cutting down the governor at a rally organized by her nonprofit for women's development. The governor had said she should leave politics to men. "Don't you dare, Mr. Olusegun Adetula!" my mother screamed, spittle gathering in the corner of her Ruby Woo-painted lips. "Don't you dare belittle the women who carry this society. We carry it!" But no, I went straight into his arms. Mine was a faltering anger: here, then gone. My mother would be disgusted to see the weakness in her spawn.

***

We're in the nursery. I am seated on the floor between my mother's knees on a folded blanket, feeding Fikayo while my mother lines my scalp with oil. The smell of the coconut oil meets the smell of formula in my nostrils. Fi is naked against my bare breasts, skin-toskin bonding my mother scoffed at the first time she saw us in this position. "Bonding?" She laughed. "Where did you read about this one now?" But this proximity to his sucking mouth, even if the milk doesn't come, has me flushed with feeling. Fi tugs on the bottle against my breasts while my mother tugs softly at my hair, plaiting straight cornrows. This is what it is like to be a mother and a daughter.

Timi is cooking okra soup in the kitchen, and when a waft strays into the room, I hear my mother's belly rumble. We laugh. A husband who shares the kitchen with me is something I am proud of, a way of life my mother approves of, preaches. She works through a tangled section, and I stiffen my neck in discomfort.

"Sorry, does it hurt?"

I shake my head.

"How's the copywriting?"

"Fine. I submitted June's calendar yesterday."

"It's stupid they didn't give you time off."

"It's fine. If I stop, they'll find some mass comm student to do it for cheaper. It's just words; I can handle it."

"And Timi's work?"

"Good. He's building a website for Coke with Deji."

"And"—she continues to plait my hair—"are the two of you okay?"

I take a deep breath and try to relax my shoulders so my mother doesn't sense the tension this question elicits. "Why?"

I feel her shrug. I wonder if she has somehow smelled the strain through my scalp. Maybe her professor friend has taught her nose a trick or two. And if so, what emotion is she identifying? Shame? Resentment? Anger? How do I tell my mother, the woman who told me never to stay with a man who disrespects me in any way, that I am doing just that? That not only did Timi disrespect me with this affair, but I couldn't even flare up in response?

Whenever we heard a story of a husband who left, who hit, who had another family in a village somewhere, my mother would joke that my father—"that one who died to escape my wahala"—knew dying was better than misbehaving. That he knew she wouldn't have stayed a minute longer, that her blood was thicker than that. He had met her on the streets of Unilag waving a placard that read *Women Are Students Too! Students, Not Maids! Students, Not Sex Objects!* He joined the protest that day, later finding out she was the last daughter from a polygamous family she never completely forgave for their lack of attention. "That's your mama's origin story," he used to say to me when I sat on his lap and pulled at his full beard, "our superhero." Joking about my father's death made me squirm, even though I recognized the dark humor as the coping mechanism it was. But she would look at me with those blazing eyes that want all the good in the world for me and say, "Women suffer enough. Don't add man problem on top. Keep your shoes beside the door."

I can't tell her now that maybe her superior blood thinned with me.

"We're fine," I say. But I have waited too long. She knows I am hedging.

She will not push it, though. Instead, she will scoot her chair away from the table later at dinner, announcing her departure, leaving a full bowl of delicious food untouched, leaving Timi thinking that he has offended her with too much salt. But I will know it is my mother bringing her protests from the streets of Lagos into my home.

***

My mother is gone and Timi wants to talk again; he wants to hammer this out once and for all. He wants to be sure we are good, are we good, are we good, arewegoodarewegood? Timi wants to know, Timi wants.

I walk into our bedroom where we have moved the cot, away from Timi's questioning voice. I want to look down into my baby's face with his always-puckered brows, to have his lustrous brown eyes look back into mine, his chubby puffpuff cheeks reassure me with their fullness, his plastered curls remind me of newness and freshness and growth.

Instead I find my baby turning blue in the face. His fingers are fisted tight; his arms are flailing little sticks. Has the strain hanging in the air of our bedroom asphyxiated our son?

***

When the doctor tells me that Fikayo has a gastroesophageal reflux, an allergic reaction to the formula, that breastmilk would be ideal at this point, I feel a sharp pain in my breasts. Can guilt be felt physically, like a blade on a finger, like a cramp in the calf, like biting your own tongue?

***

The lactation consultant's office is in the Boys' Quarters. We squeeze past two jeeps in the narrow driveway to get to the oneroom office at the back of the main house. The signage is lopsided, dusty, but my doctor said Dr. Laoye is good at what he does.

Timi and I sit on the couch while he paces.

"Have you taken any cod-liver oil?" he asks after I tell our story, that a fourth formula is being tested on Fi, that my baby is now bones in a bag of soft skin, that my auntie's agbo didn't work.

I shake my head.

Dr. Laoye reminds me of those boys I loved when I was thirteen. The older boys in our estate who looked big and tall and bounced with a swagger to buy Guinness from the shop where I would be buying matches or Maggi or cotton wool. They looked like the epitome of adulthood to me with their loud, uncontained laughter and colorful rubber wristbands, as if they knew exactly what they wanted and how to get it: beer, life.

And that had been Timi too, so dogged in his pursuit of me, his want of me. What fractured this want, insinuated a pause long enough for Abuja to happen?

"This isn't about you," is what my mother might say in this situation, as she has done before, those days I came home crying about a boy who didn't love me back, a friend who stopped talking to me, a job I didn't get. How she would straighten my shoulders and wipe my face and insist, "It isn't about you. Roll it off. Those who appreciate you will come." How she would embrace me, "my gentle, sensitive baby" whispered into my hair in a voice I thought sounded mournful or scared, and I would go back into the world trying to be less gentle, bolder, demanding more from life once I saw things through the filter of my mother's opinions.

Dr. Laoye asks me to sit on the consultation chair and take off my blouse and bra. I like that he has not looked to Timi for permission or acknowledgment, unlike many nurses at the hospital who ask about my husband before attending to me.

I look nowhere as the cool from the air conditioner tightens my nowbare nipples. Not at Timi, not at the doctor. I pin my arms down, fighting the urge to cover myself.

Dr. Laoye peers at my breasts, then cups them in his gloved hands, latex against breasts.

This is the first time a man has touched my breasts since the night of confession. That night with Timi that brought us Fi, that angry night when I allowed my nails to dig into his back, scratch at his skin, draw blood, when he held my breasts and bit them, and I arched into the violence of his mouth, asking him to press down harder, longer, forever.

Could my confused pleasure of that night have ruined me for my child?

The doctor squeezes gel into his palm and gets to work on my breasts. The gloves glide over my skin with the slippery, tingly gel, with a soft sound, his fingers moving first in an elliptical motion from the sternum, round and round, till he tugs at the nipples.

As the tugs become harder, I hunch over. Dr. Laoye lightly grazes my shoulder, tender, an unspoken *relax*. My eyes shoot up to find Timi's. His face is blank, too straight, and I know he is struggling to show me nothing.

I think: Look at another man touching me, Timi.

And then I feel it, a warm trickle out of my left nipple. The milk feels like a living creature crawling out of me. I look down at my chest, then up to share this moment with Timi, but he has turned away.

***

The hospital wants to test my breastmilk before they introduce it to Fi. *My* breastmilk. Fi's. Even while the doctor explains milk content to me, why they are testing, how the mother passes on more than fat and protein, how toxicity the mother has been exposed to can be a risk to the baby, all I can hear is *your* breastmilk. Timi's gaze keeps drifting down to my unbound breasts under the boubou.

Later, my mother shows up at the hospital with the woman from her conference, the smell professor. The woman has decided to take up a visiting professorship from Unilag, and they have just come back from lunch. I reach for my mother's hands. "We're waiting to hear," I say.

"Timi?" I can see my mother's nose wrinkle when she says his name. I will not confirm her suspicions.

"With Fi," I reply.

Another nurse comes to stand by the bed. "It's time to pump again, madam."

The nurse pulls apart the flaps of the hospital gown and starts to apply lubrication to my nipples. I do not move to help. I do not move away. I just lie there, a body. When the pump has been attached and turned on, my mother's professor friend stands to leave the room. The swish of her colorful kimono disappears around the door. My mother goes out after her.

I am now alone with the nurse, who is intently watching the liquid stream down the tubes into the bottle. *What are you looking for?* I want to ask. This feeling of milk out of my breasts is so strange, as if a string were being unspooled out and out and out. *What can you see?*

***

When I stir from sleep, my mother and her professor friend have returned to the room. My mother rushes to fuss over me.

"Mummy," I say, shifting my face away from her pesky touches. "Do you want to check on Timi and Fi?"

"Yes, yes." She hurries out of the room, happy to be useful, leaving me with the professor.

"Good evening," I whisper, remembering my manners. She turns toward me. Her face looks sunken, the wrinkles fanned around like the lines on a palm to be read. She nods at my greeting and walks closer to the bed, almost regal in carriage. She stops before she reaches me.

I am curious: What is it about me that is repellent to her? Why won't she come closer? Can her trained nose smell my shame? My failing motherhood, wifehood? My failed daughterhood, too?

She is quiet for so long that I think she has not heard. But then she takes two steps closer. When she speaks, her accent is a flavored reflection of all the places she has lived, nasal and clipped and flat and lyrical all at once. "Good evening." She shifts. "What is it?"

I am not surprised at her question. "What can you smell?" I ask, doing the Nigerian thing of responding to a question with another.

She laughs, but her face is sad. "Darling," she says, and this endearment, which I would find annoying coming from anyone else, fits. "But darling, you smell a lot like your mother."

***

My mother walks her friend out to get a taxi, and I slip out of bed. I move down the corridor, climb the flight of stairs that will bring me to my baby's ward. I find Timi asleep on a chair next to Fi's cot, a thin curtain their only privacy from the rest of the room. I stand there staring at my family.

"Timi," I whisper, and he jerks awake.

"Hey," he says, rubbing his eyes. He looks at my breasts, and I follow his gaze. There are splotches where milk has leaked onto my gown.

"Timi," I say again.

He stands and leads me out of the ward to the dim corridor. A fluorescent light farther down blinks every few seconds.

"Hey, what's wrong?" His hands rest on my shoulders. He runs them down my arms, slides them back up.

"I've forgiven you," I say. For my job, I rely on the thesaurus, finding new ways to say old things, fancy ways to turn the client's directives into copy the consumers can relate to. But for my own life, the words are flat. I can say only what I can say.

He becomes still. He swallows. "You said you had."

"I have. I swear." I raise my hands to trap his on my shoulders. While my belly swelled with our baby, I would smile at my beautiful husband, who was the first man I felt confident enough about to introduce to my mother, a man I was sure wouldn't misbehave. Surely I must have suckled some fire from my own mother's breasts, even if just a trace. I press down on Timi. Hard. "I just hate that it was so easy."

I feel him go rigid. This is the first time I am allowing us to discuss the affair since he dropped that suitcase and knelt in front of me, crying, begging for forgiveness. "What are you saying, Aduke?"

There is a scar on Timi's chin, a small diagonal line hidden mostly by his beard, and I like to rub my thumb against the slight elevation. He says he doesn't know how it got there. But what would the scar say if it could speak? If the body could tell what it doesn't forget, doesn't process? I reach out to touch it now.

"I'm saying I am angry that it was so easy," I tell him. "I needed to say that to you."

The doctor says toxicity passes unto the child through breastmilk. If I don't tell Timi these things, will my fluids flood with unvocalized coarse emotions? Will I choke my son with the force of them?

My hands fall to my side; I release Timi. He drops to a squat. He is trembling; he holds his face. "Give me something to do. Give me a list, anything. What can I do?" His voice thickens. "What can I do?" He loses balance and latches onto my knee. I look down at my husband's head. There isn't anything he can do differently. This is about me, was always about me.

The fluorescent bulb flickers again, like a flashlight panning an abandoned room, lighting up things that have stayed in the dark too long.

***

The next morning, my milk is declared safe for Fi by the doctor with the tribal marks. He smiles wide, all those scarred commas stretching.

When Fi is placed into my arms, when his lips and gums circle and clamp onto my nipple, I cannot stop crying. Emotion rises up my chest, hot and forceful, up my neck, up my head, then crashes over me. I pull him closer to my heavy breasts. I hold him tight. My wet kisses slobber all over his forehead.

Does that nose look like mine? Those eyes, like my mother's? "My sweet baby," I cry. "I love you," I weep. "I love you," I sob.

My mother sits by my head, letting me cry, stroking my braids. Timi shows up just outside the door, keeping his distance, still reeling from yesterday's talk. My mother stops stroking. She stands up, beams at me, says, "Look, my baby is a mother. Her own woman." Her voice is gentle—no mourning, no concern, no fear.

I nod at Timi to come closer, and he stumbles across the threshold to join my mother and me, my baby and me.

2024 WORKSHOP STORIES

What Happened to Aboy

Joshua Chizoma

The complaints about Aboy began small small, then became a drowning.

This was during Jide's second year away from home. Spurred by sudden gusts of loneliness, he would call his father, and in the familiar cadence of the older man's voice, the pause and cough after every few sentences, he would find home. In exchange for Jide's stories of the antics of fellow third-year law students, his father told him about the new church being built opposite their house, whose noise — accusing, unrelenting — was like it was sent from hell; about Obinna's new shop, to which even customers from Lagos travelled to buy goods; and, in benediction, about Aboy. This was how Jide learned that Aboy had tattooed a skull on his forearm, that he smoked weed for breakfast, that money disappeared when he was around, and that he did not fear their father again.

After listening to his father, Jide would call Aboy, and thereafter segue to Obinna. It was usually at the end of his conversation with Obinna that his heart would find calm. He and Obinna began each call by laughing about how it was that their father sounded more like a petulant child as he grew older, given to conveying every bit of information through a complaint. Thereafter, Obinna would tell him where their father's exaggerations ended and the facts began. They always came back to this: how weird it was that Aboy was *now* considered a bad boy.

Their father's constant refrain when they were children was that Aboy did not behave like a boy growing up in Aba. What he meant was that Aboy had no quick wit, no street smartness garnered from having to push and shove to get ahead. That was true. Aboy had been a piece of delicate china, a break waiting to happen. He was unusually gullible as a child, always being tricked by the other children; his books stolen; his clothes ripped; forever the prey. When Jide entered university, he would see his brother in the boys and girls that grew up in Lagos and Port Harcourt and Abuja. Children who could afford to be foolish, for whom means and access provided a soft landing, respite from their iberibe. Aboy was like that.

Their father had no such inclinations. He was a brawny, loud man who sold meat at the local market. In the evenings he would come home reeking of struggle, crusted blood on his clothes, the smell of death clinging to him. He was happiest when a bottle of Star was in front of him, Osadebe's music blasting at eardrum-defeating levels, and when in the company of other men, screaming at Arsène Wenger to please get his boys to play like they wanted to win a trophy.

While Jide and Obinna knew from early on how to get out of their father's way, the lies to tell to escape a beating, Aboy struggled to develop that skill. His lies were a joke. Affronted by how incongruous they often were, their father would give him a further beating for having the temerity to tell bad lies.

The night Obinna complained to Jide about Aboy, Jide was at the back of the faculty building, smoking. He sat on a bench, looking over at a wall dividing his faculty from another. He thought of where Obinna would be, perhaps shutting down his shop. He often felt weird speaking to his family after smoking weed. He felt like they could perhaps smell the stink on his breath or tell that his head felt like it was stuck in a washing machine, swirling and swirling.

'Nna, kedu?' Obinna said when he took the call.

'Udo di,' Jide replied. Highlife music pulsated in the background, the suitable accompaniment to pepper soup and happy men and a carefree Saturday evening.

Obinna listened as Jide recounted what their father had told him earlier about Aboy. His laugh boomed into Jide's ears. 'This man eh,' he clicked his tongue, 'he should leave that boy alone before he gives himself high blood pressure.'

The music was gone when Jide was done, so he clearly heard the sadness in Obinna's voice when he said, 'Jide, nwanne, Daddy is not entirely wrong. Aboy has changed. Aboy is no longer the boy you know.'

***

The year Aboy was born was the year Jide's childhood ended.

Jide had just finished his first school-leaving certificate examinations and had a long stretch of days lying bare, beyond which was secondary school. In the mornings, as soon as their parents left for work, he and his friends sat down before Jide's television. Seasonal films were the rave. *Merlin* versus *Legend of the Seeker*, *Xena the Warrior Princess* versus *Hercules*. They were not allowed to watch *Spartacus*, but they did, anyway.

In the evenings, at the field just behind his house, they would gather to play football. In those glory days they took names to themselves: Santos, Sanchez, Ronaldinho. A gathering of two boys was enough to form a team. Anything that could roll easily became a football. Yelps and cries would rend the air, as the boys luxuriated in the freedom of being just children.

Fights often erupted with the speed of a fired shot. The kindling was flimsy: a contested goal, a malicious kick, teasing that pinched too hard. Chekwube, who eventually became a police officer, would put his large frame in between fighting boys and threaten to slap anyone who swung another blow. Jide would step in afterwards, a pint-sized arbiter, asking each side to air their grievances, and then deciding whose fault it was. He'd get riled up when anyone accused him of being partial and would complain to Obinna later on, asking him, 'Was I not fair? Was I not fair?' Obinna would be befuddled by the tenacity with which Jide defended his integrity. He failed to recognise within himself a variant of this same trait, the singleness of purpose that made him certain, even at that age, that his path diverged from his older brother's: he was not going to university; he was going to be a businessman.

One afternoon, as Jide and his friends pooled in Jide's sitting room watching a movie, Aunty Ngozi showed up. She stomped to the TV, turned it off, and pointed to the door, the fat in her arm dancing to unheard music.

'Everybody, go home!' she thundered.

'Where did my sister keep the baby things, do you know?' she asked Jide. She went into the bedroom and returned bearing items their mother had bundled into a bunch. Then she went around gathering other things, ticking off a list she had in her head.

Just before she left, she came to sit on the cushion. She hugged Jide. 'Your mother is in the hospital with your father. You will soon have a baby brother or sister, by God's grace.' She looked earnestly at him. 'You are now a big boy, Jidenna. You should not be playing too much. Is this how you will take care of Obinna and your new younger brother or sister?'

She rubbed his head. 'Stay here and wait for Obinna to come back from school. Then you two should be praying for your mother so she will deliver safely. You know God listens to the prayers of children, eh?'

The days that followed were dark. In the daytime, their father would be in the market, and Aunty Ngozi would stay with Jide's mother in the hospital as she battled the complications that came with the surgery through which she'd birthed the baby. At night, Jide's father would be at the hospital, and Aunty Ngozi would go be with her family. In the sadness of the early days, the newborn remained unnamed for months. He would become 'Aboy' because Jide needed a name for the three-month-old he and Obinna and the women from the church had to take care of. He would stay 'Aboy' even after his father remembered to give him a name.

Most nights, the children would be alone. Jide, holding the baby, marvelled at the precious bundle in his hands. One night, the boy could not be pacified, his voice slashing through the night as though he wanted to wake the dead. Obinna slept, leaving Jide to conjure all the tricks he could muster, all the baby sounds he knew, none of which seemed to placate the boy. As Aboy cried, a floodgate opened up inside Jide, and teardrops rained down too. At twelve, he did not realise it, but he was letting out frustrations at the many things he could not be, at the fact that on that very evening his father had come home to say that their mother had said she was tired. 'What can I do if she is tired? Is it not two of us that are in this fight together? Tell me, what can I do if she is tired?' His face had been open, like he wanted a response from Jide. Then he had sighed and headed for the door. Midway, he had turned back and walked to the cot where Aboy lay, lifted the boy and cradled him tenderly, swaying just so, just so. He had sighed again and laid the boy back. Then he had left.

'Please, stop crying. Please, please, stop crying,' Jide said now, in between hiccups. And the boy quietened.

When the woman from the church came in the morning, she saw the two curled up, Jide enfolding his brother on the bed where they lay.

***

After he spoke with Obinna Jide knew he had to see Aboy. There was a part of him still hanging to disbelief, a latch-on that only truth could dislodge.

When he got home on a sweltering Saturday afternoon, he saw Aboy lying on the couch in their parlour, his legs hanging off the arms of the chair, his feet dusty. He was wearing a pair of jersey shorts and had his arms flung over his head, bushy armpits facing the ceiling. His snores sounded like a faulty motor engine, an assault to the quiet of the house. Standing at the door, Jide took his eyes to the boy, marvelling at the delicacy in his features, his face, his lips. Aboy was going to be taller than Obinna and he, Jide saw. If he decided to become a gym bro, girls would be in trouble. And see how innocent he looked, his Aboy. Jide contemplated what, in this familiar stranger, he could recognise.

Just then, Aboy opened his eyes. The smile that climbed to his face was the sun rising.

'Chief, welcome,' he said.

'How you dey?'

'Nothing spoil,' Aboy responded. 'Would you like something to eat? How is Enugu? You have changed o.'

The banter felt like water from a rock – unnatural, but easy.

Over the course of the following days, standing in the same place as his brother, Jide knew that the earth had moved. In the mornings, he would dress up for his university entrance examination lessons and when he came back he would sit in his room. He'd disappear in the evenings, returning late at night, the smell of all he'd inhaled announcing his presence.

Obinna came for the weekend, and the three played a match. Jide could see that even though Obinna was still the best player, Aboy played with fierce concentration, tackling with intent, purposeful in the little violences he engineered on the field. This, and the flashes of a violent streak that were evident in the fights he always got into off the field, the hardness in his eyes, the ungentle way he moved through the world, told Jide that Aboy had become the man their father wanted.

But then money started leaving Jide's wallet. It began with small notes, one hundred naira here, another two hundred there, till one time a whole one thousand naira disappeared. Jide did not talk about it but noticed that, like his father, he began carrying his wallet with him even to the bathroom.

One time Jide woke up and could not find his phone on the bed where he had left it. He called his father on his other phone, a small Nokia, scarcely able to keep the fear out of his voice.

'Aboy has taken my phone. I left it on the bed, and I woke up and can't find it.'

There was a long pause before his father said, 'I plugged it in the parlour for you. You were sleeping when they brought the light.'

Jide was filled with chagrin, but it was mostly relief that coursed through him. At no time did he feel guilt at the false accusation, or how easy it was for him to point a finger at no one else other than Aboy.

The day before he left Aba, Jide sat down with his father in the parlour, listening to the news. It was something inconsequential. The man on the radio seemed quite excited, and so sounded like he was both shouting and in a rush. Jide and his father sat, pretending to listen. Something was lurking, like promised rain riding on the rays of fierce sunshine. It was Jide who first poked at it.

'What are we going to do?'

His father looked at him.

'About Aboy.'

His father sighed his age. He said, 'You know what to do when your child is sick. You know what to do when your child fails an exam. Even if a girl comes tomorrow and says, "See this baby on my breast, your son Aboy gave me the pregnancy," it is nothing new. But what do you do when your child is a thief? What kind of burden does God place on a parent that way?'

The radio droned on.

'Every time, I wonder what went wrong. Is it because he has been home since he finished secondary school? He is not the first to do so, is he? Am I the one that gives admission to universities? Was I too harsh on him? But I was trying to avoid this exact thing. Aba is no place for a boy without a strong hand gripping him. Now look, just look.'

There were no words to describe the pain Jide heard his father speak. The older man's voice broke in several places. He heaved like he was beseeching God. He turned to look fully at Jide and said, 'Is this the child your mother died for?'

***

When their mother was pregnant with Aboy, she looked like she had eaten the sun for breakfast. She would be walking down the street, Jide and Obinna on either side, the coming child pushing out in front of her, and some stranger would stop to tell her that she was carrying the pregnancy well, that she looked like she was going to have a girl. She would laugh, lift her face to the clouds and mutter an amen. The laughter pealed in the house throughout the pregnancy. It introduced a version of their mother that did not make a fuss if the boys soiled their outfits and allowed them to eat whatever they wanted at dinner time. The laughter disappeared when Aboy came, and many other things followed the hole the silence created.

As a toddler, Aboy was Jide's shadow, tottering after him, squealing with pure delight in the evenings when Jide would come to pick him from his crèche, and nestling into his arms to sleep. Jide's was the face at Aboy's PTA meetings and inter-house sports events and graduation ceremonies. His was the hand that fed him and clothed him and cleaned him. As Aboy shed the chubbiness of babyhood, he seemed to inhabit a world in his own head, speaking sparingly and laughing even less. He would disappear into silences and reappear with questions. 'I don't know anything about our mother. Do you think she would like me?'

Jide would try to capture their mother in a glass for Aboy to drink, but often came up empty. He noticed that he could only talk about their mother using the language of loss, recounting the things that went away into the night when she died: a waiting smile after school each day, a steady hand resting on his shoulder and steering him through life, and the version of their father that was quick to absorb happiness, less prone to an outburst.

The version of their father that Aboy met lived on the settee in their parlour, had his ears glued to the radio with a bottle of beer in front of him. He was away all day, coming home in the evenings. He would listen as Aboy talked about his classes and his friends and unicorns and creatures he saw when he slept. The man would rub Aboy's head and ask him if he had eaten something, if his stockings needed to be replaced, and was it not his bedtime yet? But their father began to pay attention as more plates slipped from Aboy's careless hands, and more books were lost because he did not remember to zip up his school bag, and more injuries showed up on his skin, maps of his forgetfulness. But the beatings did not start till the day their father came for Aboy's inter-house sports competition.

Aboy had been in his last year in primary school, Obinna just entering senior secondary school, while Jide was preparing for his senior secondary school examinations. Jide's father sat with other parents in the stadium. He fanned himself in the heat, his top buttons open to reveal a hairy chest. Mothers yelled encouragements to their children, and students walked about wearing the colours of their different houses. There was a band drumming energy into the air. The arena crackled with electricity.

Aboy was to represent his house in the 100-metre dash. At the line up, he raised his hand to his face to shield his eyes from the sun, scanned the seats, and saw his father. His face broke into a thousand tiny pieces and he jumped up and down. His father gave him a thumbs up.

'On your marks.'

The children went on one knee.

'Get set.'

The whistle went off, and the boys hurled themselves forward like human-sized rockets. There were yells of excitement as someone took the lead. Then stumbled. Two others jostled beside each other. An underdog shot out from behind. A winner. Jide's father did not see any of this. His eyes had not left the starting line. He was staring at Aboy, who squatted on his haunches, watching the race. And then he stood. There was a wet patch on the front of his shorts.

***

After he got back from Aba, Jide threw himself into trying to save his brother like someone determined to put out a raging fire. He asked Aboy what he wanted to do in addition to preparing for his UTME. That began the parade of skills Aboy tried to learn. They went from welding to carpentry, tailoring to graphics design. Each time, Jide would convince his father or Obinna to pay. But they all ended the same way: Aboy would be enthusiastic at first, giving weekly reports of his progress. Then he'd do something stupid, like fight his boss or sell something that was not his to sell. More commonly, items would start disappearing whenever he came around.

One night, after yet another disgruntled instructor – this time, the graphics designer who had come highly recommended – called to inform Jide that he could no longer continue to teach Aboy, Jide dialled Aboy's number. He walked around the campus as he spoke to Aboy. From the hostel to the faculty of law, to the physiotherapy lecture halls, to Chitis Foods, where he sometimes worked on the weekends.

'My bro, what is all this? You are not getting younger. You should be thinking about your life.'

Aboy kept quiet.

'What exactly is the problem? Tell me.'

Jide could hear him breathing on the other end. Yet, he did not say anything. There was a wall separating them, too high for Jide to scale, impregnable by his entreaties.

'Am I not talking to you, my friend? What is wrong with you? Do you want to spoil your life? Why are you so foolish?'

Jide's anger was a curled whip, lashing furiously. He was unsure if the sound he heard just before he hung up was from Aboy sobbing or chuckling.

When Jide suggested that Aboy stay with Obinna, Obinna hesitated.

'Is it a good idea him staying in my shop? Is there no other option we could take?' His words were as careful as a worm wriggling through thorns.

'Nwanne, I don't know what else to do.'

'I can pay for him to do something else. Maybe he could even join the military. I hear that stubborn boys get clear eyes when they go into the military.'

'How do we go about that?' Jide asked.

'But will he even survive the military? I hear some people die from all the tests they are forced to take.'

'If he is joining bad boys and snatching bags, he should be able to survive military training,' Jide said.

Obinna laughed. 'Don't worry, he can stay with me,' he continued. 'See how we are talking about our own brother like he is a prayer point. Chai!'

'Aboy is now one of those boys. God have mercy.'

***

The first time Aboy was in a fight, it was because another kid said that he was the one who killed his mother.

That Sunday, the Sunday school teacher pulled Jide aside after service, a sniffling Aboy beside her. 'I have handled it,' she said, 'that other child had no right saying that sort of cruel thing to him.'

She turned to Aboy.

'You, if your mother was here, she would have been so angry with you. Do you know that she used to be an usher? She did not take nonsense from anybody. Your brothers can testify. Do you people tell him these things?'

The woman sputtered and ground to a halt when she saw the answer on Jide's face. Her retreat was hasty, with muttered apologies.

As Jide wiped Aboy's nose and cleaned his tears, he knew he would not tell their father about the fight. By then, he had begun devising means to get the boy to escape their father's wrath. It was the reason he had started taking Aboy with him to football matches. Aboy would hold the shirts and shoes of the older boys as they played. He soon graduated to helping them run little errands – a bottle of water, a pack of sweets, letters to their lovers. Jide did not say anything when Aboy began to be sent to buy alcohol, and when the others made jokes about the size of his penis even as such a young boy and what he would do to girls when he grew into a man. Jide convinced himself that it was because in those moments, Aboy looked like he had eaten the sun, his laughter reminding Jide of someone else who had gone away with the darkness.

The weekend before Jide left for university, Aboy had gone to play outside. It was a Saturday, which meant that their father often had good sales, which also meant that he was typically in a good mood. But that day, he wasn't. As the darkness stole into the evening, the thought flitted through Jide's mind that Aboy had not come home. To think about it further meant getting up, going outside and speaking to people, and then having to muster anger enough to scold the boy when he found him. All of that seemed too much for Jide, who was lying on the couch, playing a game on his phone. When his father came in, looked around and exploded with 'Where is that stupid Aboy?' Jide realised what a reckless thing he'd done.

Aboy eventually came back, stood by the door, his face a mask of terror, his eyes pleading, pleading.

'Where are you coming from? How many times have I told you not to be outside this house after 8pm? How many children do you see outside by this time? Is it that all the things I have been saying do not enter your head?'

He had been at their neighbour's. He had been watching *Super Story*.

'Is it that you cannot watch *Super Story* in this house? Or even, if you don't watch *Super Story*, will anything happen to you? Can't you stay in and read like your mates?'

His father reached for his belt, and just then Aboy ran and stood behind Jide.

There was no need for asking, Jide was supposed to step out of the way. But he just stood. For an interminable minute, a wordless exchange moved from father to son and back again. Then their father lowered his hand.

***

The night before their final paper, Jide's entire class showed up at the library – someone had asked the librarian for this last favour. Few had their books open before them, but the majority were in clusters, trading 'you remember when's' and laughter and phone numbers and promises. Someone played Wizkid from an MP3 player. A group outside sang worship songs, trying to drown out those inside the library. The air was heavy with weariness and with the anxious dreams of young people about to become unemployed. Jide sat alone just outside the library, yet he felt a sharp sense of kinship with his classmates, a wistful longing for what was the end of an era.

His phone rang. Excitement rippled through him as he saw Obinna's name flashing across his screen. There was a party, his father had told him when he'd called earlier. Obinna wanted it to be a surprise. Obinna, their father told him, went around telling everyone that he now had a barrister in the family; they should treat him with respect.

'Hello,' Jide said.

He could hear Obinna on the other side. He was crying.

'Hello,' Jide said again, this time a lot more deflated. Then he added, 'What did Aboy do?'

'This boy cleared out my account. I am not sure how he got my ATM card …'

Jide hung up. He sat through the phone ringing. Obinna called, his father called, then Obinna sent a text. He would call Obinna later, he told himself, while remembering how, just the last month, he'd had to send money to his father to replace a phone that went missing at home; how many times random people found his number and said Aboy took something of theirs; the girl that'd called him crying so hard, so hard; she'd given her bag to Aboy to hold for a minute. When she came back, all of her money was gone. Now, this.

The tiredness came crashing over him in waves.

The next day, as Jide stood in the queue to get into the examination hall, he was struck by several agitations: that he was not ready for the exam; that he did not have the disposition of someone who was writing his final paper, morose as he was; and that he was deliberately forgetting something.

Sometime during the exam he became very anxious. It suddenly seemed important for him to go out and call Aboy. He hurried through the questions, his words muddling together, clumping together on the page. And then it passed. He was calm again.

When he was done, he stood outside and watched all his classmates celebrating. They ran around the faculty premises, buoyed by happiness, high on the envisaged liberty that life outside the university promised. Jide sat and watched them. He was waiting. But it was not apparent what for. Just then he heard the vibration of his phone and took it out. His hands shook, his heart struggled to stay behind his ribcage, pounding, pounding.

'Nna, are you done?' his father asked.

'Yes, sir'

'You've finished all your papers?'

'Yes.'

'Congratulations,' his father said. Then followed it up with, 'When can you come home?'

'I don't know. I still have to finish my project and tidy up a few things, then I'll come back.'

'Are you sure you cannot come back and go and do that later?'

Jide knew. All of it came together and made sense. The flightiness, the tiredness – his spirit and his body were already grieving. It remained for his consciousness to catch up, it seemed.

'What happened?' Jide asked. He willed himself not to guess.

'I think it is best if you come back. This is something we should discuss in person.' His father's voice was solemn, the voice priests use during confession.

'What is it? Is it Aboy? It is Aboy, abi? Tell me. What happened to my brother?'

'The police came this morning. It was a tip-off. They said they wanted to arrest Aboy for stealing a girl's handbag. They even knew where to find the bag.'

He paused and then continued. 'Okay. I now said, "Aboy, dress up, let's follow them to the station." But next thing I knew, there was a scuffle, and there was a bang, and Aboy was on the floor. They said he was trying to escape, but I was there, I saw everything. He was still wearing his boxers, where would he have escaped to in that state, eh?'

Jide was waiting.

'He is not dead. He is in the hospital,' his father said.

***

The fondest memory Jide had of Aboy had the Virgin Mary in it. This was when Jide was the leader of the block rosary on their street. Every Tuesday and Saturday, he would lead the block rosary children around the neighbourhood, singing, one of them carrying the statue of the Virgin Mary. Women were often generous with encouragement and treats at the sight of the young girls with their flowing head ties and the boys singing 'Ave, Ave Maria.' One day, Aboy had gotten it into his head that he wanted to carry the statue. Jide refused. He was much too small, around six or so. Plus, it would be unfair. Everyone would say he was playing favourites. But Aboy insisted, relying on the very reason Jide refused to give him the statue: that he was his brother. While the other children sang, Aboy followed behind, crying all the way from Immaculate Road to Esiaba Street, and even when they entered the road leading to the block rosary venue.

'I'll stand behind him.' Obinna came to meet Jide. 'Just let Aboy carry small. Abeg.'

Jide looked at the young boy, his shoulders slumped, nose runny, and cheeks bearing the pathways his tears had created. He relented. It was the look in Aboy's eyes that Jide remembered, the tears not fully dried, unadulterated joy, the cheers of everyone as Aboy, carrying the statue, teetered and then righted himself as they went the last few steps to the block rosary venue.

All the while Obinna stood behind him, lending Aboy his strength, making sure their brother did not fall.

***

When the bus pulled into the park in Aba, the sun had given up on the day. Jide found his bag and hung it over his shoulders. He headed for the exit. Obinna was standing at the ticketing section, his hands in his pocket, his head bowed. Jide stopped. At any moment, Obinna would raise his head. Their eyes would lock. And there'd be no need for Jide to wonder, as he did now, if Obinna knew. Because when Jide had sent that text to Chekwube, just before he had packed his books and left the library two days before, Chekwube had replied, 'Does Obinna know? I no wan enter wahala. Tell him, or I will.'

Throughout the journey home, Jide examined that short paragraph he had sent off to Chekwube on the wings of anger. Guilt tore into him, merciless. When he had enlisted Chekwube's help to 'deal with Aboy,' had he not known that was a landscape that accommodated many things? Had he not known calling the police on someone, especially a brother, was an act of treason? When the shooting happened, was he not the unseen hand holding the trigger, saying, 'Kill my brother for me even if I can't?'

But what of when cold air had blown over his anger? There had been time to withdraw the message. He could have called his father or Obinna or even Aboy. He could have sent out a warning. At any time, he could have made sure he was not the reason his brother lay on the floor that morning, a bullet eating into him. But he hadn't.

Obinna looked up and saw him. His face was cupped in its usual half smile, like he was afraid of smiling too much. He walked up to Jide and put his arms around him. The hug held.

After a lifetime, Obinna pulled back, but did not let go of Jide's shoulders, looking into his face, like a lover.

There, Jide knew Chekwube had told him.

When Obinna spoke, he said, 'Let's go and see our brother.'

Soldier Soldier

Ekemini Pius

1.

The man's Alzheimer's grew worse when Hotdog died. Hotdog was a German shepherd into whose grooming the man had invested so much: monthly trips to the vet, expensive dog care products, and feeding so regular Hotdog had looked perpetually pregnant. His gruff baritone would filter into our apartments in the evenings when he sang to her – he gesticulating like an orchestra conductor, she whining along to the rhythm of his song.

We – the residents of Chief Magnus Apartments – loved Hotdog and knew all her songs, sang them to her whenever she wagged her furry tail to welcome us back from work, and bought her treats when we could. We saw her every other evening chasing chickens and lizards and basking in the rust-coloured sunset. So we were surprised when the man trudged into the Amazing Grace Cathedral service one Sunday morning with Hotdog's collar dangling from his hand. The cavernous cathedral was agog that day because it was the annual harvest thanksgiving–women in flamboyant lace and stylishly wrapped gele, men in too-tight suits, children in oversized clothes and iridescent eyeglasses, heaps of freshly harvested food items at the altar.

Beads of sweat clustered on the man's neck despite the gusty, dry December Harmattan that cracked our lips and shrivelled our skin. His lower lip quivered and bloodshot eyes darted around the church in search of us. Once he found us, he hurried over and joined us in the creaking pew. Shoulders hunched. Head bowed. Avoiding the arrows of our gaze. Caressing Hotdog's collar like prayer beads.

The choir started a hymn – 'It Is Well with My Soul' –
followed by a sensational rendition of the piano, and then the
man became a puddle; he sank to his knees, buried his head
between his thighs, wept loudly, and snorted till the ground
before him became a melding of tears and snot. At this point,
we shifted uncomfortably in the pew and flirted with the idea
of lifting him off the ground to prevent the further soiling of
his white trousers and to refocus the stares he was receiving
from uneasy congregants onto the choir. While we were still
conspiring among ourselves in voices drowned out by the
soloist's soprano, the choir warbled the hymn to an end, and the
service was over. The man picked himself up from the ground
in one crisp movement, like he was never there, dusted off his
clothes, thrust Hotdog's collar into his large, sagging breast
pocket, and sauntered out of the church, hugging himself, not
sparing us so much as a glance. Like we were not even there.

Once his figure faded into the distance, we sat back in the pew
to debate what may have befallen the man. Emem said maybe
Little Mary, his house help, had run away with all his money.
We immediately dismissed her suggestion because Little Mary
was fiercely loyal to the man and loved and protected him as
though he were her own father. She once slashed an agbero
boy's wrist with a swishing knife as he attempted to pick the
man's pockets, and the man loved to recount with glee–as much
as his Alzheimer's allowed him–how the penknife glinted in
the sun and cut tantalizingly through the boy's veins, drawing
squirts of blood and a pubescent scream.

Dr Funmi suggested that Hotdog had gone missing and the
man had brought her collar to church to enlist God's help in
finding her. We laughed off this suggestion, too, because no
one knew our street or the surrounding streets better than
Hotdog. She had mating partners in each of the four streets
that connected our neighbourhood, and the dogs never came
to our compound – she went to theirs. She sometimes brought
home strays from other streets so that the man could feed them
–which he did because he would not deny Hotdog anything he

had the wherewithal to provide. *No way in the world did Hotdog go missing.* We snapped our fingers over our heads to dispel even the slightest possibility that this could have happened. As we oscillated between opinions, Dr Funmi's phone chimed; it was a call from Uduak, the only resident of Chief Magnus Apartments who was an atheist and made Sunday his laundry day. She put the call on loudspeaker because our ears were primed like a rabbit's.

'Hotdog don die,' he said over network static. 'I just say make I inform una.'

'Jesus! What killed her? Oh, my Jesus!' Dr Funmi screamed, hushing a group of congregants making small talk nearby.

'I no sabi wetin kill am,' Uduak said. 'You go ask the man or Little Mary.'

Uduak hung up before Dr Funmi could utter another word. The cathedral was fast emptying now. We joined the last throng of people, wishing that the three-minute walk back to our compound could be shorter.

***

We found Little Mary watering the man's potted plants when we got back. She was a small woman with a shaved head who scurried about like a mouse. Like she would rather not be seen. In clothes at least three sizes too big. Rumour had it that the man had employed her several years ago to clean his house three times a week, and her work rate had impressed him: the way her very gait seemed to vacuum filth, the way she spun brooms and dustpans in her hands while humming a song. Then her husband had thrown her out of their young marriage, and she had nowhere to go. So the man let her live in his house, and from then on she had become like a daughter to him.

We asked her what had happened to Hotdog, and she did not reply. Instead, she hosed down an ixora flower. When she realised that we would not leave without a response, she dropped the watering can and took off her rubber gloves. She rolled her eyes and folded her arms across her breasts. Then clearing her throat, she told us that Hotdog had taken the man's shoe and ran off to play with it. That was not the first time Hotdog had taken the man's shoe, but this time when she brought it back, there was no fondness in the man's eyes, no snapping of the fingers to invite her to a dinner of baked beans and fish. Instead, he had picked up his hammer and struck Hotdog on the head. Little Mary said it was only when she had dug a grave and lifted the corpse to bury it that the man shook his head violently and stared at the corpse wide-eyed, as though some scales had fallen from his eyes. After he realised what he had done, he threw some rumpled clothes on, removed Hotdog's collar from her neck, and ran with it to the Amazing Grace Cathedral.

2.

The man was a cobbler and had his stall ensconced behind the security post at the compound's gate. The stall was made with planks and rusted zinc roofing and a door that would not shut. Dedicated to his stall for at least three hours every day, he sorted out anyone on our street who needed to repair their shoes. It did not matter what kind of shoes they were or how bad you thought they were, you only had to bring them to the man. He understood the communion of foot and insole, the symmetry of toe and toe box, how to appease and tease leather to do his bidding. He made his glue by dissolving Styrofoam in petrol, sharpened scissors to glistening point against smooth stones, spooled eclectic colours of threads on pencils. We went into his stall with our shoes in our hands and waited till he repaired them because if you left your shoes and came back the next day, the man may have forgotten who the shoes belonged to and what work he was supposed to do on them. He once called Dr Funmi a thief because she claimed a shoe on his shelf which he swore she had never brought to him.

On one side of the stall, he had used straps of leather to glue the name 'Ukeme Effiong' in cursive to the wall. And no matter how many times he was pressed to reveal what that name meant to him, he said nothing. Instead, he would bend his head lower into his work and tighten his grip on the sewing needle or sandpaper some soles with more force than necessary.

But no sliver of information ever escaped Thomas, our town's newspaper vendor for the past fifteen years. He held everyone's history in the crook of his arm as he did his newspapers. It was he who told us that the man was a retired soldier who had fought in the civil war. The man had been at home at the start of the war when Biafran soldiers swarmed his neighbourhood in search of able-bodied men to conscript into the army. They caught him just as he had been about to slink into some thick bush behind his house, gave him a proper beating, and flung his pulpy body into their van—and he became a soldier.

Ukeme Effiong, a soldier who had been conscripted one year before and had attained some ranking within the battalion, had empathised with the fear in the man's eyes and eased him in by allowing him to spend his first few weeks mending the tired boots of soldiers. Then the man began active combat operations just when the Nigerian army invaded Enugu and began to shell the city, displacing families and firmly planting dread in the hearts of the people. The man fought side by side with Ukeme Effiong in the Biafran army's attempt to stem the raging tide of the opposition. A grenade landed in front of them, and it was too late to run, so Ukeme Effiong pushed the man aside to safety and fell on the grenade, embracing his explosive, instant death.

Now, the man glued the epitaph 'Hotdog' to the wall with leather strips in italic script, just below 'Ukeme Effiong.' When someone came into the stall and cast a glance at 'Hotdog' written on the wall, the man would look away and blink rapidly, tears welling up in his eyes. He said he always wanted to be reminded of what he had done.

3.

It seemed like Hotdog's death had swung the man's heart open to a gust of loneliness. We had never seen the man with a woman while Hotdog was alive, no history of a wife anywhere, and even when a few women on the street had wanted to spill themselves all over him, he had paid them no mind. But now, from our windows, we could see him swinging the hands of women when they came to mend their shoes, laughing too loudly at their jokes, peeping from the stall to ogle the ones with ample behinds. And a fair few of the women did fall for him because, Alzheimer's aside, the man was a fine man. He was light-skinned, with a bald head he oiled to a shine, and a beard that wrapped his chin in soft, wavy tufts. His voice was husky, but that didn't matter much because his dreamy eyes sucked you in.

The man's romance with Sister Bulldozer began like a fledgling thing. Like a newborn calf with wobbly legs. Sister Bulldozer lived at the shoulder of our street and was renowned for her loud midnight prayers. With a voice so thunderous you'd think she was born with a microphone in her larynx, she would bind forces of darkness, clapping her hands and punctuating her prayers with 'I bulldoze! I bulldoze!' She came around the man's stall every few days with a different pair of shoes to mend, and we giggled and gossiped about the possibility of having so many bad pairs of shoes. Was she destroying her shoes intentionally just so she could have an excuse to come see the man? Then she stopped coming with shoes, only with an elastic smile plastered on her face and a perfume so piquant it announced her presence and serenaded the compound. The man did not take to her at first, but her persistence won him over, and they would spend long hours at his stall even when he had closed work for the day, laughing and slapping tables, and later going into his house for dinner. Sister Bulldozer told anyone who cared to listen that she would pray for the man's full recovery, that whatever ailed the man was too small for her God, that she would partner with Little Mary to take care of him, that she loved the man and that was all that mattered.

And then one Saturday morning – while the compound was abuzz with people washing clothes, wiping down their window netting, and making small talk – the man's door burst open and Sister Bulldozer spilled out, followed by the man and Little Mary. Sister Bulldozer hung her handbag on her shoulder and gripped the straps as though she was ready to flee at any moment. The man held a clothes hanger in a combat-ready rifle posture, pointing it at her. The compound held its breath.

'Commander Ukeme, the enemy is here. We can't let them take Enugu. Should I open fire?' he turned to ask Little Mary, who was standing behind him. He cast side glances at Sister Bulldozer as though to prevent her from escaping.

'Darling, you need to relax. It's just me, your Dorothy,' Sister Bulldozer said, trying hard to even the tone of her voice and appear relaxed.

We exchanged furtive glances, questioning why she was Dorothy in this moment and not Sister Bulldozer. No one called her Dorothy or even remembered that was her real name. She took pride in being called Bulldozer, anyway.

The man furrowed his brow and stared down Sister Bulldozer. 'You think you can capture Enugu while we are here? You think it is possible?' Turning to Little Mary, he asked, 'Commander Ukeme, I am awaiting my orders, sir. Should I open fire or not?'

Little Mary cracked a wan smile and turned to look at us in our different perching postures, as though she was expecting us to help her answer the man. Then she turned back to him. 'Hold your fire, soldier. We will open fire but not today. Enugu is still safe,' she said, moving close to him.

'But if we don't open fire now, this soldier will go back and gather a thousand of his fellow soldiers to attack us while we sleep tonight, and that means they will take Enugu,' the man said, lifting the clothes hanger to his eye level to measure the range of his target.

'I promise you that none of that will happen, soldier. Put your rifle aside.'

'At least, let me detain this soldier, just to make sure,' the man said. And without waiting for Little Mary's permission, he made a dart for Sister Bulldozer. Now, we knew Sister Bulldozer for her prayer prowess but not for fleet-footedness, so imagine our shock when she wheeled around and sped toward the gate, her gown billowing in the morning breeze. The man followed in hot pursuit but gave up as soon as he went through the gate because Sister Bulldozer outpaced him, and there was no way he was catching her. But the tenants who lived on the fourth floor and had a lofty vantage point said Sister Bulldozer did not care if the man had given up halfway, she ran until she reached her house. The man returned to the compound gasping for air and clutching his chest. Little Mary held out a glass of water in one hand and medication cupped in the other, which he eagerly flung down his throat.

'Easy, soldier. Breathe. This is Biafra. Enugu will not fall today,' Little Mary said. The man nodded repeatedly and allowed Little Mary to lead him into his house.

4.

You'd think the man had rounded off his romantic adventure. Well, we thought so too. Until Little Mary told us that he was asking his customers at the stall who knew Sister Bulldozer to help him beg her to consider returning to him. But the street gossip had it that not only was she unwilling to go anywhere close to the man, she also shot a menacing glare at anyone who asked her why her prayers could not cure him, why she had scampered to safety that morning instead of bulldozing.

The man cut his losses and moved on just as Nurse Titi moved into our compound. She was soft-spoken, in her fifties, and had a generous hand that endeared her to the tenants. She told us that she had no children and had lost her husband sixteen years ago in a car crash; that she worked in the private hospital where the man received treatment, just a few kilometres from our street. The man first took a liking to her for her kind heart–how gracefully she helped Little Mary administer his medication, enquired about his visits to the doctor, and even suggested extra care tips from her wealth of nursing experience. Then he became besotted with her, enduring the tedious flight of stairs up to her apartment on the fourth floor just to see her when she returned from work every evening. And although she seemed genuinely pleased to be in his company, we did not think he could persuade her to want him romantically. But we should have known better, because a few weeks down the line, we caught her looking at him the way a woman looks only at the man she loves–with consuming tenderness.

Nurse Titi said, much to our delight, that the man's treatment was progressing well, that she had spoken to his doctors and they had sounded confident. We were inclined to agree with her claim because the man had not manifested any new symptoms in a long while. We believed this assurance played a role in convincing her to embrace his love.

Despite all the man's romantic entanglements, we were happy that he was finally with someone who seemed like she could handle all the sides there were to him with equal measures of grace. Someone who could douse fires. We also agreed that she was certainly a better person than Sister Bulldozer. So what could possibly go wrong? We teased and called them love birds when we saw them together, and Nurse Titi blushed like a little girl every single time.

But one day she knocked on the man's door bearing a cooler of food, and instead of being invited inside as usual, the man filled the doorway like an immovable object.

'What do you want?' he asked, scratching his brow.

Nurse Titi chuckled. 'What do you mean by what do I want? Are you going to step aside for me to pass or what?'

The man folded his arms across his chest. 'You are not passing. I don't want you any more. I want Hotdog.'

'You know Hotdog is dead.'

'I know. But she's the one I want. I don't want you.' The man slammed the door in her face.

5.

Little Mary did not take the man's rejection of Nurse Titi lightly. She told us that although she had been unfazed by the man's illness over the years, this one struck a nerve because Nurse Titi's involvement in the man's treatment had relieved her of so much pressure, as she had been solely responsible for his care. Nurse Titi had stopped visiting because the man was firm about not wanting to see her again. This surprised us because his public manifestations were episodic, and he usually sought peace with anyone he spooked. Now, Nurse Titi greeted us curtly, perhaps ashamed because we had witnessed her rejection, and because the man had gone back to his old ways and was not recovering as well as she had told us he would.

It was on the day of the man's weekly doctor's appointment, a windy public holiday that swept dust at our window netting, that Little Mary bared her mind and told the man what she had told us – that she would take him to his appointment today, but he would have to hire a carer soon so that she could focus on housekeeping, because there was no more Nurse Titi, and she didn't want to break down. The man, who was walking toward the cab that pulled up to take him to his appointment, stopped dead in his tracks as soon as Little Mary finished speaking. What happened next shocked us so much that we analyse it to this day: the man picked up a jagged stone from the ground and flung it at Little Mary. Maybe she didn't duck because she had never felt she would need that reflex around the man, that it would ever come to this point where he would attack her. The stone hit her square on the head, and blood streamed down the side of her face. We ran to her, wrapped her head in the bandage that Dr Funmi provided, and Dr Funmi rushed her to the hospital in the cab that came for the man.

The man huddled on the ground beside his stall, shaking his head and staring at the patch of Little Mary's blood that had soaked into the fine sand. He jerked up, went into his house, and for about thirty minutes there was a great rumbling noise, as though he was knocking the furniture against each other. Then the man appeared with a small, packed Ghana-Must-Go bag slung across his shoulder. He went into his stall and swept his shoe-mending equipment into a smaller bag and left the compound. We asked him where he was going and what we should tell Little Mary when she returned from the hospital. But the man paid us no mind, hailed a cab, and went off.

When the man did not return after a few days as we had hoped, we organised a neighbourhood-wide search for him and took turns attempting to comfort Little Mary, who wailed in our arms, inconsolable. The search yielded only a sliver of hope and nothing more – some people said they had seen him at the Amazing Grace Cathedral just a few minutes after he left our compound, standing in front of the locked building and staring at the sign of the cross hoisted atop the building; others said they had seen him at the motor park much later on the same day, but when we went there, the park manager said that there were no ticket records bearing the man's name.

***

Little Mary now works as a house help for a family on the next street. Sometimes, on her way home from errands, she stops by our compound and stands in front of the man's stall for a few minutes, fingers bunched at her sides. As though in silent supplication. As though willing the man to return home.

Wema

Cherrie Kandie

Sadeeq had settled in this strange country without meaning to. After a long layover had clued him in on some of what Nairobi had to offer, he had come back once or twice, scoping out opportunities for his gold business. But even after he had shuttered that, he had still visited, just to see. The lions and beaches and beaded trinkets and all that tourist stuff were interesting, but ultimately, something about the air had appealed to him. Finally, he had bought a small, whitewashed house on the outskirts of Kasarani when parts of the area were still a forest and a clean river ran through.

For how quiet they were, Kenyans easily and vehemently found fault with their homeland once you got them to open up. Like fish in water, they could not appreciate how the place was almost perfectly made. Not perfect, but perfectly made.

The weather in Nairobi was gentle, not too hot and not too cold, no heatwaves and no Harmattan. The food was bland, but that alone would not kill him. Besides, fresh pepper was abundantly available.

Kenyans were a lot like the British who had created their country. They were dull and proper. They kept things going. Their beautiful women did not make their beauty the centre of their lives. There were very rich men walking around like ordinary people, in worn shoes and regular cars and medium-sized houses. Underneath the middling propriety, however, was a submerged propensity for sudden violence. Sadeeq had read about the Mau Mau. It had taken him a while to locate that spirit among the people. It was hidden, but it was there.

He had fit into this place like a puzzle piece finding its space, because places like this allowed parts of him to stay hidden.

He had grown up a poor village boy, the child of a single mother. She had somehow loved him through every circumstance. She had sung to him throaty songs. She had fed him with her last coin and her last breath. He had hazy childhood memories of laughter and elation, of skinny-legged playmates just as dirty as he was. But what he had never forgotten was the silence after his mother's death.

He had made peace with silence on one end and with noise on the other. Each had a role to play. But them coming so close together – the crunch of her body when she was crushed beneath a car; then the pin-drop silence; and then the wailing, the crowds, and the loud tales; then the clean pocket of silence when they realized that he was right there and had seen everything; then the swarming sympathy and condolences; and then the silence later at her funeral – had been too much to bear. It was around this time that he had begun to sit in quiet corners, slap his ears repeatedly, and bury his head in between his folded thighs. He was trying to find a balance between the silence and the noise.

A distant senior aunt had swooped in. She was a widow; she was regal and Francophone. She had a mischievous gold canine and a frame as wide as her ready and welcoming smile. She had raised seven sons, and they had all left her for faraway lives. Her large house was empty and calling. She weaned him away from the oily, heavy, and peppery foods of his childhood. He developed a taste for coffee and baguettes, even for supper. He found silence without having to hide or slap his ears or bury his head in between his thighs.

When they went to register him for school, they realised that he did not know his birth date. He had never had a birth certificate. He knew only the name that his roving father had left him: Abderahman. They had looked him up and down, asked him to hold out his hands like he was a bird or an airplane, telling him to turn around just for laughs. They decided that he looked about eight years old. He became eight years old.

Name: Sadeeq Abderrahmane
Parent/Guardian: Wuraola Yetunde Adeyemi
Date of birth: 01/01/80

During the four years they spent together before she died, she taught him the power of *other places*. She took him on all her trips to gorgeous, exotic places like Abidjan and Marrakesh. She sent him to an international school, where he met children from all over the world.

She said, 'The world is enormous. Do not be afraid of it. You don't have to stay in one place. You don't have to stay in places you don't like.'

When she died, he was ready for the silence. He walked into the night.

Sadeeq travelled all over the continent trading gold and became very wealthy, but not in a straight-and-narrow way, not in a way that made him eligible for something like a newspaper feature. Before he became wealthy, he had been poor and hungry and homeless and stateless, stowing away between countries in the backs of pickups and lorries, hiding in the cargo, sometimes slinging a gun, sometimes nearly dying, sometimes finding new languages on his tongue.

He saw that rich or poor, you were nothing. Wit and brute force were slippery gods. They got you somewhere but never really got you there. And they always brought ghosts that trailed you to your death.

He had spent most of his life on the other side of doors slammed shut, breaking them down and adorning himself with all he had never had, only to see with his own eyes that it was all more empty than the nothingness he'd come from. And this – this cynicism – had nearly killed him. He had always been a bit impatient but grew more so. He carefully considered human folly and decided that he did not forgive it. He did not forgive the puffed chests, the ill-fitting leather jackets, the condescending looks, the upturned noses, the over-rouged lips, and the bottomless pits of lust for fame, money, and other bodies.

He decided to respect only goodness. Not kindness and not niceness. Only goodness. And the weak could not be good.

***

Wema bent forward. Her mouth pursed in concentration. Her eyes became tiny slits. Her customer's head lay tilted to the right, supported by a fluffy light blue pillow that matched her hair salon's blue decor. A long, thin, loose shaft of hair rested in the space between her left thumb and forefinger. Just before finishing this cornrow, she paused to stretch out the cramped fingers on her right hand. She spread them out like a duck's webbed feet and then bent them like she was scratching something. With her fingers bent like that, her hand looked like a claw. She liked to hear her finger joints crack when she did this.

It had been a long Saturday of washing heads, oiling scalps, blow drying out the knots in hair, and entertaining the entire spectrum of her customers' emotions – children, teenagers, and adults alike. The children screamed. The teenagers preened. The adults complained about the economy. She hadn't noticed how dirty her salon had become, or how late it was, or that she was so hungry that she felt a bit dizzy. She could be one of those hairdressers who sneaked in bites of food as they handled their customers' heads, but she was too good for that.

She stood up straight to rotate her neck, which eased her shoulder and back muscles. Out of the corner of her left eye, she spotted an unfamiliar shadow that had lingered for one moment too long outside the lonely window at the back.

A person she had never seen before then appeared at the salon's front door. Wema looked at him, her hands still on her customer's head. He sported a perfectly tailored brown suede jacket over a black T-shirt. He smiled and waved as if to put her at ease. But Wema was glad that this last customer was still around. She estimated that she had about three cornrows left.

'Welcome,' she said, despite herself. She had leaned closer to engage this new person, but she remained focused on the three remaining cornrows.

He sat uncomfortably on one of her small curved-back chairs. Despite his composure, the dark solid lines of his tall frame looked out of place in the cramped space. The white walls were livened up by full-hearted splashes of light and navy blue.

After an extended period of silence, he pinched at his hair and said, 'I want to start dreadlocks.'

His Kiswahili was odd. Not Sheng', not coastal, not upmarket, but technically proficient.

'You're not from around here, are you?'

At this, he smiled. This time he showed his teeth and chuckled. The gap between his two front teeth was striking. She felt more at ease. She had one cornrow left.

'How much?'

'I don't often do dreadlocks.'

'But you know how to do them.'

'Yes.'

'Then how much?'

'Ten thousand.' She said this almost as a joke, laughing and looking down to finish plaiting the final cornrow, anticipating a haggle.

By the time she looked up, he was gone. She did not hear him leave. She was stunned to see a stack of crisp notes on the table she used for accounting.

She counted the notes. One, two, three … ten. She gasped. That was her salon's monthly rent.

***

Sadeeq knew all the thugs and whores and cops, all the jaba spots and their layabouts, all the shopkeepers and tax collectors and MCAs, all the mama mbogas in their neat wooden stalls, all the nduthi guys, and each watchman. He knew every critter on the street, every genuflecting dog, and every hole in the wall. He even knew where the graffiti had come from and who had cut down the trees way back when.

The nduthi guys began to lean closer when they saw Wema passing by, a knowing in their eyes. This fractional leaning was almost impossible to detect because they did not greet her. Still, they knew her now because of Sadeeq.

With him, Wema realised how narrow her life had been. She ascribed it to being a woman. She was not scared to walk around at night as he regularly did, watching people and places, finding out new things. She simply was not curious enough. She was tied to her paraphernalia, the things in her home and her salon, and the people contained within. These were a lot of people: she was a popular hairdresser, and she lived with her grandmother and her cousins and their brood of children. But she understood her relationship to them only in terms of duty. She was obligated to all these people, and she could not be curious about them, because when duty becomes too curious, it falls apart.

She would have been a regular churchgoer, but Sunday was the day that most of her clients scheduled their appointments. Weekends in general were her busiest times. She found herself attending morning Mass every day even though she did not take communion. She was not born a Catholic, but the consistent cock-crow presence of the priest gave her comfort. The flamboyant Pentecostal preachers that her grandmother adored would never wake up so early.

In the beginning, Sadeeq had felt like the air. Everywhere, unyielding, imperceptible. He always said that she was good and beautiful. He said this one day when she was on top of him, swaying and almost at climax. It ruined it, and she collapsed next to him. She looked at him and asked, 'Why do you always say that? Good *and* beautiful? What do you even mean?'

'Because you are the goodest person I know.'

'Goodest?'

'I am trying to make a point here.' He laughed and added, 'Wema. Goodness.'

She had never thought about her name before. She had always had it. Just like she had always had herself.

They talked about their mothers. Wema told him about how hers had been a good-time girl with endless legs and a pretty face. She had been an excellent mother when she was around. The problem was that she was rarely around. The only framed picture of her mother was in one dusty corner of her grandmother's house. Her childhood make-believe had included stepping on a stool to unmount this picture, talking to it like they were mother and daughter again, sisters even. Sometimes she had truly lifelike dreams of her mother cradling her like a baby, even if she was already 27 years old. She would wake up in a cold sweat and pat the bedding around her, looking for her mother and finding only her sleeping nieces. The thing that kept her sane was her work. She plaited all this disharmony into her clients' scalps, and the resulting geometrics pleased her.

Wema was certain that if she slipped and fell into the slightest bit of chaos, she would never recover, just like her mother never did.

Sadeeq listened intently. He sat up with his back against the bedpost. He looked down at his hands. His palms were arranged the way she had seen Catholics hold out their hands when receiving communion, with one hand over the other. He sucked his cheeks in, looking frustrated, then sad.

He said, 'I don't know what my mother's face looked like. I've forgotten it.'

At this, there was silence.

Then, unable to look straight at her, he surprised himself by blurting out, 'I had an aunt.' He'd never told anybody about his aunt before.

He went on at length about the way she had shown him a secret gold stash months before she died, when she'd realised she was diminishing. She had known that her children would not want him, that nobody would, so she had made arrangements. That stash had kept him alive for years and later led him into the gold trade.

Traces of an old accent strained through. It was musical. She was curious.

She didn't know what to say, so she hugged him, and they held each other like that through the night.

***

Sadeeq called her beautiful so seriously and frequently that Wema had no choice but to believe it. The gifts were small and infrequent at first – a valentine bouquet here, a pair of earrings there. But then he bought her a phone, and it was like a vault had opened. He gave her gold jewellery, expensive clothes, and anything she wanted. For her cousins, he paid fees, bought school uniforms, paid for doctors' and dentists' visits, and gave many other favours. Some of her cousins had never been to the dentist and had to have many rotting milk teeth pulled out.

When he bought her grandmother a large couch, Wema thought that it took up too much space.

"The other one was just fine. Where did you take it?"

He said nothing. Her grandmother was crying and laughing and sitting on the couch and thanking Were Khakaba and blessing Sadeeq by raising her hands to the sky and letting them fall in his direction.

They would come back to his apartment staggering from nights out and barely make it to bed. Then they would fuck and have a weed cookie to keep the high going. He would order a KFC bucket for her because of how ravenous the cookie had made her. He taught her how to smoke. Then he taught her to roll the perfect joint, how to use a grinder to gently crush the dry marijuana leaves, and how to hold the rolling paper together with a dash of honey.

She sold everything in her salon and closed it. The items that she had loved had begun to look like trinkets: her adjustable chairs, shampoo bowls, mirrors. She surveyed the chest of drawers that she had walked through all of Gikomba to find. It looked too earnest, too solid, too light blue. She wanted to hack it into pieces. She ignored her clients' calls. She stopped looking forward to things. Time stopped passing by; it became something that fell backwards and devoured her. It was all because there was so much money.

She moved into his apartment. It was in a gated community – high-rise and luxury, overlooking the Thika Highway, with four extravagantly large rooms. Three days after she moved in, and without consulting her, Sadeeq cut off the beautiful two-year dreadlocks that she had always worked on so tenderly. He did not even go to a barber shop. He cut them badly in the bathroom and came to join her on the couch.

She was incensed. She tried to say something, but the words melted into a hot puddle at the base of her throat. She began to gesticulate and weep like she was at a funeral.

Sadeeq had never seen her so angry. He looked at her quietly. She saw him tilt his head slightly, fascinated.

She finally managed to exclaim, 'Why would you do something like that?' These words expressed upset more than they asked an honest question.

Wema asked the driver to take her to her grandmother's house in Huruma.

'You are crying over a man's hair.' Her grandmother spoke this utterance slowly, mixing it with concern. Wema looked at the lovingly sewn pink tablecloths and began to sob again as she leaned on her grandmother's shoulder. She envied her

nieces' faraway laughter and wondered who she was as she
rubbed her face clean.

***

Her first two children came very quickly. Wema was glad to
have them, to dote on them. Sadeeq and she no longer did
exciting things or had deep discussions. The silence between
them was the worst thing.

Sadeeq felt grotesque and unknowable, like a cavernous
lake. This feeling never went away; it had lodged itself deep
between his ribs. He did not have the words to understand
himself, let alone to communicate himself to Wema. This was
neither here nor there, because he did not feel the need to make
himself known to her. He only knew that he loved her because
he wanted her to remain the same. It was never this way
with anybody else; he knew that people's lurking wants and
imperfections usually found their way to the surface somehow
to destroy everything, so he always made provision for people
to express their lowest, worst possible selves. But he wanted
Wema to remain the same, and in this he was vulnerable.

Sadeeq did not allow the gateman to let her out and
instructed the driver to take her only for scheduled spa, salon,
and shopping trips. No money touched her hands; he made
ample deposits at every place she went and paid any balance
afterwards. Her grandmother was content to receive money
from Sadeeq and to stay away from their luxurious apartment.
She would say that the way the windows ran from the ceiling
to the floor scared her. Apparently, windows should not be
so large, every house needs a few secrets, and that much light
would bring bad spirits in.

One day, Wema asked to go to the spa but sneaked out through
the back door of the establishment to sit in a quiet corner of a
bar for hours, feeling dazed and free. More people began to
filter in as it grew darker. What happened next made her wish
for her gilded cage; she wanted to be silent, unknowing, and

pampered again. She saw Sadeeq coming in with his friends and all their new young things, the tails of their long weaves fluttering right above their thin waists, laughing like they owned the bar. Those women were so beautiful. She pictured herself laughing and walking in with them, then suddenly she felt old and ugly. She had never felt that way before. She had no proof that he was cheating, but somewhere inside herself, she felt certain that he was. She darted out before he could spot her. She went back to the spa and left wordlessly through the front door, leaving the attendants confused.

'Madam, leo umekaa sana,' the driver said in a measured way, looking at her through the front mirror. *You've been in there too long.* She knew that he would report her to Sadeeq, but she was more dispirited than scared.

When he came home, he found her watching TV and asked, 'Where were you today?'

'The spa.'

'Do not lie to me.'

'They gave me a special service today. I was tired. I just needed something special today.'

'Tired? But you hardly do anything.'

She said quietly, 'You used to love me.'

The look of fascination in his eyes made her feel like a zoo animal. He said nothing.

She desperately wanted him to say something. She whimpered, 'I gave you everything.'

He scrunched his face and responded, 'No. I gave *you* everything.'

This irritation hurt her. Her face cracked. He paused. She looked so small on that plush, humongous couch. A lost bird.

'What do you want, Wema? What more could you possibly want?'

She wanted to say, 'I want you.' Instead, she said, 'I saw you.'

'What?'

'I saw you at the bar today. I saw you with all those girls.'

'So that's where you were.'

'You want to kill me, Sadeeq.'

'All this money will kill you, eh?'

She looked down at her body, noticing how it had changed after three children. It's surprising how quickly things fall apart when they want to. It felt as though from the moment they had met, they had played ring-a-ring-a-roses, and now they were falling down. No, *she* was falling down. He seemed fine. He was the same, and she did not have a self. She wanted to hurt him. She dug deep within herself for the last pocket of truth present within her, something lemon-bitter that was hostile to duty, curiosity, or anything that could be called love. She said, 'You are a miserable animal. Even if I died tomorrow, you'd still be miserable.'

Wema's contempt did not hurt Sadeeq as much as it made him feel that he had nothing to lose or protect. He called her an ungrateful prostitute, and she lunged at him and scratched him, drawing blood that matched her red manicure. Then he beat her so badly that it split her lower lip. She grabbed a knife and ran towards the main gate, telling the gateman that she would kill either him or herself if he did not open the gate immediately.

She spent a fitful night at her old priest's servant's quarters in Huruma. He had opened the gate to find her bleeding and barefoot, her feet caked with mud, and vaguely remembered her from years past. It was against parish policy to let people into the rectory, but he'd done it because Wema's state was extreme. The next morning, the priest called the domestic violence shelter hotline. When they said that they needed a police report, Wema knew it was over – Sadeeq knew all the cops. So she asked the priest for money, waylaid her children on the way home from school, and took them with her to her grandmother's.

Her grandmother wept. She cupped her hands over her scalp and cried out that she had always known it was only a matter of time before something bad would happen in that house. She surprised Wema by saying, 'He will come looking for you. You have to go.'

'But the children ...'

'Leave the children. Go. Here's some money.' She fished out a brown envelope from a crack in the wooden wall unit and pushed Wema out into the night.

***

It took a couple of weeks of staying in lodgings, a misguided one-month stay at a one-room shack that she loosely furnished, and a frantic call to an old client whose number she hunted down, but Wema finally found a place on the far outskirts of Kasarani that was both functional and affordable. The stacked apartment building stood alone; parts of the area looked like a forest. Sad, angry, and euphoric, she dragged herself over her new balcony to light a joint, rolled just as Sadeeq had taught her. The haphazard Nairobi nightscape dotted with yellow lights like stars, met the starless sky on the horizon. The moon was full. The night dazzled. Below her were rare patches of land filled with trees and bisected by a grimy river. Nestled in there was an antique-looking whitewashed house.

For a moment she wondered what it would take to be part of the river or the moon, to be smaller than an atom, to be nothing once and for all, and she cried and cried and cried. But the crying did not feel futile, as it had felt in the past. Tomorrow she would send for the children, who were still in Huruma.

She was naked. The tiny fourth-floor bedsitter had no furniture but the mattress and bedding she had brought up for the night. She would bring the rest of her belongings tomorrow: her Meko gas, her sufurias, her curtains, the glasses, the other mattress.

She could smell the slapdash renovations that the landlord had done for her. The paint fumes were overwhelming. The cement was new. There was dust and dirt everywhere, and she could feel their granules beneath her feet. She would make arrangements for water tomorrow.

She leaned forward. Her nakedness thrilled her. The weed made her giddy. The breeze was perfect for how hot the night was. Then she felt a rush of goose pimples running from her right shoulder down to the hand that was holding the joint. It almost fell, but she steadied herself. She looked to her right but saw only blackness and distant lights. Sadeeq was there, somehow. Near her, somehow. She knew it. She felt the sudden urge to cover herself. To extinguish the joint, lock her doors, and hide beneath her covers. Then she reminded herself that it was the fourth floor and scolded herself for being crazy. She let out a laugh that was much too loud for the modest night. But she decided to go and sleep. Her front door was locked. And she would lock the balcony door. She had two sturdy padlocks.

As she turned around, a voice yanked her out of the minutes of safety she'd found in her body.

'Wema.'

She screamed, and Sadeeq went on.

'Did you think you were going to lose me? I'm right here. I'll always be here.'

A tiny, strong white light appeared and washed over her. It most likely came from his phone. The man was on the balcony next to hers, craning his neck to talk to her.

Love is Enough
and Other Lies

Erica Sugo Anyadike

Faith couldn't be certain what *exactly* she saw Mike doing to Lucy in that shadowy hallway off the main party room, but when she glimpsed them – Lucy's face up against the wall, her dress twisted and bunched high on her thighs, her limbs floppy and loose; Mike's huge hand pinning Lucy in place, his trousers pooled around his ankles, his movements furtive and frustrated – her chest tightened, and she struggled to breathe.

Mike stopped abruptly and pulled up his trousers. He half-dragged, half-carried a stumbling Lucy further down the hallway to one of the rooms, using his arm to support her as she leaned on him, and looking over his shoulder, as if he sensed that they were being watched. He opened the door to the bedroom with his free hand and shut it behind them. Faith remained frozen in place, moving only when an insistent flash caught her eye – Lucy's phone, on the floor of the hallway where she'd discovered them. Someone was calling, but the ringtone had been muted. Faith emerged from the shadows and peered into the hallway. Mike and Lucy were gone now. She doubted they would appear any time soon. Still, she tiptoed down the hallway, retrieved the cell phone, and placed it into her bag. A distant part of her, a part not yet hardened, whispered at her to intervene.

She moved towards the room and stood outside the door. Pressing her ear to the door, she listened for voices, but the loud music coming from the party made it impossible to hear anything. She hesitated. Mike was Joseph's right-hand man. If she caused a commotion, Joseph would find out and be furious at being associated with a party where bad things (maybe even *criminal* things) might have happened. He had too much riding on this election. Money had exchanged hands, prayers had been recited, rituals performed, and cows slaughtered for the ancestors. Like his namesake's, Joseph's coat had many colours. He understood the pleasures of the flesh, the pull of earthly things but he had no time for scandals, for being the subject of lurid gossip. That's where Faith came in. Almost as if she'd conjured him up, Joseph sent her a text.. Startled to see his name appear on the screen, Faith stumbled back from the door and read it.

Where are you? Musa needs a distraction.

A variation of the same text he always sent her. The multiple ways he expected her to be at his beck and call. To entertain him or his friends. She allowed him to order her around because he paid well, but she was starting to find his demanding nature oppressive.

The last time, she hadn't responded fast enough, and he had sent a furious message saying he was outside her Rosebank flat. It had been six o'clock in the morning. He'd insisted she come down and they talk immediately. Heart hammering, she had rolled out of bed, thrown on her dressing gown and gone downstairs to his car.

As soon as she shut the passenger door, he pressed the central locking. He turned to face her. 'Musa said none of the girls were his type.'

Faith pretended to flick lint from her dressing gown. 'I don't know what his type is.'

Joseph slammed the steering wheel with the palm of his hand. Faith flinched.

'It's *your job* to know. Research him. Find out what he likes. Or – I don't know – provide a variety!'

Faith nodded, swallowing her anger. How was she supposed to know everything about his fellow MPs? She ran an event management company, not a detective agency. But when he got like this, it was better to appease him.

'I'll get on it.'

Joseph leaned back in his seat and looked up at the ceiling. He rubbed the bridge of his nose. 'Musa thinks he's the second coming of Mandela. People have been encouraging him to run against me. He's convinced he's better than everyone else.'

'In what way?'

'In every way. Morally, more money ... whatever.'

'Every man has his weakness.'

He chuckled. 'See, that's what I like about you. Find out what his weakness is. Girls, booze ... boys?' He laughed at his own joke.

Faith wanted to end this as quickly as possible, so she finished his sentence for him. 'And make sure he indulges.'

'Exactly.' He reached over and squeezed her hand. She squeezed his back. 'I apologise for this morning. I was in a bad mood. I hope you understand.'

Faith had understood perfectly. Joseph's campaign was in full swing, an orchestrated dance of rallies and photo ops, handshakes, and backroom deals. This had been a bad year for his political party, divisions widened, rifts grew. Backstabbing, once done in the dark, was now carried out in the light. Faith's parties allowed Joseph to connect with influential individuals, build alliances, and secure support away from media scrutiny. The alliances were especially important. It was harder to betray a man when you shared the same vices.

Right now, she wanted to barge into the room, to startle Mike into stopping, but if the sordid details of Mike's behaviour became public knowledge, it would deal a fatal blow to Joseph's ambitions. Faith's dreams of power and influence, the networks she'd painstakingly cultivated, the contact list of powerful people who owed her favours, the information and assets she'd accumulated – all of it would be useless, gone, in an instant.

And for what? A situation she wasn't sure about? A girl who had always disliked her?

She had stumbled upon this scene because she never danced at her own events. She always wandered, worrying, making sure everyone was having a good time. She could go back, join the crowd, pretend this never happened. That was the best way. Perhaps the only way.

She retreated from the hallway and headed back to the party.

***

Faith grabbed a glass of champagne and a bottle of sparkling water off a passing tray. Self-loathing rose in her throat, but she drank it down.

Gqom music pulsed through the air. She kissed cheeks and stroked egos with practised ease. She could almost forget that she'd grown up in Alex, eating pap and mogodu instead of the sushi she pretended to like now, dreaming of the celebrities she saw in discarded *True Love* magazines, cutting out portraits and photos of their homes. This penthouse – with the exclusive Sandton address she had chosen as the party venue – took her breath away with its unparalleled grandeur, luxurious furnishings, and tasteful décor, more magnificent than anything she had seen in the magazines. It struck her now that she loved this place because it reminded her of herself, nothing too much or too little, every piece curated, controlled, compartmentalised – in its place. If the apartment had been a person, she thought, they would have been best friends.

Faith took in the young, nubile women arranging themselves artfully next to powerful men seated on plush, oversized leather sofas. She heard the clink of champagne flutes and saw the bubbles sparkling in the refracted light from the enormous chandelier, shaped like a protea. A man stumbled into a plinth displaying an intricate sculpture of twisted metal and wood, and Faith's heart leapt into her throat. He'd almost knocked it over, but it remained in place. Security had appeared and led the man away with minimal fuss. She surveyed the rest of the penthouse. Everything else seemed intact. But she worried about the masks. Would someone lurch into them and bring them crashing down? All those masks with enigmatic faces like silent sentinels, as if they were watching … or waiting. But for what?

She laughed at herself for being ridiculous. She had never been superstitious. She was not about to start now.

The group of girls she'd recruited for the party were fresh-faced, naïve, and awed by the opulence surrounding them. They could not afford designer labels. Most of them possessed questionable style. Faith insisted on approving their outfits, going to great lengths to explain the difference between classy and trashy. Low necklines and mini – trashy. High necklines with mini – classy. Only expose one thing at a time. Lace fronts were excluded. Left to their own devices, the girls would no doubt wear skimpy outfits in Lycra or polyester, content to let it all hang out.

Mike always wore designer athleisure: tracksuits from Dolce & Gabbana, Gucci bucket hats and pool slides, LV sneakers and bags, logos on blast. Joseph wore custom-made suits. The lines were clean, the colours muted, and the fit perfect, conveying an air of understated elegance, hinting at the attention to detail that defined his every move. All of Joseph's shoes were made in Italy. He eschewed the garish gold Rolex that Mike favoured, opting for a stainless steel Breitling instead.

Most of the men wore suits of varying quality, all of them straining to project an image of success and belonging. Their shirts were too bright, their ties too bold, their watches too flashy. They dyed their hair with Bigen. Although her guests liked the girls young (early twenties, eager, grateful), most didn't want to be reminded of their teenage daughters.

She called the girls over, gathering them to her like ducklings, and leaned in, her voice low and conspiratorial.

'Stick with Mr. Mashaba, ladies. He's generous. So are his friends – that group he's with. Kodwa, watch out for Mike. Wandering hands, that one. Can't take no for an answer.'

The girls giggled. One of them lifted her glass, while holding a bottle in her other hand. '*Right?!* I told Mashaba I only drink Moët Nectar Impérial, and he had his driver go out and buy me a whole bottle.' She placed the bottle triumphantly on the table beside her.

Faith frowned at Bottle-girl, whose name she couldn't remember. What were these pretentious habits? The girl hadn't known anything about Moët Nectar two weeks ago. She pronounced it *Moh-way* for goodness' sake, the mark of a novice. 'What did I tell you?'

'About?'

God help her. 'About pacing your drinks? About never letting a glass out of your sight? Now you're boasting that a man bought you a whole bottle from outside? You think that's a good thing?'

Bottle-girl put her glass on the table and averted her gaze.

Faith sighed. She had shown them how she watered down her wine and diluted her champagne. She taught them to watch out for the men who insisted you *go hard or go home* and sprayed spittle in your face while singing elder millennial songs about booze by Rihanna and Jamie Foxx. She had demonstrated how she did shots when called upon by overzealous partygoers. After every shot, she drank two large glasses of sparkling water, garnished with lime, disguised to look like a gin and tonic. Now, it seemed, she would have to remind them again.

'These men can be generous, yes, but all of them – *all* of them – only want one thing. You give it to them and you give up all your power. They will lose interest, instantly. You've seen my pictures on Instagram right? The trips, the bags?'

All the girls nodded.

'Good. If you want more than a bottle of booze, keep your eyes open and your legs closed,' Faith said, scowling as she repositioned an errant, flimsy piece of fabric, a side boob cut-out about to become a full boob display on Bottle-girl. 'If these men wanted hoes, they could easily get them off the streets. You're here to get money, or at least gifts you can resell. Give them the girlfriend experience. What did I tell you about the girlfriend experience?'

Bottle-girl piped up. 'Smile. Listen. Act like you care. Let them do the talking.'

Faith nodded, mollified. 'Thank you for remembering. Do not get drunk. Do not embarrass me. Or you won't get invited again. Now, go mingle.'

Chastised, another one of the girls, a willowy yellow bone, began to tell Faith that she'd exchanged numbers with Musa. Faith smiled and sat down. She patted the seat on the couch next to her.

'That's excellent,' she said. 'Tell me all about it.'

***

Out of her peripheral vision, Faith watched as Mike appeared at Joseph's elbow, his clothes dishevelled, the tracksuit top worn backwards, as if he'd gotten dressed in the dark. He leaned in and whispered something, gesticulating with his hands, his movements emphatic and agitated. It looked serious. She looked openly now, scanning the party. No sign of Lucy. Her stomach lurched.

Joseph's expression hardened. He turned away from Mike, shaking his head, and then turned and whispered something back to Mike. Mike flinched, nodding, his earlier bravado wilting under Joseph's stare and walked away, looking chastised. Joseph locked eyes with Faith and beckoned to her to come over, his eyes flicking to the hallway that led to the room where Mike had taken Lucy.

Faith excused herself from the girl - the Musa story was unimportant now - and hurried towards him. As she approached, she noted the tension in Joseph's jaw, the flicker of fear in his eyes.

'Look, I'm sorry to ask you this, but Mike did something stupid. That girl he was with earlier ...'

'Lucy?'

'Yes. They had a misunderstanding.'

Faith's hands began to tremble. She stuffed them into her trouser pockets, hiding her hands so that Joseph wouldn't see.

'What kind of misunderstanding?'

'She's upset. Hysterical. Can you talk to her? Get her to drop all this talk of rape charges.'

Faith looked at him and then turned to stare at Mike. He watched them from across the room.

She shrugged. 'If she wants to go to the cops, I'm not sure I can stop her.'

Joseph shook his head and gripped her shoulders so tightly it hurt. She thought he was about to shake her. She froze.

'I don't want that to happen. It would be a disaster for me. He'll pay her whatever she's asking for. Actually ...' He let her go and took a swig of his whisky. He offered her some. She shook her head.

'*Actually*, Faith, it would be a disaster for you too. We've been doing business for a couple of years now, right? And it's worked out well, wouldn't you agree? Hasn't it been great for you and your family? Can you imagine if this gets out? This would affect both of us.' He adjusted the strap of her Louis Vuitton Pochette, even though it hadn't been falling off her shoulder. He called Mike over. Mike came and pressed an open envelope, thick with wads of cash, into Faith's hand.

'Mike will do whatever it takes to make this go away,' Joseph said.

Mike began to speak, but Joseph silenced him. Mike skulked back to his corner, a dog disciplined by its master. Joseph called someone and made arrangements to have Faith's car waiting at the back. Just as she was turning to go, Faith stopped to face Joseph, her skin uneasy, as though ants were crawling all over her.

'*Did* he rape her?'

Joseph paused, the whisky glass midway to his mouth. 'No ...
I don't know ...,' he said. He took a long swig. 'You know Mike.
He gets a little carried away sometimes.'

Faith didn't know Mike, but she knew what men like Mike
were capable of; she had seen the signs, heard the whispers. But
there's knowing, then there's seeing, and seeing makes things
real in a way that can't be ignored.

She steeled herself and headed for the hallway.

***

Outside the bedroom door, hand hovering over the handle,
Faith took one deep breath, then two, and opened it.

The smell hit her first, eggy and metallic, ammonia and blood
– a nauseating cocktail of bodily fluids and the sharp, sweaty
tang of fear. It clung to the back of her throat. She forced herself
to breathe through her mouth, shallow and steady, as the air
thickened with each step. And then came the sound: a low wail,
desperate and animal. She wanted to cover her ears, to never
hear the sound again. It was pitiful and primal and full of pain.
A hurting that could not be denied. Finally, when Faith's eyes
adjusted, she saw Lucy – curled up in foetal position, dress torn,
panties around her ankles, eyes glassy, mascara streaking her
face. She lay crumpled on the bed, a broken doll discarded by a
careless child.

Faith cleared her throat and sat beside her. She wanted to
place her hand on Lucy's back. She wanted to comfort her, to
say something kind. But what could she possibly say? *I'm sorry?
I should have stopped him? I know how you feel?*

All of these were woefully inadequate.

Instead, she reached for Lucy's hand and held it. Lucy let her.
Her hand was damp. It felt small and warm.

'Woza sisi,' Faith said. 'Let's get you out of here.'

Lucy looked down at her torn dress and shook her head.

'You don't have to see him. We won't use the main entrance;
we won't go through the party. I promise.'

Lucy stared at her for a long, suspended moment, chest heaving with silent sobs. Then gingerly, she levered herself off the bed. Faith dressed Lucy, wrapped a blanket around her, and led her down the back stairs, through the deserted kitchen, into the service lift and out to her car idling in the alley.

***

Office towers loomed overhead, empty and ominous, the windows dark and lifeless. In the passenger seat, Lucy sat hunched and silent. Faith stole a glance at her. The streetlights on the M1 highway streaked past the car windows, illuminating her face in intermittent flashes, casting shadows that accentuated the hollows of her cheeks and the dark circles under her eyes. They sped past billboards advertising townhouses worth millions of rand, pristine facades and landscaped gardens a stark contrast to the settlements on their outskirts; past glossy posters touting the latest television shows, their airbrushed stars smiling with perfect teeth and empty eyes; past sleek watches worth several months' rent, their glittering faces promising a good life that seemed as out of reach for most people as the stars above; past Nelson Mandela Bridge, where a giant sign said 'Call Your Mother,' which made Faith sad and made her smile all at the same time, this reminder to balance love and duty. Love was a verb – a doing word – to simply say it would never suffice; you had to back it up with action.

Their eyes met, and Faith offered a small smile, a tentative gesture of comfort and solidarity, but Lucy looked away. They paused at a traffic light to let other cars pass, but Faith was on edge, her senses heightened, hyper-aware of potential carjackers, reflexes ready, foot on the accelerator. A man appeared out of nowhere in front of the vehicle. Lucy screamed. Faith revved the engine and almost ran him over. The man jumped back – fast for a guy whose glazed eyes looked like he was high on nyaope - and yelled at her to 'voetsek!' It was only as they drove off and her hammering heart began to slow, did she look in the rear view mirror and notice the spray bottle of soapy water still in his hand and the rag cloths sticking out of his pocket. She began to laugh, a jangly sound full of nerves and lacking mirth.

'Lucy, ngiyazi ubuhlungu,' Faith began, when the adrenaline had receded. 'What happened to you was terrible, and I'm so sorry. But going to the cops? It's not going to end the way you want.'

Lucy stared at her. 'And what way is that? With that bastard behind bars where he belongs?'

Faith sighed. 'I wish it were that simple. Look – Mike has money. Way more money than your parents. He'll hire the best lawyers. They'll tear you apart.'

The tension hung in the air, heavy and malignant, full to bursting with things unsaid. Lucy continued staring out the window, facing the road only when Faith took the Milpark off-ramp to the university. The silence stretched between them, broken only by the hum of the engine and the distant sound of traffic.

Faith drove into the university, the sprawling campus a welcome sight after the claustrophobic confines of the car. She parked outside Lucy's residence, empty at this time of night, except for a few students at the other end of the lot, holding cans of beer in their hands, their conversation punctuated with laughter as they gathered around a red VW Polo, Black Coffee blasting from the system.

Faith pressed the electric button to lower the window. It was only then that Lucy spoke. 'So, what are you saying, anyway? That I should just let him get away with it?'

It was the way Lucy asked this question, her tone belligerent and challenging, that reminded Faith of all the times Lucy had cut her down with a snide comment or a dismissive once-over, the implication clear: *You're nothing. You'll always be nothing.* It had stumped Faith at first, because Lucy came from a comfortable family but was nowhere near wealthy. Sure, Lucy's family had some small business dealings with a few politicians, but she was definitely not political royalty. Her family's connections were just enough that Faith couldn't ban her from her events altogether – Lucy was a determined hanger-on who always found a way to get invited, and Faith didn't want to make a scene – but Faith had done her research, and Lucy was not that much better than she. So why, Faith wondered, was Lucy always making subtle digs about her humble beginnings and her 'questionable' moral compass?

Despite Lucy's accusations – and there were many – Faith was not a pimp. Lucy had never been one of her girls. Faith had attempted to recruit her only once, and she had been relieved it didn't work out when she'd discovered how argumentative Lucy could be.

She had wanted nothing to do with Lucy. Not then and not now. Something about her rubbed Lucy the wrong way. Maybe, as the saying went, 'their blood just didn't agree' – and Faith had lost interest in trying to figure out why.

Lucy would find some way to blame her for what had happened to her, Faith was sure of it. But Faith had made a promise to Joseph, and here they were. She would put in an Oscar-winning performance.

Faith reached over and squeezed Lucy's hand, her palm clammy. 'No, of course, he shouldn't get away with it.' She forced a note of reassurance into her tone. 'We'll make him pay, I promise. We just have to be smart about it. I've got some money I can give you. Enough to disappear for a while, get you away from all this. We can arrange a doctor's note. For your absence from varsity.'

Faith took out the envelope, stuffed with so much cash she hadn't been able to seal it. She held it out towards Lucy.

But Lucy was already shaking her head, her eyes flashing with indignation. '*We* can arrange …? Who the hell is *we*? I don't want your hush money. I want Mike to go to jail for what he did to me.' Her voice rose, and a couple of the students turned towards the sound.

'Keep your voice down,' Faith said.

Lucy reached for the door handle, ready to leave, but Faith lunged across the centre console and grabbed her arm. 'Wait. Just listen to me, please.'

Lucy hesitated, her muscles tense under Faith's grip. Faith scrambled for a new angle.

'Uyamkhumbula uBusi? That girl who used to come to the parties, the one with the butterfly tattoo?'

Lucy frowned. 'Yeah, I think so. What about her?'

Faith closed her eyes as if it pained her to remember, the lie rolling easily off her tongue. 'She accused one of Joseph's friends of assaulting her, just like you. She went to the cops, pressed charges. I'm sure you can guess what happened?'

Lucy shook her head.

'She disappeared,' Faith said. 'Dropped out of school, deleted all her social media. Udumo yilokho ukuthi uthole i-"scholarship" to study abroad. But we both know what that means.'

Lucy's face was ashen in the dim light. 'They ... they paid her off?'

Faith met Lucy's gaze, unflinching, driving the point home. 'I've seen what happens to girls who don't play ball, Lucy. They end up as cautionary tales. Is that what you want? If you ask me, take the money. Ask him for more if you want.'

Lucy stared at Faith. The seconds dragged on. Then she began a slow clap. 'That "cautionary tale"? Nice touch. You think you can make all this go away with a payout and a free vacation?'

Faith bristled. '*I think*,' she said, enunciating every word through gritted teeth, 'Ngizama ukukusiza. To shield you from how cruel this world can be to women like us.'

'Women like us.' Lucy laughed, the sound harsh. 'You mean the women who become the victims of your so-called friends?'

'I mean *survivors*.'

The word hung between them, heavy with implication. For one wild moment, she considered supporting Lucy, helping her get justice, burning it all down: the discreet payouts, the glamorous parties, the trips to exotic locales, the fancy clothes – all the shiny false idols she'd worshipped for too long.

She thought of her mother, hunched over the sewing machine, the resigned slope of her back bent from domestic labour, the callouses on her fingers from additional work taken on to make ends meet. A life of thankless labour with nothing to show for it at the end. Her mother couldn't even afford to own her own house until Faith had paid for it.

The moment passed.

Lucy leaned towards her, closed the distance between them. 'Ungangisiza uyazi,' she said, her voice hopeful, her eyes searching Faith's face. 'If there were two of us, the case would be strong. If you helped me, we could stop him from hurting other –'

'Awukuqondi yini?' Faith cut her off. 'This is bigger than you or me or Mike. You go to the cops, and everything falls apart. The parties end, the money dries up, people are investigated, careers jeopardised, and families torn apart. Now, maybe you're well off, but some people –'

Lucy turned on her, eyes flashing. 'Yeka. Stop it! Listen to yourself. Awuyena uMother Teresa. Don't pretend this is about anybody else except you.'

The accusation stung.

'You don't get to judge me,' Faith hissed, her composure cracking. 'You think you can enjoy the good times and then clutch your pearls when things get ugly?'

'You don't even like Mike,' Lucy said.

'I don't,' Faith agreed.

'Then why?' Lucy said. 'Is it because of Joseph? He's married, and even when he's at the parties, he doesn't even see you. He makes you organise women for him and his friends. He doesn't care about you – he only cares what you can do for him.'

Faith's face warmed. Lucy's words cut her, but she kept her features still. 'This has nothing to do with Joseph.'

'I'm just saying – even at the parties, he chooses –'

'Exactly. He has a choice, and right now, so do you. What's it going to be?'

Lucy placed her hand on the door and turned to look at Faith, her jaw set. 'I'm going to the police, and you can't stop me.'

Faith's voice was ice. 'Hamba. But remember you were on camera. You went with him. Despite what you might say, I bet the footage in the corridor looks like you agreed.'

Lucy shook her head. 'I didn't agree. I was drunk.'

'Maybe so. But "drunk" and "reliable witness" don't really go together, do they? How do you think that'll play out with the judge or in the media? And that's before they find out about your little tendency to dance on tables.'

Lucy's laughter was shocked and a little forced. 'Dancing on tables doesn't make me—'

'You're preaching to the choir, babe. I mean, *I* get it. But most people won't. Drunk, dances on tables, had a couple of abortions. Maybe one of those things is fine. But all those things together? Ja, neh? It's not a good look.'

She watched as Lucy's shoulders slumped.

'You're a monster,' Lucy whispered, but there was no heat in it. Just a weary, wretched sort of acceptance.

'No. Mike is. I'm not the one who did this to you. I'm the one who's trying to help,' Faith said. She believed what she was saying, so why did her voice lack conviction, even to herself? She thought about giving back Lucy's cell phone and decided against it. An upset woman with a phone at her disposal seemed like a bad idea.

Lucy said nothing. She seemed to shrink with each passing second. She reached for the door again, and this time Faith let her go, watching as she disappeared into the residence, leaving the envelope of cash untouched on the passenger seat.

The money sat there like a mute accusation, a silent challenge, a gauntlet thrown. In a world where everyone had a price, Lucy's refusal to accept bribes was admirable.

But admiration was a luxury Faith couldn't afford.

Faith calculated the risks, the potential fallout. She'd warned Lucy of the consequences, painted a vivid picture of the public humiliation, the character assassination that would follow. In a society all too eager to blame the victim, people would shred Lucy's reputation, dissecting and condemning her every choice. Faith hoped that the fear of such scrutiny would be enough to convince Lucy to remain silent, even if her integrity couldn't be compromised.

I'm sorry, Faith thought, a lump forming in her throat. *But better you than me.*

She started the car, the engine roaring to life, and turned up the volume on the radio, drowning out the sound of her own conscience.

***

Faith stepped back into the chaos of the penthouse, the heavy bass pulsating through her bones like a second heartbeat, the strobe lights threatening a migraine. That odd sensation again, the masks watching her. A few people clung to bottles and each other, stumbling towards the exit, while others stayed, lured by the never-ending alcohol.

Pills and powder circulated discreetly. Faith tolerated the ecstasy. It made it easier for the girls to feign interest in the men. The cocaine she disliked but could do nothing about – everyone partook, young and old. It made the men confident, if you were lucky; garrulous, if you were not. Up close, the movements were too frenetic, the laughter too shrill, pupils blown wide. From afar, the party looked like paradise, the ugliness with Lucy airbrushed out of the picture.

Mike materialized at her elbow. 'Uyilungisile le ndaba?' he asked.

He was the last person she wanted to talk to. His voice in her ear, his hot breath on her skin made her queasy. 'It's done. I took care of it,' she said, not looking at him. 'Excuse me. I need to check on the other guests.'

Faith sensed Mike watching her as she walked into the crowd. She pushed through the writhing bodies until she reached the balcony. The Joburg lights glittered below. She gripped the railing, gulping the cool night air, remembering the hopeful pleading in Lucy's eyes, the purpling fingerprints on her wrists.

'Here you are,' Joseph said, coming up from behind her. He slid his arms around her and nuzzled her neck. She stood perfectly still, inhaling his scent. Something expensive that smelled like suede and oud.

She kept her eyes on the skyline. 'Just needed some air.'

'Thought you'd abandoned us.'

'Never,' Faith said. She turned to face him. Peaty whisky and Cuban tobacco enveloped her. He was drinking and smoking and flirting while she grappled with the consequences of his friend's behaviour. Irritation flared, but she suppressed it. She adjusted his suit, smoothing down the sharp edges of his lapels, and smiled. 'Just a minor hiccup. Took longer than it should have. But it's sorted now.'

'Glad to hear it. I knew I could rely on you.' His hand lingered on her lower back.

'I need the bathroom,' she said, the words distant, as if spoken by someone else. He turned his body to give her space to pass. She left without looking back.

***

In the marble bathroom, Faith reapplied her lipstick. She traced the contours of her lips, the crimson a slash of war paint, to ward off the demons clawing at her edges, the undertow of melancholy she struggled to keep at bay. She looked at her reflection, and it was like staring into the face of a stranger.

She let herself imagine, just for a moment, a different path. A quiet apartment high above the city streets. A desk by a window. No 'shopping trips' to Dubai. No discreet visits to doctors. No more young girls with hollow eyes. In this alternate reality, she was fulfilled, content with her work, and loved by her family.

The faces of her imagined children danced before her eyes, their laughter echoing through the halls of a home untainted by secrets and lies. A partner was harder to imagine.

She had grown up without her father. She hadn't missed him, not really. It was hard to miss something you never had. He was a mirage, someone who appeared sporadically in her memories of her childhood, who gave her gifts and held her briefly, only to disappear into the distance, never to be seen again after she turned four years old. Her mother always assured her that he loved them, but love had not been enough. It was the only lie her mother had ever told. Many years later, Faith had seen him crossing the road with his other family. She'd followed them for thirty minutes before turning back.

If he'd recognised her, he hadn't shown it.

Faith straightened her spine and lifted her chin, donning her mask once more. She'd sold pieces of her soul, but the essence remained, a glowing coal buried deep. One day, perhaps, she would excavate it, blow off the ash and watch it spark back to life.

But not tonight.

Tonight, she would break her own rules.

Tonight, she would dance until her feet bled.

Tonight, she would drink until her heart numbed and her senses dulled and the world blurred soft, soft, soft at the edges.

The Black Dog

Ndongolera C. Mwangupili

Evening was fast approaching. Downcast, the man sat on the veranda of a thatched hut, waiting for nothing. Inside, the woman whimpered, carrying a baby tied with a piece of cloth on her back. A woven reed mat lay on the floor, covering almost half of the room. On it lay a torn blanket, a greyish bedsheet and a pile of clothes folded like a pillow at one end. Propped up against the back wall, a dirty sack bag, bulging with more clothes, faced the door. Just above it hung an outdated blue calendar with a photo of the state president's face, smiling. In the other half of the room, pots, a wooden cooking stick, plastic spoons, plates, cups, a plastic bowl, and an empty metal bucket were scattered all around, a layer of dust on them. Their purpose almost forgotten from disuse. Dry pieces of nsima lay on the floor, attracting an army of ants and cockroaches. Above, cobwebs formed a ceiling, spiders dancing in them. Sunlight penetrated through holes in the thatch. During the rains, it leaked mercilessly.

The baby girl's yellowish-brown hair was plaited, and she stared out with darting, anaemic eyes. Bones on her cheeks protruded like swollen boils.

With the child on her back, the woman paced around the tiny room. She was of average height, but thin, with cracked and bleeding lips. Though she was dark-skinned, she bore some paleness and ridges on her face, and veins were noticeable on her bare arms. A chitenje cloth was wrapped upside down around her waist, showing the president's face across her backside, surrounded by cobs of maize.

The man, seated on the veranda, could hear the woman's whimpers and insults from that round-shaped hut. Yonder, on a section of raised land, the affluent community was visible – mansions, flower gardens, children playing and riding bikes on tarred streets ... But down here, there were only ngomi huts made of mud. The grass around his hut was overgrown and littered with dead leaves and dog shit. A few steps away from the man, a skinny black dog was lying fast asleep. Green flies hovered around it. Once in a while, it woke up from its sleep and made frail attempts to bite the flies. Just like the woman and her child, it was weak and starved.

It was a house of famine. A house of dearth.

Now, the baby was crying in her weak voice.

The sun was sinking below the western horizon. Darkness, black as the dog which lay asleep, was creeping in. Crickets had started to chirp on top of the thatched hut, and dark clouds were gathering over the land from all corners of the earth. The man could see flashes of lightning along the skyline and hear thunder from afar.

'Where's food?' the woman asked, at the top of her lungs, from inside the hut. He knew the question was directed at him. He had nothing to give. Not even answers.

'Where's food?' she asked again.

Silence.

'Where's food, chimunthu iwe?' she asked, this time punctuating her question with an insult.

Still, there was silence, dead silence, from the man. The baby's wailing filled the silence.

The man lowered his gaze. Shame mixed with despair. His eyes rested on his slippers of different sizes and mismatched colours, then on his overall jeans, torn at both knees. This was his work suit. A long-forgotten memory ago, he might have been a muscular man. But, as age ran faster than time, fatigue mixed with desperate hunger, his muscles lost firmness, his gait stooped, eyes bulged, until he became a shell of the promise of his youth.

It had been months since he had last worked. Not since December at Shang Hai Supermarket, where he had been a security guard. He had arrived at 5pm on the twenty-third and gone to meet his boss inside the shop. The supermarket was full of customers, and the tellers were busy serving those buying.

'Here ess your Deceeembeah pay.' His boss spoke with a strong accent, throwing the envelope at him.

He picked up the khaki envelope from the floor at the door and began counting the money.

'Go do dat oudside. You're smellin' and filtfy. Get outta heeere!'

With empty eyes, he looked at his Chinese boss. He was a small but fierce man who had a strong presence in the supermarket. With a move of his hand and flick of his hair, he would tell his workers what to do or not do. He was hated.

'I sai' get outta and go to yor bench!'

He turned, walking away. He wondered how he could not be filthy with the payment he got monthly. K50,000 for feeding himself, his wife, and their baby. Being its resident, his boss was aware of the poverty in the city; it was visible in his community. Several times the boss complained of fuel prices; the man, at least, had little to do with fuel. Unlike his boss, he walked to work, and he never travelled to his village, as he could not afford it. Surely, goods required fuel to be transported, he knew that. He, and all the people, were feeling the rise in prices. And he had heard the president say this rise was worldwide due to one big country in Europe occupying a neighbouring small country. And people said trade between countries was affected as the war was being fought. One minister singled out flour to blame for making bread expensive. Party cadets repeated these things several times. Those in the opposition had their own stories, too. It was all confusing, he thought. They said this. They said that. The man knew only one thing for sure. Every day was a struggle to survive to the next day of struggle.

He sat outside the shop waiting for closing time. People came and left the shop, carrying plastic bags with groceries. He envied them and wished he had some. He held tightly the khaki envelope in his pocket, his hand refusing to release it.

As they locked the shop, he went to his wooden bench, his bed. He had no blanket, so he made do with his overall jeans. Every night he lay on that bench, trying to court sleep, while night drunks passing by called him names. He never answered them back. He knew the limits of his job.

In the morning, he returned to his family. Nearing their hut, he found his wife sweeping the compound, the child on her back. She stood straight, welcoming him with a smile. It was payday, she was joyed. He gave her the envelope.

'Did you get a Christmas bonus this time?'

'Those goats know no bonus. But we've enough for Christmas shopping, mother of my child.'

'May you be blessed, father of the child.'

December 24 was a shopping day. The woman had wanted to have a Christmas shopping spree. And here the man had honoured her wish. It was his wish too. Every man desires to make his family happy. If not daily, then at least at Christmas. Every man longs to be the head of his house, even if only once a year. He gave her the money, and she shopped and shopped. On Christmas day, there was eating and eating, drinking and drinking, dancing and dancing, merrymaking and merrymaking ...

***

The black dog barked at the flies that would not leave it alone. The man came back to his senses. Here they were now. The Christmas festivities had passed, the house was overflowing with sobs and wails.

Weeks without a proper meal seemed like a long, long time. Having little food, or missing meals, was not new to them. They had gotten used to that, but now they had no food. The man, the woman, their child, and their black dog were wearing out. They saw themselves slowly dying of hunger. The man thought about the Bible. In his sorrows, he always found solace in the holy book. *Man shall not live by bread alone.* Yes, for he shall live by other types of food apart from bread. But what? He and his family had no food, no bread. Nothing could be called food in their house. His mind wandered. He was in church, holy communion. God's presence is in bread and wine. That is God's body and blood. Food is the body and blood of God. Thus, food is life. Without food, they were dying physically and spiritually... Food is life, and the absence of food is the absence of life. A man shall thus live by food alone, for it is life and living...

***

The man sat mute outside the hut. Coming from the upper land, a gentle breeze caressed his face. It carried the sweet odour of freshly cooked rice, reminding him of Christmas. Kilombero rice and chicken was what they had eaten on December 25. His belly growled. But he remained motionless in his thoughts.

The woman suddenly stormed out of the hut. The baby on her back continued howling. It was a howl of anguish. A howl of distress. A howl of hollowness.

'Where's food, you fool?'

But there was no response from the man. He just sat there, his hands supporting the weight of his head, holding his lower jaw, his elbows resting on his legs. His thoughts had drifted again...

He was back in his village. He felt the rawness, the virginity of the land, the greenness of the vegetation, with the freshness of rain-wet soil. He saw her there, in that village. She was a village girl again, dark, with dimples when she smiled, her body shaped like a Coca-Cola bottle, large breasts, tight waist, and big hips. She was a beauty, but innocent and young, full of hope, hope of being married to a man working in town. She had heard that in town, married couples shopped together, ate together in fast food cafés, walked in parks while holding hands, bathed together, and slept on the same bed. True love existed in town, not in the village.

They had fallen in love. It had been quick. He thrilled her with his talks and, during their courtship, he had told her town stories. Stories of buildings on top of each other. Stories of cars cruising along the roads every second. Stories of streetlights dancing with possibilities. Stories of town life, day and night. But he had also told her stories of tricksters and conmen. Bottle store stories, church stories, and workplace stories. Stories of prophetic miracle money. Stories of money being everywhere on the streets like litter. Ghetto stories and suburb stories. Stories of factory workers and construction labourers. These stories had built in her a vision of town-life paradise. A life of adventure and fun. When he asked for her hand in marriage, she could not say no. She wanted to experience that life of bliss with him. She dropped out of school, form 3, to marry him.

But that girl was long gone. In her place was the woman, standing over him, breathing heavily, the baby on her back. She was angrily tense. He looked up, staring at her. She had changed. She was not the woman he had married. Now, with her hips deflated and dimples gone, he blamed himself for what he had done to her, for soiling her. He sighed. Love? Love is stupid, and people are stupider in love. They had fallen in love, stupid love, and it had made them stupider. Now, here he was, failing to provide the life he had promised her. He wanted to curse God. How had He, the all-powerful one, allowed this in their life? Was he an evil man to deserve that? Was he not religious enough? Had he called upon his family the wrath of God? Was poverty a punishment on him for things he had failed to do in his life?

His thoughts floated further... Every Sunday, he knelt before the statues of Christ and Holy Mary, receiving the holy communion. He had never stolen or been in any fight with neighbours. Was he not a good man? Praying and being good are not the same. One can be prayerful but not do good to people, or be good to people, but not prayerful. Blessed are

those who have both. He pondered... he knew it, he had both.
But why the poverty in his family then? Was it a sin of what he
had failed to do?

They were silly thoughts. Yes, what else could they be, but
silly thoughts? He lived in a silly country, surrounded by silly
people, and lived a silly life.

***

The woman could see the protrusion of collarbones above her
man's chest, and two ligaments stretching up from them on the
sides. He was no longer the strong man she had feared before.

'Where's food, you lazybones?'

Silence, dead silence, from the man.

The woman was on him, shaking him and beating him,
whimpering and repeating the same question, 'Where's food?'

The man was immersed in thoughts... This was not the life
he had dreamt of living with his family. He had not dreamt
of violence. But here it was, and he wondered if poverty and
violence were in their lineage, their blood.

He was back in his childhood village, his mother cooking, his
father seated on a stool under a mango tree, him close by on
the ground.

'You've finished schooling. We expect you to support your
siblings now. Find a good job in town,' his father had told him,
as if the town had jobs that people plucked like mangoes from
a tree.

And, indeed, he had been fortunate and had found his job as
a security guard without many struggles. But the money was
little; he wanted more for his family. They deserved that kind
of happiness, he had assured himself, especially at Christmas.
Was Christmas not supposed to be a day of happiness? Was
God not a God of happiness? Could he deny his family a godly
happiness on a godly day? So he had given out all he had,
knowing God provides food for birds that have no farms. God

dresses mountains and valleys in beautiful colours of vegetation. Would the same God fail to feed and dress his family?

That reflection hit him hard. He saw God as a leader, leaders as gods of their country, and his family as a country; God failing, leaders failing, and he, too, failing. He was a failed leader of his family, his people. A leader of promises and lies. Leaders in his country were as stupid as he was. Promising miracle money, miracle progress, and miracle food ... It was a country of people believing in a religion of miracles ... a people praying for miracles...

The man's heart burned with anger. It was not anger towards his wife. It was not anger towards himself. This was anger towards his country and his people, of which he was one. He felt cheated by his country. He felt cheated by his society. Everyone seemed not to care about where they were coming from, where they were, and where they were going. The motionless movement of daily activities. The aimlessness of action and inaction.

He had questions no one could answer, questions about freedom, about the power of the people. He was going crazy. He was dying; he was bursting with thoughts. The thoughts were killing him, eating him up, silly thoughts. He was silly, as he lived in a silly world.

The man stood up from where he had sat and she stepped away. In silence, he walked towards the door. As he opened it, the woman pushed him from the back. He fell forwards, onto the utensils inside, scattering them. His hand hit the sack bag. Clothes spilled out. His head hit the metal bucket in the room, leaving a cut on his forehead. He was bleeding. Blood dripped down, forming a stream on his face, down to his overall jeans.

He stood up, and, picking up a cloth from the mat, wiped blood from his face. He fumed and foamed. Boxer-like, he turned around and released his left hook. It caught the woman on the lower jaw where she was standing at the door. She flew back, and it was like she really was flying, like she had become a feather, floating slowly through the air, before toppling on her back three steps away, hitting the ground with a thud. He watched in shock. He did not know he had the strength to punch his wife so hard. He was amazed by the energy he had. Despite the hunger and his weakness, with his punch she had flown weightlessly like that. And then, for a moment, the man wished she had fallen on the black dog lying on the ground, wished it could have cushioned her, protected her and the baby from a crash landing. But he saw the dog jump up in fright as the woman landed on her back. There was a sharp cry from the baby. Then silence. Dead silence.

In a state of confusion, bits of memories and thoughts flashed by him like fleeting bursts of light... His life... His family... His country...

The dog barked again, rousing him from the passing horror of his thoughts. Here now, they were hungry and fighting. And now their baby, their only baby, lay motionless on the ground. Overhead, heavily pregnant clouds had gathered above them. Some small drops of rain began to touch down. The soft breeze was gone, and now a windstorm was developing.

Swiftly, the man picked up the lifeless baby in his hands and began running to the hospital downtown, miles away. The woman dragged herself after him, still whimpering. The piece of cloth she had used to wrap the child now hung slackly around her waist, covering the smiling face of the president. The black dog followed them. And the darkness swallowed them the way the black dog had swallowed the flies around it.

Too Long for Home

Yanjanani L. Banda

It is the news of your younger sister's sixth pregnancy that sets everything for breaking. You are just from work. Your handbag, a purple Chanel knockoff, along with your kaunjika high heels and the eight-inch monstrosity of a hair piece line your way to the kitchen where you guzzle a cup of tepid tap water amid laboured breaths. *Freedom at last.* Until your mother's call comes in. Right as you scratch at the itch on your ample behind, your mind on the dinner you are yet to put together before your husband walks through the door.

"Your sister has done it again," she says, and you want to ask what, but hold your tongue. The mixture of excitement and disapproval in your mother's voice reminds you of two years ago, when she called to announce Nelia's fifth pregnancy. You feel the distance between you constricting. Her words charge across the invisible cell phone lines like a suffocating tornado, displacing the calm you had anticipated for your long weekend ahead.

"That girl – tsk! I told her I would not tolerate this behaviour, but did she listen?", she says, adding fuel to the fire already burning in your chest.

Your eyes roll of their own accord. You can tell her playing at disappointment has improved with the years. Even with the exaggerated sigh, you can picture her smiling, shaking her head in disbelief for good measure. Your tongue itches to silence the rehearsed theatrics.

Only when talking to you does her voice take on the tinge of reproach. Perhaps letting you know she is trying to be a mother in her own way, so you do not feel too deprived of the warmth that should have existed between you. But you know it is your monthly support that makes her act the disapproving mother. Nelia is her baby. The one who stayed. It absolves her of any missteps in your mother's eyes.

And you? Well, you bear the weight of your father's sins against your mother. You are your father's daughter, after all. The one he carried along in his carousing. And certain sins, however polished, have a way of shining even brighter behind their manicured exterior.

"Who's the father this time?" you ask, careful to hide the animosity in your voice. You succeed a little, but the edge is there, wrapped in the questions you dare not vocalise. *Why not me?* Your good deeds and six years of marriage have not smoothed the folds of your shrivelled womb where a seed should pucker to life and grow.

Your mother prattles on. Short, successive bursts that bleed into one another, barely registering in your mind. For once, you wish she would remember you are her daughter too – that your sister's fertility mocks your own lack of fecundity. To force your enthusiasm feels inhumane.

You do not say these things out loud. For even to your ears, the words seep with an envy uncharacteristic of your curated front. You have worked too hard for the space you now occupy in their hearts and minds, however small. Instead, you clutch at the burning in your chest and nurse the saltiness that trickles into your mouth.

Good daughters hold their tongues, you remind yourself. Good daughters do not take a life. At least, not one so close to them as the one you snuffed out.

***

There was nothing eventful about your birth, you have been told. You greeted the world on a Monday morning. Bright and early, without a fuss, as though privy to your father's impatience to leave you and your mother behind. And leave he did, after holding you in his strong arms and bestowing upon you a good name.

You were meant for consolation.

In the years of your father's absence, you were a reminder of both joy and pain to your mother. When the sting of abandonment overwhelmed her, she would pinch your high cheekbones and only fell short of gouging out the eyes you had inherited from your father.

She had fallen for the sincerity in the depths of your father's eyes once upon a time. A sincerity she had not known was only temporary, masking your father's impatience to conquer his prize.

You cried with the pain she induced even as you ran to her for comfort. She curled into herself at your touch, sometimes swatting you away from her side. The anguish in her eyes was something you did not comprehend. To you, she was *Mama*, and that was just the way of love.

When joy descended upon her, your mother would whirl you around in her arms, planting noisy kisses on your cheeks, eliciting squeals and childish laughter. It was a happiness of its own kind – a well many inches deep, yet leaking on the sides. Mother and daughter playing at dissociated lives, but you did not know this then.

Your father returned when you were five years old, a smile on his lips. He was a tall, handsome man who put beauty to shame with a mere gaze at his frame. He walked through the gate of your M'chesi home that Saturday afternoon like a man who owned the world, raising dust under his feet. It was your mother's gaping mouth and fixed gaze that drew your attention.

He stood there, all limbs, with an intensity that made the wind stop to listen. He crouched and beckoned to you with his open arms. For a moment, you stood in place, staring between him and your mother, searching for confirmation in your mother's distorted face. She nodded lightly. Visible enough that you knew you did not imagine it.

You took slow steps towards him, turning to your mother again and again, waiting for the moment she would bid you to retreat. Even as she urged you on, her face wore a look you could not decipher. It was fear, pain, and relief rolled into one. When you were at arm's length, your father plucked you from the ground and threw you in the air. You landed back in his arms. Too quick. Too soon. Like the distance between you had never existed. Like he had never left.

You laughed cautiously at first. And then heartily. The little cackle that made everyone within earshot smile. He laughed too, and it was beautiful to your ears, like the beating of a drum with its accompanying echoes. It was that laugh that warmed your mother's insides. Made her head hang in surrender to his buttered words as he promised to love her better.

"I need you," he said, your muddy body plastered to his chest as though it were a lifeline. Your mother softened at how you patted his cheeks and giggled at the prickliness of his sparse beard.

He must have seen her smile right then, as she watched you bouncing in his hold with childish pleasure. He studied her like a hawk. And true to the man he had always been, he shortened the distance between them stealthily, still cradling you in his arms. He reached for her hand slowly, but held it tightly once he had it in his grip. Like one who would never again let go. Once again, she dared to look into those eyes. Deep brown eyes with the calm of the sea, the brewing storm underneath hidden perfectly. And once again, it would be to the undoing of you all.

For a while, your mother believed he would stay. That he had tired of a life without roots burrowing deeply into the ground. He had always been a son of the streets, playing house to tame the animal inside.

Eager to keep him, she cooked and cleaned and bent to his whims. Two years he stayed, teaching at the primary school which was always desperate for learned men. And on the day Nelia came along, your mother left you in his care. You were her insurance. She imagined he would not leave you alone in her absence.

Your mother knew you had become his world. The one whose babbling pried laughter from the recesses of his soul and brought a shimmer to his eyes, illuminating the handsome dark face she had fallen in love with many years ago. You rode on his shoulders or walked hand in hand with him as he kept pace with your small strides. Sometimes, she caught him watching you, a contented smile clear on his face. For you, he would chase happiness to the depths of the ocean or the peak of Sapitwa. For once, she believed him a changed man.

As she wailed and pushed Nelia into the world, your mother tucked the fear that threatened to undo her deep in her chest. If not for *her*, he would stay for *you*. But when she walked into the two-bedroom house a few days later, her stooping grandmother cradling Nelia in wiry arms, stifling silence greeted her at the door.

He had done it again. This time, taking even her insurance plan with him.

For days, your mother refused to hold Nelia, her sorrow mingling with crazed laughter. In the mornings, she sat on the verandah, staring at the front gate, willing him to reappear, wishing she had loved you better. At night she whispered into the silence, proclaiming on him a thousand deaths even as she prayed that he would return you into her arms.

He did not return, so neither did you; all her waiting and searching yielded nothing.

Once again, she loathed the sincerity she had spied in his eyes on the day he reappeared. Now she knew better. His sincerity had not been meant for her. You had been the prize all along.

***

The woman with the gap teeth and skin rich with the sun's warmth was the first of the many you remember. For months, she bathed your body in scented lotions and mothered your stomach with succulent meats enticing to your seven-year-old eyes. She had learned quickly that you were the door to your father's affections – and had accepted it. Until a year down the line.

You lounged on the worn leather grey couch mirroring your father who sat comfortably on the opposite sofa as though he owned the place. Tom and Jerry played on the screen, their murderous antics diverting your gaze once in a while. The woman sidled close to your father, brushing his arm the way she did when she wanted something. She stole wavering glances at you before launching into her desperate pleas.

It was his pronouncements of love she wanted, and he gave them noncommittally. Until she begged for the one thing she should have never dared to ask.

"Tell me you love me more than her," she said, gesturing at you with skittish eyes.

It was the first time you saw your father's eyes bulge in anger, his nostrils flaring as though gasping for breath. The first time you witnessed the marks your father's hands left on a woman's body. Though you wept for the mothering touch you would miss, you learned the most important lesson about your father: the pleasures he sought in a woman's embrace were nothing compared to the place you occupied in his heart.

She was the only woman you had loved outside of your mother, so you promised yourself never to love your mother's replacements again. Instead, you broke their expensive perfume bottles, burned favourite dresses, threw car keys in the trash, and made loved animals disappear, hopeful that, with every indiscretion, you drew closer to returning to *Mama*. You bore the battle scars of the women's anger on your body proudly. But even after replacement number seven, you were not returned to her. It was just you and your father again. You were now fourteen years old, learning to live with the marks your father's hands had started to leave on your body. In this, you were loved and unloved all in the same breath.

***

"How is this so hard to understand!" You throw the wig that was clamped in your fist to the floor, the distance from one end of your bedroom wall to the next feeling too short for your pacing. "I wear all this cheap stuff just to take care of them. Forget buying myself a new pair of shoes. And what do I get in return? Do my sacrifices not matter? Shouldn't they matter to you at least?"

Maziko sits upright on the bed, staring at you through sleepy eyes as you re-tie the chitenje around your bosom. You have not slept since your failed attempt to talk through your angry tears the previous night. Your eyes are still red and puffy from the effort.

"Self-pity does not suit you," he says, and you wish you could take a dagger to his chest.

Maziko reaches for his cracked Tecno on the weather-worn stool you purchased a week before your wedding at the second-hand store you had patrolled for months after you and Maziko had agreed to marry.

"Can't we do this in the morning? You know, when we don't have to *wake* our neighbours?" He gestures to the switched-on light from your neighbour's bedroom window.

His voice is soft. Placating. He has never been one for a fight. He's a soft-spoken man, your Maziko, a man of peace. But today, it raises your ire. You wish for a hint of your father's cruelty in him. The thing that made him cut ties swiftly and efficiently.

"No," you hiss.

There's an urgency in your voice. A spurring on you do not wish to die down. You have been at the mercy of your sister and mother for sixteen years. Believing, with every good deed, you cancelled your father's debt to them. *Your* debt. But with each passing year, you have felt the noose tightening around your neck.

When the first child came, you agreed it was a mistake. That you would do your best to care for them on your secretary's salary. Two years later, Nelia was at it again. You protested this time and spoke firmly so it would not happen again, calling on your mother to exact some discipline. It was to no avail.

"You should have modelled better behaviour to your sister," said your mother. "But how could you, when you were not even here for her?"

You had been too dumbfounded to ask how Nelia's misbehaviour was your responsibility. And with your silence, you had signed off on everything that followed.

You stop short of the other wall and turn to stare at Maziko whose eyes have followed you in your nervous pacing.

"I can't wait." Your eyes are pleading, but there's a cutting edge to your voice.

"OK." He raises his hands in surrender, patting the space beside him. "Then sit down, at least. I'm on your side. You know that, right?" he says, and you wonder if nothing would change if he knew.

You wonder if he would look at you the same way. If he would stay. You have beaten yourself up about it for far too long. Two thousand six hundred and fifty-five days to be exact. You wanted to be loved. When he came along, he cared for you in a way that erased everything that had gone wrong in your life. Everything *you* had done wrong. With each passing day, it grew harder to own up to the part of you that you feared he could never love.

You steal a glance at him one more time and let out an anxious breath. He should be the first to know. Freedom must come at a price.

"No, I'll stand. I'm too anxious to sit."

He nods and rests his folded hands on his crossed legs. You rub sweaty palms on your hips, leaning against the wall. Your tongue feels heavy in your mouth. You can feel the twitch in your upper lip as the air between you solidifies. Finally attuned to your own racing heartbeat, you begin to speak.

***

Your father kept souvenirs from all the women he left behind: a necklace here, a bracelet there, a picture, a scarf, a ring, and many other things you did not much care for. Each bore a tag with the name of its owner scribbled in meticulous calligraphy by your father's hand. The conquered, on display. A museum of bodies worn and destroyed. Your mother's name was not among them. There was nothing of hers to hold on to.

***

You remember it like yesterday – the day your anger calcified into a tangible thing. You had just taken a ferocious beating to your side from your father's belt.

"Why do you make me do this?", he asked in that soft voice that always made your skin crawl. He was a different man on such days. Transported back into his street-roaming years. When only ruthlessness guaranteed survival. And you had to survive, just as he had.

The gag in your mouth ensured that the only thing you could do was grunt. You had to keep up appearances, both of you. To your neighbours, you were a father and daughter left behind by a scornful woman. You played your part, clinging to the hope that one day he would release you back into your mother's arms just as he had promised the first time he left belt marks on your skin.

He often told you he knew of your little schemes to get him away from the women who had made both your lives easy. He told you the belt was a witness to both his love and disappointment in you.

"We were supposed to be happy" he said, tears running down his cheeks. "You made me want to be a better father, a better man. That's why I took you from her. Because I wanted to be good." He sobbed like a child.

Every time those tears fell, you wanted to believe him. To believe that you had hurt him much more than a daughter should. That if you had endured, if you had not tried to get him away from your mother's replacements, you would have had more of his love and less of leather scalding skin, leaving welts mapping every part.

You crawled on your other side. Each effort made your body shudder with the pain. You froze at the door's threshold when his bloodshot eyes finally registered your retreat.

"You shouldn't have behaved like your mother. She thought she could save me."

He closed his eyes, deep in contemplation. When he opened them again, the wounded man was there. The words were like venom on his lips.

"You were supposed to keep me good, but no no no no! You thought you could get me back to her with your little scheming."

He was still ranting when he wobbled his way to you and knelt at your feet. You loathed the prospect of his help to make it to your bed. You did not wish him to wipe your tears as if you were the child he still thought you were, in need of his protecting hand from a cruel world.

It was Mama Charity's fault, for reporting your innocent conversations with the boy from three doors down as something dangerous and unbecoming of a 'cultured' man's daughter like yourself. You had seen the way she looked at your father. She was not his type, you knew that, but it did not stop the woman from trying.

For the first time, it occured to you that your father would never forgive the meddling of your childhood years. It had made you a tainted thing in his eyes. Incapable of bringing goodness out of him. With every misstep, he would take you back to it. You realised then that to survive, one of you must cease to exist, just like in his stories of street triumph.

He helped you to your feet and guided you to your room with care. With every step, tears fell hot on your cheeks but you bit your tongue. In his eyes, you were still his little girl. Not ready

for the world and all its vices. He watched you like a man ready
to lunge to your rescue as you lowered yourself onto the bed.
For a moment, you were like two frightened children staring at
one another, each grasping for security in the other.

"Tomorrow you can do better," he whispered loud enough
for you to hear and the spell was broken.

When your eyes closed with the heaviness of sleep and pain,
you prayed that if you woke again, you would have been chosen
to survive.

Something fluttered in your belly. It felt like the end of
something.

***

Eight days have gone by since Maziko walked out the door. In
that time, you have turned your words upside down and taken
shears to their wings. You have cried for innocence lost, eyes
glued to the living room door, waiting for him to retrace his
steps into your home and back into your life. You have watched
the sun rise and dip into the horizon, felt its warmth on your
skin, your heart impenetrable.

As day number nine dawns, you are wide awake from a fitful
sleep. You taste the heaviness in your mouth and the mingling
smell of sweat and urine staining your sheets. Today you
promise yourself a new beginning. Freedom from a past you
have guarded closely and paid for dearly with your life.

You busy your hands, wash and clean until the surfaces shine,
and adorn your body with oils for your journey home where
everything began. Where you were once a little girl stolen from
her mother. Where you returned once upon a time, hoping for
relief, but found closed fists and hearts that could no longer
take you in. With every step, you feel the weight get lighter.
Having now lost what you feared most, you know nothing else
will grind you down.

***

"He fell sick and died," you had told your mother when you arrived at her door after days of travel, weeks after your father's death. She held you in her embrace, and for a moment, you were happy you had come home. Until her body stiffened, as though transported back in time. *Could you be any different from the man who had stolen you all those years ago?* You knew right then you could never say what you had done.

***

When you stood in your mother's compound on the day of your return at seventeen years old, you did not know that years later you would walk over the threshold of your mother's home one more time as a cleansed thing. Ready to unburden yourself for the last time.

The sirens of the police car will not have to announce their arrival. They will come for you a little after 2pm. You will hold your arms out without a fight, your mother convulsing with her tears. She will enfold you in her embrace, kissing your cheeks the way she had when it was just you and her. "My baby has come home" she will say, and for a moment, you will think, *This is love.*

Midnight in the Morgue

Foster Benjamin

'Hello, Inspector D.Q?'

The voice stabs me awake. I toss my blanket, as one will when a snake comes visiting. A thick blackness settles over my eyes, like a monster's shadow.

'Jessica!' I call out, my voice thick with dread. I stretch out my hand to feel her. To wake her. To alert her to this stranger's voice.

My wife isn't here. Where is she? I swallow a curse. Damn! I kicked her out eight days ago. I couldn't stomach her accusing tongue over my beer voyages.

'Hey, Inspector D.Q.?'

The voice is back. I slam it against my memory, trying to uncover the owner. Am I dreaming? I catch the voice again – this time it clicks. Grandpa Matebule! My long-gone grandfather who's been haunting my kinsfolk. Tonight, it seems, it's my turn to encounter him.

I sit up. 'Gogo?'

'I'm not your Gogo. It's me.'

The voice breaks through the darkness again, this time rising from the corner. Instinctively, I reach for the gun tucked under my bed. I grope for it – nothing. Jesus! A chill numbs my veins, and I feel a thumping in my ribs. I rub my sleep-encrusted eyes again to make certain I'm not in a nightmare.

'Who are you?' I try to keep my voice even. I'm sweating.

'I am the Dead Man,' the voice says.

'Dead man?'

'The one you killed. Killed twice.'

'Killed? Twice? Me?' I'm wide awake now, like a stray frog in a snake kingdom.

I spring to my feet, peering in the direction of the voice. I dash to switch on the light. Brightness floods the room, almost blinding me, revealing the man behind the voice. He's standing in a corner, next to the main door. He's of slight build, with a small potbelly beginning to protrude through his bloodied blue shirt. In his hand a pistol flashes. My gun! He's pointing it at me. Immediately, my balls shrivel. I feel them creep upward, deep into my intestines; then release tentatively. When I speak, my voice comes out like a child's.

'Don't kill me sir. Please, don't,' I cry, throwing my arms in the air.

'I'm not here to kill you, officer.'

'Please, don't, please.'

I sink onto the filthy tiled floor. Something wet pools around me. It's a minute before I realise it's my own urine.

I close my eyes and pray silently: 'Oh Lord, bury all my wrongs under the mountain. Throw them deep in Lake Malawi. Or even faraway Zambezi River. Receive my soul.'

I open my eyes. The Man is still pointing my own gun at me.

'What I need is my money, nothing else. My two hundred dollars, the one you took from me. Remember?'

Embarrassed, I whisper, 'Yes, sir.'

'If you steal from the dead, you're the worst criminal, all right?'

'Yes, bwana. Sorry, sir.'

I steal a look up the wall, my eyes resting on a cobweb-stalked clock. Ten thirty. I creep on all fours, grab the dollars from their drawer, and guiltily try to hand them over, like a child caught stealing chicken from his mother's pot.

'I'm not taking this money here, you moron.' He lowers the gun, placing it on a nightstand much to my relief. 'You'll bring it to me where I am.'

'Where?'

'The morgue.'

'The morgue?' I nod my head vigorously. 'Hm—mm.'

'Put on your uniform. Then take your gun and bring it along with you. Just in case.'

'Just in case?'

And just like that, he's gone. As abruptly as he had torn into my dreams.

My body is numb, every inch of it shaking as I stare at the wall where the Dead Man has just disappeared. Heart pounding, I back into my wardrobe and fish out my uniform. I put it on, my eyes still glued to the corner, as if awaiting the man's return, his second coming. I take my handcuffs and insert them between my belt and trousers.

Something rattles the window. Gun now in hand, I rush to check. I stare out the window. Nothing sinister stirs. Just the darkness beckoning me out. I pluck my white headdress off the nail beside the window. It smells bad. Just then a bottle of beer catches my eye. I grab it, prise off the cap, and down it in one breath. It gives me the courage I need to make for the door.

Outside, the biting cold seeps into my skin. Stars crown the sky, and they watch me as my boots eat into the asphalt. The road is deserted, except for a few frogs that have taken over. Their croaking is drowned out by the humming of the tea factory nearby.

I move on.

Now I begin to picture my encounter with the Dead Man at the morgue. How will it be?

I idly look up into the sky. I see the moon back in full glare, as though watching my next steps. Or as if it's my escort on this journey to the morgue. For the first time, I wish the whole thing were a nightmare. But it is not. It's reality. In my twenty-year career as a cop, I've never been haunted by my clients: road accident victims.

Piipiiii! A horn blares ahead, jolting me out of my reverie. I step off the middle lane. Lights flash through, and the car speeds down the road. Another car trails it, full lights on. I cover my eyes with the back of my hand. 'Idiot!' I blurt out..

'Inspector D.Q.?' The voice echoes back all of a sudden. I look around. Am I imagining things? I look about again. An air of familiarity washes over me. I realise I'm at that scene again. The accident scene.

I listen hard, attentive. 'Inspector D.Q.? Step over here.'

I follow the voice and bump into the Dead Man. He's leaning against the wreckage of his car, one cheek cupped in his palm. On his face hangs a look that alternates between sadness and anger. I can see it under the bright stares of the moon. The other arm is shot out, palm spread out like a beggar's.

'You remember this place?'

'Yes. This is Lauderdale Market.'

'The place where you killed me twice, right?'

'Not twice,' I protest. 'It was once. Once.'

'Look, you stopped me at arm's length, too close. I slammed on brakes. It was too late. I plunged head-on into the minibus, which was overtaking a tea tractor. Then chaos. Death. My death. Isn't it?'

'Yes, sir. I remember.'

'As if that was not enough, you came over, and preyed into my pocket, and took my money. Two hundred dollars.'

'Ye – ye – yes – sir.'

'My brother, if you kill a man and you steal his money, you become a double killer, a worst murderer. Your victim becomes a twice-dead man. So, I want my money back. You don't know where I got it, do you? I got that money from the devil. It's the money under the covenant.'

My fingers quickly dip into my left pocket for the dollars. What I find turns my intestines inside out. My heart is pounding. I search over and over. Nothing. I twist my face like a one-million-kwacha-bet loser. Where is it? Have I lost – ? Adrenaline shoots into my temples as my eyes lock with his, the owner of the dollars.

'I – I – put it …' I stammer.

'What?'

A stroke of recollection brushes my face. I plunge into the breast pocket, and out come the dollars.

'Here's your money, sir.'

'Are we in the mortuary?'

'No.'

'What did I say?'

'I should give you back your money.'

'What did I say, you government dog?'

'I – I – should – give – give – at – the morgue.'

'So?'

Silence.

'Don't get on my nerves, man,' he says, folding his arms together. 'Start off to the morgue. Go NOW!' he shouts.

I make an about-turn, and march back to the tarmac road. A guilty conscience makes my shoulders droop.

The tragic scene floods back into my mind. It plays out like a movie in slow motion.

The sun hangs low in the sky, catching us all here. We have poured our souls into the day: directing traffic, beating some sense into reckless minibus drivers. These drivers! They're twin brothers, carved from the same wood, raw. Unkempt. You tell a minibus driver not to exceed capacity, he breaks it and packs travellers like sardines; he even mans a vehicle that chokes along the way, one with tyre strings sticking out ...

Just now, out of the blue-gum trees arching over the road, a car emerges as if dropped from that *Mad Max: Fury Road* movie.

Barely twenty metres away, I jump into the middle of the road. With an audible snarl, I hail the bouncing car to a halt. In the same breath, I leap and land on all fours on the pavement.

Phwaaa! An ear-splitting crash ricochets off my back, followed by a single word – 'Maayoo.' I shake in utter horror as I feel a pair of hands on my shoulders, raising me up.

'Are you OK, bwana?' A chorus from my junior officers – two sergeants – reaches my ears.

'Yes,' I say in a low voice, concealing pain. I sweep a look back at the road. The spectacle I take in slashes my heart apart, and I recoil in shock. A minibus and a Toyota Sienta lie battered off the road, with the Sienta seemingly written off. Out of the minibus, wailing and screaming rise. My fellow cops turn, running into it. I head down to the Sienta with a slight limp. I still ache from the fall. "I see my juniors busy, helping the victims into the ambulance from the tea estate."

As I approach the Sienta, a gut-wrenching sight comes into view. The driver, eyes shut, is trapped behind the steering wheel. Trickles, crimson red, seep out of his mouth, nose, and left ear. I look away, close my eyes, and breathe in and out, face skyward. In the moment's darkness, *It* returns, whispering into my ear: *Into his pocket. Check.* I peel my eyes open, intrigued by *It*, my long-trusted partner who appears at every accident scene when duty calls, when the hunting urge strikes. *Delay not, or you'll be seen.* I dip into the driver's pocket. Something crisp sticks to my fingers. I pull it out, my heart full of expectancy. 'US dollars,' I almost exclaim at the sight of two hundred bucks.

I straighten up a bit, sweep a stealthy look around, first at my fellow cops, then at the gathering spectators. I see their eyes are all glued to the minibus. Except one man. He's just ten metres away, his back sagging under a long bamboo basket. He must be one of those tea pluckers. His long stare is fixed on me. I turn him a frosty mind-your-business look. *Into your pocket now. Fast. You've hunted nice nice.* It is *It* again, doing what it does best. The instant I sneak the dollars into my side pocket, a muffled cry breaks loose from the car.

'My money, please give it back,' the driver wails, blood all about him.

'I don't have your money, Mr Driver,' I answer back, my teeth gritted, voice low-pitched.

'I'll tell your friends when they come for me.'

'Tell them, tell them. I don't care. If you're dying, just die in peace. Ugh.'

'If I die, my blood will haunt you. Haunt you, really.'

'Why?'

'Don't you see you've caused it all? Why stopping me at arm's length? So close? Why stealing my money?'

'Enough!' I raise my voice, inviting more eyes on me. I can see one sergeant stepping over.

'Return my money. I should die with it. Or – '

I fish out the money, throw it into my mouth and gulp it down my throat. I sure as hell will withdraw it from between my buttocks. Yes, I'll hold myself hostage in the toilet. Guzzle down a bucket of warm water. If it won't work, then piripiri chillies will do. Tomorrow, dollars in hand, I'll head down to a black market. My calculation pegs the dollars at half a million kwacha. Half a million kwacha! I'll get two bags of maize. Pay Alex's school fees. Get three pairs of underwear ...

'Halt!' A shout echoes in my ear, ushering me into the present.

A police officer, too short and too small for his warm jacket, emerges from behind the roadblock at Mulanje Golf Club, his gun cocked and at the ready. 'Friend or enemy?'

'Friend.'

'May I know you, sir?'

'I'm No. B3978 Traffic Inspector Dambo Qachepa, fondly called Inspector D.Q.'

'Oh, bwana. Sorry.' He immediately freezes to attention, saluting me.

'Stand at ease, officer.' I unfreeze him, and he lowers his K2C rifle, illuminated by the faint light from the sentry.

'Sir, where to this night?'

'I'm off to the hospital,' I lie. 'My wife's admitted there. Malaria.'

'Oh, sorry, bwana,' he says, turning his head towards the sentry and shouting, 'Machaka, take boss to hospital on your motorbike.'

'Oh, no, no. Thanks, my brother. I'm just walking. It's part of the physical fitness, you know. Moreover, I'm almost there, just two hundred metres, not so?'

I trudge on, eating into stretch after stretch of the road.

I branch off the tarmac and step into the light along the gravel path. I follow the light further, and it takes me up to the old morgue. Without a moment's delay, I sneak through the fallen barbed wire, casting a cautious eye around. From behind a big concrete pole, near the main entrance into the morgue, comes a sound. A snore. I pick my way towards it, my boots barely touching the floor. I see the watchman sitting, face upwards. He's snoring deeply. Stumps of teeth glitter in the light. A plastic plate sits on his overalls, with half-eaten nsima and bonya fish on it. By his side an old panga knife and a weather-beaten club lie. I take the weapons away.

'Hey, madala. Wake up.' I tap him gently with the side of the pistol.

He jerks awake in a violent manner, reaching for his missing panga knife. Cockroaches flee from him. Blinking, he jumps to his feet and salutes me.

'I need the keys, madala. The keys.'

'Keys for what, my boss? For where?'

'For the mortuary.'

'Oh, no, sir. I don't keep the keys.'

I pull the pistol and train it on the old guard's head.

'One ... two ...'

'Oh, no, no. Wait, wait.' Immediately, he rushes to dip into his bag. He takes out the keys and eases them into my palm.

'Your hand – give me your right hand.' Immediately, I pull out the handcuffs and throw one cuff around the watchman's wrist. I tighten it hard; he growls in pain. Then I drag him to a metal bar, cuffing him to it with the other end.

I insert the keys into a giant padlock, and the door flies open.

'Dare not shout while I'm in. Or you'll join others inside. Clear?'

The watchman nods assent, his face a mask of fear.

Inside, a dim light pulses. A biting coldness breaks out on my skin. I look around, hoping to see the Dead Man standing or sitting somewhere. Waiting for me. I don't see him. I head towards the left side of the chamber. He could be there, I tell myself. I trip over something and almost lose my footing. Glancing down, I spot a six-pound hammer and a hacksaw hugging each other, like twin brothers. I wonder what kind of job they are working inside among the corpses. Thinking deeply, I recall those morgue tales. Stories about corpses rising back to life in the sight of the mortuary caretaker – and the caretaker wielding his hammer to perfect the job, knocking the corpse back into the chamber, to the place where it belongs. Those tales.

. I move to the first storage container, my brows gathered together for courage. I push aside the lid and see a small corpse wrapped in white. *This must be a child, not him,* I tell myself, placing the lid back. Immediately, my eyes fall on the second storage. Instinct tells me it must be him. With one step forward, I'm there.

'Are you the one?' I speak to the corpse, all bound in white, its height just like his – the dollar man. He doesn't respond.

'Bwana, here I am. Inspector D.Q., your friend.'

I get no reply.

I close my eyes, rub my forehead, and open them again. Now, I look up at the wall, and my eyes perch on the clock. Three minutes to midnight. I stare back at the corpse. A new thought occurs to me.

My fingers begin working on the Dead Man's face, unwrapping it. To my relief, I make out his face. Pale. Waxen.

'I'm here, sir. As you told me,' I say, smiling into the still face, expecting a smile out of it. 'I've brought your dollars, sir. The whole of it. Two hundred, just as you demanded.' I speak aloud, shaking the dollars before his closed eyes. My confusion turns into anger as the Dead Man's silence grows thicker.

'Speak to me now, you useless corpse,' I shout, throwing the money onto his side. 'That's your money. Take it. And never haunt me again.' My voice echoes back and forth.

As I make my way out, I stop dead in my tracks. I can hear voices approaching. Four detectives storm in, shouting, 'Hands up!' with their rifles steady. I set my pistol down and raise my arms, shivering.

'Inspector D.Q.?'

'Y – e – s …'

'What the hell are you doing here?' the voices chorus.

'N – o – t – h – i – n – g …'

'You're under arrest for criminal trespass!'

No Child of Myne

Beaulla Likambale Ng'ombe

'Mr Myne, could you please come into my office for a moment?' the doctor asked.

'Certainly, doctor,' I replied, quickly rising from my seat to follow him.

For the last thirty minutes or so, we had been in the sterile, dimly lit waiting room. My wife, Carolynn, had clasped her trembling hands in her lap, stealing glances at the clock that seemed to tick more slowly with each passing moment. Neither of us had spoken.

We had both given our blood and were now hopeful, yet anxious, as we awaited the verdict on whether I could donate to our son, Jack, who was battling a possibly genetic disease. My wife's recent diagnosis of high blood pressure had disqualified her as a donor – not that I would have allowed her to endure more after everything she'd been through with our three children. Now, it was my turn to shield her, to be the pillar, as any father would when called upon to protect his family.

The doctor gestured to the seat across his desk as he settled into his, unravelling his stethoscope from his neck and putting it aside. I was uncomfortable. Since we started this ordeal and Dr Stewart had taken over Ken's case, I had found him to be forthright – sometimes more than necessary, causing Carolynn and me quite a lot of anxiety when we had to meet with him. But he was the best, we were told. So we forgave him and focused on the task at hand. A task more important than anything else, even the good doctor's brusqueness: saving Jack.

He cleared his throat. He was uncomfortable, so I was even more uneasy. Since he didn't like wasting time, I was a bit taken aback when he stated the obvious. 'You volunteered to be a donor for your son.'

'Er, yes,' I answered, frozen in anticipation, the sound of my racing heart loud in my ears.

A deep sigh, and finally, after what seemed like hours but must have been less than a second in real time, his eyes locked with mine. 'Unfortunately, the situation is more complicated than a simple blood test. Your blood type didn't match Jack's, which led us to conduct further genetic testing. The results were quite unexpected.'

He paused, ensuring I was following. 'You and Jack are not biologically related. And unfortunately, your bone marrow isn't a match either. This means you cannot be his donor.'

Each word was like a slap. 'What?' my voice croaked, as though it were coming from someone other than me. A sudden dizziness swept over me, and my skin became clammy. In the distance, a migraine loomed, approaching like a thunderous train.

Dr Stewart continued, his tone steady. 'Since your wife is not an option, the best course now is to find his biological father or any biological siblings for the transplant.' He paused, considering his next words carefully. 'Given Jack's condition and his age, using a family member would significantly reduce the risk of complications in the future.'

'What complications could come from a donor who is not biologically related to him?' The words slipped out before I could stop them. I didn't want the answer. Tears welled up, stinging my eyes – perhaps it was the onslaught of that migraine. My body felt alien, and I was grateful for the chair that held me upright. I might otherwise collapse.

Dr Stewart's response was clinical, his voice a stark contrast to the turmoil inside me. 'The patient could develop a condition known as chimerism. This occurs when the individual's body contains two different sets of DNA.'

My heart pounded furiously, a mix of fear and confusion coursing through me.

Dr Stewart looked at me with concern. 'I take it this is the first time you are hearing about this?'

'Yes,' I whispered. A lump clogged my vocal cords.

'I'm sorry to be the bearer of bad news, but as you can see, this is urgent, so I would suggest that we start working on identifying another donor as soon as possible.'

As he spoke, his voice seemed like it was coming from a distant place, retreating further from me, hurtling me towards another time in the recent past.

***

'The boy needs a bone marrow transplant,' Jack's doctor at Hope Private Hospital had told us after he had been diagnosed with immune deficiency disorder. This new diagnosis threw us off balance because it meant that we had been given wrong diagnoses and advice for a long time.

'Unfortunately,' the doctor continued, 'the procedure is only done at King Martin Central Hospital. Already there's a long line of patients on the waiting list.'

A glimmer of hope brought relief. Finally, someone seemed to know what they were doing. Having a terminally ill child in the home had chased away all the happiness, all the smiles. Our joy had been suspended, and we had been walking on eggshells, because it would have seemed inhuman to have our spirits lifted when our small boy spent most of his time groaning in unending pain. As appreciative as we were to the doctor, we still needed to be assisted quickly.

'You can't help us jump the line?' We had hoped the doctors would make our son a priority.

'No,' he answered, as though he expected the question. 'Those lives on the waiting list are equally as important and deserving as your son's.'

I was quickly learning a valuable lesson: Money could do many things except pay our way to a quick medical procedure... We had to go through the normal process, just like anybody else.

Ethics. Integrity. Honesty. Words that would ordinarily make me respect this doctor became nonsense in the face of my desperation.

'Alternatively,' he said, 'you can get this service in South Africa. I can give you details of a hospital where my friend works,' he continued. 'Bone marrow transplant is his speciality, so if it's your wish, I can link you up with him ...'

***

'Mr Myne?' Dr Stewart's voice was loud, with an echo that pulled me back to the present. His hand was on my shoulder, steadying me as the room spun slightly. I blinked, struggling to anchor myself in the present. Had I fainted? The walls of his office seemed to close in, oppressive and too real.

Denial clung to me; I half-expected him to chuckle and admit it was all a terrible joke, to reassure me and then explain the procedure as planned.

But he wasn't joking. And he wasn't smiling.

'I know this is hard on you, and I understand why it's difficult for you to accept. If I were you,' he continued, 'I'd be talking to my wife right now. I am sorry, but we are running out of time.'

'Could we perhaps, er, run the tests once more?' The words came out a desperate clutch at hope. I knew it was a long shot, an attempt to shield myself from the reality of my wife's betrayal and unburden the weight of a lie spanning over a decade.

Dr Stewart's eyes met mine, his a blend of professionalism and pity. I felt small.

He sighed, his next words measured and heavy. 'Mr. Myne, with all due respect, we've already repeated the test three times.' His pause was laden with reluctance. 'If there was any ambiguity, any at all, I wouldn't have brought you this conclusion. Understand, please, that Jack's time is running out. The more we delay, the more we risk his chances.'

The finality in his voice was a cold splash of truth. The doctor's office felt colder, the sterile smell of antiseptic sharp in my nostrils as the reality set in: Jack, the boy I raised, loved, and called my own, was another man's son.

'I don't get it,' I managed to say. 'I am his father. I have to be.'

'I know this is tough,' Dr Stewart replied, his voice softening. 'It's a lot to take in, and it's hard to face. But you might want to discuss this with your wife now. We're really pressed for time.'

She had gone back to continue her vigil outside Jack's room in the ICU. To avoid infections prior to the procedures, only the parents were allowed to visit, after going through a sanitisation process.

'Are the lab results out? When can they perform the transplant?' Her questions came on top of each other.

I immediately recalled how her facial expression had changed when the doctor back home was telling us the procedure for the bone marrow transplant. The mentioning of blood tests had terrified her, but her facial expression had returned to normal in seconds. She had known then. She must have been afraid, but she couldn't say no to the procedure either.

'We need to talk outside,' I told her, ignoring her questions. I couldn't afford to look into her eyes. I needed answers.

'Myne, what's going on?'

I turned around and faced her. 'Is Jack my son?'

She blinked rapidly. There was the slightest of hesitations before she shot back. 'What kind of a question is that?'

'I'll ask you one last time, and God forgive me what I'll do to you if I don't get a straight and honest answer.'

We had been married for twelve years, and I knew all her mannerisms. I knew she was cooking up a good story. She had the most expressive face I had ever seen. It was one of the things I loved about her.

'Just tell me the truth.' I hated the plea in my tone. A drowning man begging for a lifeboat.

'He is your son,' she said, but her face was still, as if unconnected to her voice.

I didn't need her to take a polygraph to know she was lying.

'Are you sure about that?' I lifted her chin up and asked, softly this time. I saw her trying to get her mouth and her eyes on the same page. She failed.

'Yes.' She looked down as she whispered.

'Then you and I should go to the doctor to explain this phenomenon, because according to Dr Stewart, Jack is not my biological son, and that being the case, I cannot be the donor.'

She looked disoriented, like someone about to slump to the ground. I knew it was all an act. I quickly grabbed her.

'You are not fainting on me. That won't work, my dear. I will ask you again: Is Jack my son?'

She shook her head, her face still cast down.

'I want to hear you say it.'

'I am so sorry, Myne, but I can explain.'

'Sorry about what? Explain what? I want to hear you tell me in plain words whether Jack is my son or not.'

'He is not yours.' She lifted her head up. False bravado was written all over her face.

Although I had wanted to hear the truth from her, I wasn't prepared. I moved towards the nearest bench and sat down.

'I am so sorry,' I heard her say.

'When did you know?' Before she could respond, I said, 'That was a stupid question, don't answer it. You knew even before he was born, because, I mean … How could you *not* know?'

My body started shaking, and beads of sweat could be felt on my temple. Early symptoms of the betrayed.

'I am so sorry,' she pleaded. 'But let's concentrate on Jack; he needs our immediate help.'

'Yes, Jack, *your* son,' I sneered. 'You better talk to the doctor about the procedure and how to find a donor.'

I suddenly felt stifled. I didn't want to be anywhere near her or the hospital. I got up and began to leave. Still, I had one more question to ask her.

I stopped and turned around.

We almost bumped into each other, her words in my face, 'Myne, can we please –'

'Are the other two children mine?' We both spoke at the same time.

She stepped back. 'Why can't we discuss this when we get back home?'

'Which home? There will not be a home for you to go back to. Whoever Jack's father is can easily take you in,' I said, caustic. Bitter.

'Myne, please ...'

'Just answer me, damn you! Are the other two children mine?'

A group of people coming out of the hospital looked at us in surprise. I had not realised that I had spoken so loudly.

'No.' Again the bravado was back in her eyes, but this time, it was real – with a dash of arrogance. I don't know whether it stemmed from being angry for being caught out or whether it was because we were busy fighting about paternity issues when Jack lay helpless in his hospital bed. Whatever it was, it gave her energy to stand up to me. This was a side she had never shown me before.

'None of them are yours! Happy now?'

It finally dawned on me: None of the children looked like me. The thought alone was enough to make my heart stutter several times in quick succession, like the tripping of electricity back home in Lilongwe.

I wanted to crush her. She had embarrassed me, belittled me, and made me a fool in this strange country. I had come from so far, spent so much, just to hear such news?

I felt worthless.

I felt alone.

'How could you –' I started, but she cut me off.

'You did this to yourself, Myne. I told you to drop the subject, but you couldn't.'

How could she turn around her guilt and make me look like I was the one in the wrong? Apparently, I hadn't known her at all.

'So it has all been a lie?' I choked as tears welled up for the third time in less than an hour. What had life been like before

Dr Stewart's announcement? For the life of me, I couldn't remember. Twelve years had crashed and burnt in sixty minutes or less. 'All these years, three children later, and you tell me now none of them are mine?'

She just shrugged.

'Care to tell me whose children they are?' I knew it was perverse, standing in that Pretoria hospital, with people walking past. The sick and the healthy looked our way, bound by their curiosity. But I needed to know.

'It doesn't matter now.'

It mattered to me. But I couldn't bear to look at her any more. So I did the only thing I could. I walked away.

***

There was no getting out of this. There wouldn't be any closure. Three children? Three frigging children, and none of them were mine? I tried to understand how she could have pulled that off without me having any clue. There had never been a time when I suspected her of cheating on me. Smooth criminal.

Just thinking of them together in bed, their legs intertwining, their breaths mixed as they passionately made love, made me want to put my hands around her neck, choke her until life was snuffed out of her useless body. Choke her until the light in her eyes faded …

I was feeling murderous. I had never felt like that before. I had never even considered killing anything before, not even a chicken!

I imagined her writhing and moaning in pleasure as they lay on a bed. Panting after a marathon of pleasure … spent … fulfilled …

I wondered whose name she called in the heat of their pleasure …

I was going insane.

***

This betrayal had cut too deep into my heart.

I so much wanted revenge. 'You're not the only one to have secrets,' I turned around and said as I walked back towards her, 'I have a grown-up son with a girl I dated in high school.'

Even though he had never visited us at our residence, my son Ken and I had a very good relationship. When his mother had informed me of the pregnancy, I had accepted it, despite not being in love with her. But I had loved the baby then, and I loved him now. I had looked after his needs ever since ... I was so proud of him. At his recent graduation from university, I had presented him with a brand new Mercedes Benz, latest model, to show what he meant to me.

She chuckled at my revelation. Not the reaction I was looking for.

'You think I didn't know about your big secret? Well, here's another secret for you: You should ask the mother of that boy who the *real* father is,' she said as she pushed me aside, heading back into the hospital.

I grabbed her arm so strongly that she winced in pain.

'You're hurting me.'

'Not as much as you've hurt me today.'

She had just delivered another bomb. *What was she talking about?* I asked myself, trying to convince myself that it was a slip of the tongue. *Of course, Ken is my son!* I told myself over and over again. *How could he not be my son?*

'What did you say?' I shook her in annoyance. 'Tell me what you mean. What are you saying about Ken?'

Silence. Her face was blank, no emotions. She was beyond caring. Evil. Pure evil.

'Just tell me!'

'It's simple. I hope you still remember the tough times I went through with you when I couldn't get pregnant the first one and a half years of our married life,' she started. 'You went wild. You were sleeping around with anything that wore a skirt. Complaining to your parents and siblings just added to my pain. They mocked me for being childless. I was delaying them in having a grandchild, they said. Your sisters threw jabs at me about you having a son, and how I was "not so much of a woman".'

'So how did you conclude that the infertility was on my side?'

'Because I have a daughter I birthed while I also was in high school.'

No, she is lying, I thought to myself. *She just wants to hurt me further.* 'If what you're saying is true, where is this daughter of yours?'

'My sister adopted her as soon as she was born. I was still in school, young and naïve.' She shrugged.

What a man can do, a woman can do better... These words kept on ringing in my mind. Never had they been truer. More true was the saying, 'When a woman decides on revenge, even the devils stop to take note ...'

Even though my heart couldn't take it any more, I still had to hang on, just a little longer.

'So, essentially, Tadala is your biological daughter?' I knew I sounded stupid, but now it made sense ... It was like puzzle pieces coming together.

She just shrugged as she continued, 'I tracked down Ken's mother on Facebook. I used a fake name and made friends with her, and eventually we started talking about our children. That's when I got to know about Ken's real father.'

This was the talk of someone who had nothing to lose. She was holding back nothing.

'Mavuto, that's who she told me was the father of her child. But he had dropped her, so she pinned the child on one well-to-do young man named Myne ...'

I remembered Mavuto. We had been in the same class. He wasn't bright, just full of trouble. He'd spent half of his school time serving punishments. Last I heard of him, many years ago, he had dropped out of school and had become chidakwa cha m'mudzi – the village drunkard.

I was the biggest fool.

'Instead of being angry with me, you should thank me,' she said. 'I did you a favour. I covered your shame.'

My grip on her arm relaxed. Any ounce of energy I had in my body was gone. She looked at me with pity, then left.

***

I had resorted to leaving on the next available flight. I couldn't stay any more. I wanted to see Jack for the last time before walking away. I stood in the corridor and peeped through the door window. My wife was nowhere in sight, which was good. It gave me a few minutes to savour the moments before I left for good. I cried, seeing Jack's body covered with tubes, monitors hanging on his side walls. Still, there was nothing I could do for him any more. He wasn't my child.

I had been very close to the children, and I loved them with all my heart. I believed I was the best father. This revelation broke me completely. I didn't know how the children would take it once they were told, but I couldn't stay to find out. As much as I loved them, I wasn't strong enough to stay in their lives. Just then my wife appeared. Without looking back, I left the room. The hospital. And South Africa. On the next available flight.

***

Ken picked me up from the airport. We drove straight to another private clinic in the city for genetic testing. I had told him that I was coming home because I needed a wide pool of Jack's potential donors, in case, for some reason, I couldn't be one...

For the sake of the little respect and dignity I had left, I was avoiding the hospitals we had used before. I felt like I had been enough of a fool for one day, and now, whatever the results, I wanted to receive them in private.

For the first time since Ken was born, I looked at him with renewed interest as we were having our blood drawn. My heart sank further when I couldn't see any resemblance between us. I don't know what I had been seeing before, but it wasn't there any more. I had died a million deaths in one day, and this was a million more. With my head bowed, I silently cried. Ken moved closer and held me tight. I held on to him with a thin – very thin – hope that maybe *this* time my wife was wrong. That her cruelty and guilt had made her throw one last untruth at me.

After all, not all children look like their fathers, the voice whispered in my head. Like a taunting. I wanted to believe it.

***

'Mr Myne, could you please come into my office for a moment?' the doctor asked.

My heart sank. I felt like I was back in the South African hospital all over again. *What is it with doctors and this phrase?* I asked myself as my legs reluctantly took me to his office.

'Are you ready for your results, sir?' The doctor's face was expressionless. I couldn't read anything on it.

'No, but tell me anyway.'

'The percentage of relatedness is 0.000 ... You are not biologically related. I am so sorry that I couldn't give you the results you hoped for.'

It was like a cycle. The same words, delivered differently.

I felt lightheaded, like I was floating and my body was not mine any more. I looked down and saw my body slumping to the ground. A crumbling rag.

'Are you all right, Mr Myne?'

The doctor's voice came from a remote place as the abyss welcomed me.

To Breathe Again

Morabo Morojele

By then, we were accustomed to the pandemic. We had buried people and knew to walk tight to walls, as I was doing in a corridor with my sister. I had no idea where we had come from, or where we were going. I could barely lift my feet as my sister pulled me along, her hand on my arm, her words telling me to hurry, hurry, as if I would die if I didn't.

There were people behind me, coming after me, and people ahead of me also, who didn't care to turn around, rushing along the corridor to get home, I suppose – their only place of safety – to put the dying behind them, smelling all of them, of what they are when they are home.

If I could have seen myself, I would have seen that I was feet scatting, bent at the ankles, in my hippy boots. I had a scarf coiled around my neck, though it wasn't cold. The air was a pumped heat. The light was neon and antiseptic, and everything had been sprayed to die. If I could have had it my way, I would have fallen to the floor and put my back to the wall and my face to the hurry.

But I didn't and instead spied a black shape at the bottom of the rushing passage, hunched, squeezed against the wall, and yet resilient, and I thought it was following me. It was a cat-like thing with frazzled tresses, a bent back and old eyes lifted towards me.

I tapped my sister Bophelo on the arm. 'Look. Do you see?'

She didn't see, but I bent down nevertheless to lift the thing. It purred against my chest, and I felt the warmth of its life and turned to my sister. 'Can you see, Bophelo?'

She pulled me faster into her car, and then we were at her house. The cat was no longer in my arms, but I didn't worry; there were stairs in front of me that my heaving chest would barely allow me to climb, and I had a pain that was persistent and everywhere, as if I had been born with it, and yet not so bad that I needed the mercy of someone to tell me to go away and die.

People arrived at my sister's house. I didn't hear knocks on doors or see doors opening, but suddenly there were people there in her living room.

They were not her friends or her acquaintances, of that, I was sure. The first to arrive were four mahogany-coloured, identical young adults who sat or stood where they could, at different corners of the room. They lifted their chests to breathe, but otherwise barely moved and did not say a thing. They were well coiffured, with slacks and button-down shirts. They looked like junior managers with prospects in banking or IT.

I went to Bophelo in the adjoining kitchen and told her that the boys were here and the cat, too. She smirked and continued preparing our meal. When I returned to the room, neither the boys nor the cat were there any longer.

A minute later, the cat returned but with an elderly white man with long grey hair. He had thin glasses and bent his head to look over the rims at me. He wore a faded denim jacket and unpolished cowboy boots and looked like a person of old comfort and wealth. He, too, did not say a thing, and when I looked back at him after some distraction, he had also simply disappeared.

Others arrived also, preceded always by the cat: an old woman with knitting needles; a young boy with a rapper's backwards-facing cap; a woman in a sari with her hands together and her head bowed as if about to say 'namaste'; the four young men again; and Old Grey Hair also returned, but was suddenly a whiff of white dust, and was the first to disappear.

I told my sister and, though she smirked once again, I didn't think her heartless.

The next time, only two of the four men returned. I didn't ask. They didn't say. They sat at opposite ends of the room, neither frowning nor smiling. They came again the next day, though the next day might have been only an hour later, or even the next minute. My sister being out of the room, I could not know. Then they turned to powder and, just like the old white guy, they were simply and suddenly gone. More dying again – my own private pandemic – but this time, there was no one to bury.

And days later, which might have been hours, or even minutes, I missed the ebony black boys because they had been like my children. I missed the woman in her sari. I missed all the many others, and old Grey Hair most of all, because he might have told me whya thing had come and tapped me on my shoulder and said kindly, gently, 'Please, please, please, come with me.'

I'd trusted him like I trust old black men and women who wear their intestines inside out, to whom I rushed for comfort, for love. They told me that the world turns daily to a blinding, hubristic sun, whereas the moon lights footpaths that I should take to walk alone to places only I would know.

Whether anticipated, or suddenly, dying comes. One dies alone, diminished and in private. I had anticipated kicking and balking against the trailing ends of life and that I would find nothing there – no love, no emptiness even, no horror, no succour. But I was too close to poetry and to song, and so, to love. I'd brushed the round sides of the universe and had seen my mother after she'd died, flying, flying through space-time and through multiverses until she reached a place where she stood upright in her white gown and spread her arms, twirled around, and said simply, 'Ah.' I'd also seen her under the ground, with family there, who roiled and mumbled, but were brown and happy. If I could, I would be with her in either place, but having taken that moonlit path, I had rounded the round, round world and had returned home instead.

***

When Bophelo helped to unload him from the ambulance, he blurted, 'The world isn't turning fast enough. I thought it had turned a half, but it's only turned a quarter. Not in time but in the way it's inclined. The moon was up and to the right, and to the left, I could see the land to infinity. The world is round after all and deserves to be looked at.'

The nurses accompanying him said he'd shouted at them to jack up his gurney, because if he was going to die, he wanted to see the world through the tops of the windows, uncovered by posters of numbers to call and procedures to follow.

Bophelo's brother Motsomi was always one for poems and language that often didn't make sense. Growing up, she and the others grew used to this and would just let him be. But he could also tell a good story, and the kids from the neighbourhood would stand around him, engrossed, as he spun them tales such as the one about how, walking with his white friend through a small forest not far from here, they'd found a pond, decided to go for a swim and had taken off their clothes. Herd boys had suddenly emerged from between the trees and jeered at them, 'White boy, black. Black boy, white boy,' and then started throwing stones at them before taking their clothes and disappearing into the forest.

'We had to wait until it was dark,' he said, 'and dogs chased us. My mother beat me with her slipper when I got home, but my friend's mother didn't hit him; white people aren't like that.'

All nonsense, of course.

Or the story he told about how he and another friend had jumped on the back of a van as it stopped at an intersection, sure that it would halt at the next one, but it hadn't, and by the time they got off, they were far, far away from home.

All lies and made up, of course.

And once, on an evening, while boys and girls clustered together outside a neighbour's gate, he came bounding up to them, breathless. 'I've just seen the devil.'

'What? Where?' they chimed back at him.

'I came across a group of men in blankets standing in a circle at the side of the road. As I approached, they turned towards me, and the one in the middle was naked and pink. He had green eyes. I ran away.'

'Rubbish,' they chided him for this latest nonsense.

By now, when he wasn't at home, he was smoking dagga with other boys behind an abandoned shop or up and down our township somewhere. He had become the meaning of his name Motsomi and had become the seeker, the hunter.

When he got home, Mother asked him what the smell about him was.

'Sulphur. The smell of the devil,' he said, stoned, giggling, before running off to his room.

So Bophelo wasn't surprised when he said the world wasn't turning fast enough, whatever that meant. Neither was she surprised when he shouted, 'Wine, or whiskey, please, if you would,' at the two nurses sitting behind the reception counter at the hospital.

'He clearly needs a doctor,' one of them said, as orderlies lifted him onto a hospital gurney to his cries of pain, and she didn't know if the nurse meant a doctor for his body, his mind, or his soul. And though she was frightened for him, she was comforted that the meaning of her name, life, would bring him firmly back to this earth.

She visited him every day after he had been admitted, and for two weeks, he didn't say a word. 'You've been very ill, Motsomi,' Bophelo explained. Her voice was tender. 'The doctors had to operate.'

He would look at her with an empty gaze and stare at the bandage wrapped around his torso and at the tubes and plasters they had stuck to his body.

They hadn't shaved him, nor cut or combed his hair, and with his grey, sunken, dull eyes, he looked like he belonged shoeless and standing, perhaps with other men, on the side of a road.

After his third week, he started talking.

'I don't know you. Who are you?' He would turn and face the wall. 'Who are you?'

'Who is that?' he would ask, pointing with his chin at a man in an opposite bed. 'Turn the television off,' he would cry. 'That woman is talking to me. She is telling me to go home. But they've tied me, and I can't get up,' he said, pulling at his restraints.

'If I was not here, I would be not here. But if I was, I would. What could I do? Walking. Talking. There was a man with a yellow beard. He only wore one shoe. And also my teacher, Mrs Uhm.' He thought for a moment and then continued, 'She used to use the other shoe to hit me.'

He craned his neck to look out of the window and then said, 'I was with the devil,' as if on the streets out there. 'He doesn't have eyes.'

He tried to raise himself, but his hands were tied with restraints to bars on each side of the bed. He kept pulling at them until I had to tell him to stop – that he would only hurt himself.

'Am I in prison? Why have they tied me? What did I do?'

He opened his mouth as if to shout, but he couldn't, and a garbled cough was all he could muster. He used his elbows to try to remove a tube attached to his belly. Defeated, he lay back in the bed and shook his head violently from side to side. Tears sprayed onto his cheeks from his eyes.

They sedated him, the poor fellow, and Bophelo didn't know if he would ever be the same again. She would cry herself to sleep in her bed at night and think, *What a waste if this is what he will be for the rest of his life.*

'I want to go away. Go away, go away, go away,' he would repeat, making the words into a song.

'Where do you want to go?' Bophelo asked.

He jerked his head towards her, stuck his tongue out and wrinkled his face.

'Go away,' he said.

'Should I go away?' she asked him. He turned to the wall. She stood up to leave, telling herself that visiting hours were over, anyway, though they were not.

***

Bophelo never imagined how many medicines someone as ill as her brother would need, so she had taken an old six-pack cooler bag to keep them in on a cupboard next to his bed. Medicines for his chest – expectorants and dilators; pumps for air; treatments for his liver; pills to thin his blood, to loosen his bowels, to dim pain, to decalcify his bones; and creams to apply to his wounds and plasters and other things. She was most surprised that of all his pills, the ones the size of a baby's little fingernail were for his madness, and that a person's whole mental being could be turned by such a tiny thing.

At work, she made a table with columns of days of the week and rows of hours of the day, and typed which pills he had to take at what time, and left space for him to mark with a pen every time he took them so that she would know that he had.

Bophelo had looked at his medicines and read their inserts to see what they were for. She wondered also why they were named – probably by a man in Switzerland or a woman in India where they made the generic – to so trip your tongue, with enough Ks and Zs and Rs to crumple your brain behind your cranium. She wondered if they had retired that wizened old man who had once, many years ago, written a standout novel, who had a way with words they'd said, whom they'd hired to come up with names for the new drugs they were making, telling him first their purpose – for mind, body, soul (though there is nothing you can ingest that actually works for soul) – and then their 'target market,' and then that he needed to name the medicines to rhyme with ditties composed by a man dressed in a wrinkled white suit and stains.

He'd named the medicine for the tubercular illness 'Rifinah,' and had adroitly, he'd thought, added the phonetically unnecessary 'h' to the appellation; he might well have been reminiscing about a hot love affair with a woman from Malawi or from Spain when he'd coined it.

When she came in from work, she relieved the carer she'd hired to stay with him during the day, scanned his medicine checklist and briefly talked to him before going to prepare the evening meal. Afterwards, she sat in his room and asked him about his day. Lonely, his long day with the carer, with a scratchy television, books he didn't open to read, birds he saw out of his upstairs window, and a UFO he said, that had parked itself in the sky. He had been terrified that it had come for him. She listened the way she'd listened to all his stories over the years. But this time, she listened for his presence, here, now.

Motsomi hadn't fully returned to himself and would say strange things, like asking if she'd heard from long-dead so-and-so, or if she still rode a motorcycle – which she did not have – to work. He told her he'd had sex with their domestic worker, she sixteen, he fifteen, and how afterwards, he'd cried. Bophelo remembered her and recalled being envious of her nipples, like thimbles pointing through the skin of her dress, and of the smell of the sweat from her armpits and from between her thighs when it was hot.

One evening, he spent minutes explaining the difference between the colour yellow and the colour orange, and how red was, in his words, 'implicated' in there somewhere, in case she ever considered art; the sunset had been particularly masterful that day.

But he was much improved, and they would talk about the news on television or how family and friends were faring in the world outside. They wanted to come and see him, but he refused. 'No. Not until I am who I am,' and she was taken aback by how emphatic he was for someone so frail of body and mind. But then, no one wants to be seen at their worst, she thought; that is why they dress dead people in clothes they rarely wore when they were alive.

One evening as she entered his room, he did not turn to look at her but lay perfectly still, looking at the ceiling with tears in his eyes.

'I nearly died.'

The pearly gates for him. 'Yes, you almost did. Your brother used to say you were quarter to twelve. Thank god we brought you to the hospital.'

'What did he mean by that?'

'He meant that of your twenty-four hours of life – everyone is given twenty-four hours – you were at your last fifteen minutes.'

'That wasn't very nice.'

'No, it wasn't.' The statement had been an amusement but had no compassion.

'I almost burnt to death,' Motsomi continued.

'Where? At the hospital?'

'Yes. They had tied me to a cot. I couldn't get up. It was in the middle of a room.'

Bophelo remembered his hospital room: pimpled walls, first painted a colonial prison green years ago, and then a more optimistic independence green, then a spring green (the colour of a scarf a man had once given her, who had wanted her to love him), and finally painted white. The floors too were painted white so that every abrasion, every little spill of urine, every spurt of blood, every scuff on the tiles made by old fathers and aunties visiting would be noticeable, for cleaning.

'There was another room next to mine with women talking. They talked a lot, all day and never stopped, and I couldn't hear what about. And then slowly, I started smelling smoke. Not the smell of burning wood and burning things made from the earth, but the smell of plastics and of man-made things on fire. Then I saw a thin grey cloud floating against the ceiling above my bed. I tried to look behind me to see where the fire was, but I couldn't sit up. They had tied me.'

He paused for a moment, to remember.

'I shouted for the women to come. No one came. They continued talking in the next room. Then there was more smoke, and I started coughing. I shouted again, and this time a woman came. She said I should stop making noise or they would inject me. I didn't know with what and why.'

'Was the woman a nurse?' Bophelo asked.

Motsomi looked at the floor and blinked, to remember. 'Yes, I think so. I told her there was a fire, but she didn't do anything. She just left the room. Though I couldn't see it, I knew the fire was growing, because the smell, like that of tar when they have just sprayed a road, was getting stronger.

'I couldn't breathe. I was gasping for air. But I didn't want to breathe, because the smoke was going into my lungs, and it pained. I tried to turn my head against my pillow, so that I would breathe through it. But it didn't make any difference.' He paused to dredge up the memories of going to die such a death.

'Then the nurse entered the room. With a man. They didn't seem to see the smoke and what must have been the raging fire crackling behind me. The man had a bag with him, out of which he took a mask, which he put on my mouth and nose, and slowly, slowly, I could breathe again. There was a strange taste and smell to whatever it was they were pumping into me, but I didn't care. I could breathe.

'The man then pushed my bed into a corridor, and I remember going along it past shut doors and then into a lift, I think, which made a whirring sound, and it felt as if we went down, down.

'The nurse then gave me an injection, and I don't know what happened after that. All I remember is my whole body being very numb. I couldn't feel myself lying in the bed, or my one leg on top of the other. I couldn't feel anything, except the air around me, a breeze almost, for which I was thankful, because there is no life without breath. Then there was a bright light in my face, and I thought that maybe I had died. You know how they say you see a light when you die?' He chuckled.

Motsomi had been to the edge of the world. He'd stood at the precipice and looked down at all the things underneath it, but couldn't tell me what he had seen because he didn't have the words.

***

On the other side of a tall hospital-green curtain hanging from railings on the ceiling, a man was screaming. I'd never heard a cry such as that, so I knew it was of terrible pain. People talked hurriedly around him, and he gradually stopped shouting and started whimpering and gasping instead.

'It will be all right, my son,' I heard a voice say. 'But they'll have to take off your leg.'

Another voice asked, 'What happened to this patient?'

'Motorbike accident,' someone replied. 'We have to take his leg off.'

'Let's move him to theatre then.'

There was a shuffling about behind the curtain and the squeak of a bed with a limping wheel being pushed out of the room.

There were curtains on both sides of me. In front was a beeping machine with lights on a tall pedestal. To the side of it was a television. A man was mouthing what I assumed to be the midday news. There was a mask attached to my face, through which a white mist seeped out. There was a tube inserted in my arm, fixed with a dressing, and monitors plastered to my chest.

A male nurse entered. 'Good morning,' he said. 'We have to start shutting you down now.'

He turned around to the machine and pressed a button, which emitted a beep.

'One at a time,' he said, disappearing behind the curtain.

I felt quickly deflated, weak, as if the air had been taken out of me.

Minutes. Hours. And then more shuffling about on the other side of the curtain.

'This patient?' someone asked.

'Suicide, we think.'

'Why are they bringing them in here?'

'Emergency is full.'

The nurse returned. He pulled the monitors off my chest, rolled up the tubes affixed to them and put them in a cupboard below the machine. He then pressed another button and left as unceremoniously as he had before.

I felt decompressed, and that I might implode, not all of a sudden, but slowly, preciously.

There was more scuffling about and hurried talking on the other side of the curtain. They were trying to bring a life back. Then someone said, 'We've lost him. Let's close it down.'

The nurse returned. 'I'm taking you out of here now. There is nothing else to do,' he said with indifference, and I thought, he has done this many times before. He pressed a switch, and the machine was silent.

He then lifted my arm and pulled out the tube injected into it, and then pushed my bed beyond the curtain, and turned it past the neighbouring space.

'Don't look,' he said, but I did, and saw a body on the gurney in there, uncovered, and it looked like a young person with a blue bruise on his neck from when he had hung himself, and liquid stains on his pants.

The man wheeled me along a corridor – I knew corridors now – and parked me in a white-walled bay with nothing in it. I tried to get up to get away, but my arms were bound to the bed.

'Why am I here?' I asked.

'This is how we do it,' the man answered.

'Do what?'

'Let a person go.'

'Go where?' I asked.

'Nowhere. Your family is coming now, so be still,' he said, walking away.

My sister entered the bay with my brother and my son, and then cousins and some of their children, until there were about fifteen of them standing there. They were talking and laughing amongst themselves as they would at a family gathering but did not say a word to me. They then stopped talking and stood there as if about to take a family portrait, the tall ones at the back, the short ones in front of them, and a cousin's two children thigh-high at the very front.

Days might have been hours, or minutes even – time had shrunk and dilated, and I did not know what day it was, or even where I was in the day – and so I did not know how long they stood there, staring at me and snivelling. And then as suddenly as they entered the alcove, they shuffled out, my sister leading, holding my son by the arm, then my brothers and finally the others, until they had all left. I heard them walking away, laughing and joking as if it was any ordinary day.

They were gone, and I was all alone, tied to a bed, with white walls around me, white tiles on the floor, and a single square light above.

Three female nurses entered the cloister. They stood about for a moment without saying anything and then started to softly sing a hymn.

It was a common enough psalm, played nightly on the radio after they had read the daily notices of the dead.

'That's enough!' I suddenly exclaimed. 'Why are you singing to me? And why am I tied up?'

They stopped singing, and the nurse who had come before said, 'Sisters, let me be with him to talk to him for a moment. I'll call you back so that we can pray.'

'Why?' I asked.

'At a time like this, this is what is done,' she answered.

'And what kind of time is this?'

'You are no longer for this earth. You should prepare yourself,' the nurse said coldly.

'I am still here, and I would get up and go away if you unfastened me.'

'You must ready yourself for what is to come.'

She crossed her hands and patted her chest. 'When we die, we go to one of two places. It's your choice to make, although it's probably too late.'

'What do you mean too late? Do you mean heaven or hell? How would you know? There is no heaven and there is no hell,' I tried to bark, nearly depleting the last of my air.

'There are no two options. If there is anything at all after this, it is a little more or a little less of the one thing or the other.' I tried to get up to lean on an elbow.

'And anyway, what is to say that we aren't already somewhere along that line; I nearer to your hell than you, because you have me trussed up like an animal, and you there in your shoes, and if you let me go, believe me, I would be closer to the good place than you could ever imagine.'

I was feeling strangely chirpy, but also combative, because there was nothing left.

'You still have time,' the nurse said, looking at her watch. 'Let me go and call the others so that we can pray.'

'What for?' I asked again. 'I am not interested in prayer. I do not know these women and what difference their being here would make, if, as you put it, I am no longer of this earth?'

'Your family and friends? They will pray for you. Afterwards. I saw them when they came. There are many of them, and you probably have many more family and friends. But in the meantime, we will do what we will.'

'You pray to God, I take it?'

She nodded.

'Does God listen harder if more people pray, and that's why you want the others to come? So that he listens to your pleading for me?'

'I am not sure, but sometimes the whole nation is called to pray for rain when there is none, and –'

I interrupted her, 'And then it doesn't rain afterwards, does it? Ever.'

'That is why we have churches. So that we can pray. And priests.'

'Would a priest being here improve my chances?'

I tried to laugh, but there was no air inside me; one needs air to laugh, and to do most every, every other thing – like walking to a place to make love to a woman; her rooms perfumed; a beer in a bucket to make it cold; chicken pieces from the Chinese shop to fry with onion and orange-coloured tomato into a sauce; and then at four o'clock in the afternoon, because she works tomorrow, and so do you, her coy, dimpled smiles, sitting on her bed, and the family next door, with no ceilings, so you can hear them and they you; their school talk, their prayer, the father shouting at his radio soccer match, the mother banging spoon to pot. The father hears and goes outside to roll tobacco into a torn piece of newspaper.

I needed to laugh to continue with what was left.

A quarter to twelve, my brother had said. The bastard.

Bophelo had pushed the hands of the clock back, to a quarter past, and that was enough. Because days are only as long as they are, and anyway, I had dilated and condensed time, so that things happening were only simply happening, and time only matters if there is a beginning and an end.

The nurse had said, 'This is how things are done.' I had balked and had not let it be.

***

These months, these weeks, these days, I don't know, I've walked corridors to visit the bugger. I always thought I'd brought him comfort by the things I carried in my tired arms, after work. They were not heavy. They were a slice of cake most days; dried meats; sweet biscuits – I would eat some before I came to him, to push salt away – and as we masticated the gifts I brought, I would tell him stories of the ways of the earth, because the world had continued to spin, without him.

When we were young, it was Motsomi who used to turn this
tiring orb for us. He would come from the streets to explain a
yellow sunset, or to predict the coming rains, or to point out
to us the push-me-pull-you of a neighbour's dalliance with
another – a widow, for god's sake, and we would put our chins
to the windowsills to watch as he arrived, to watch the woman
as she flounced, opening the door to him, and how for the rest
of the year, he would come, for sex, obviously, and, we hoped
at least, for love. Fat Martha (her panties crept up her buttocks,
which made her walk sideways on the road) said sex was a
rough thing, and no one would return to it if there was no love.
She knew this, Fat Martha, because the boys had fucked her,
and she'd had a baby at fifteen.

Motsomi was a ne'er-do-well and did not have sufficient soul
muscle for the world. At least, that's what I used to think as we
were growing up. I knew that life was short and narrow, and
that one must decide which future, which path, if you will, to
choose. My brother had applied himself to many things, was
capable of all of them, and didn't know which one to choose. So
even now, I don't know what he does. Granted, he lived his life
and was never a burden to the rest of us who had chosen paths
and were all of us along them somewhere.

His life was as apocryphal as were his stories. He had
disappeared for years, and though he always kept in touch,
we never really knew what he did and how he survived. He
had odd jobs, some of which paid very well, so that he could
buy a car, second-hand of course, having written off previous
ones, and he would travel, not far, but at cost, nevertheless.
He started building a house and hired a truck to bring cement,
aggregate, and bricks for its build, but stopped when he ran
out of money. He once took me to see it, and all there was, was
a concrete foundation and walls half-built, encircled by high
weeds and neglect.

He had women, but he hid them from us, and we never, ever
had the chance to ask them about their lives with him. He said

once that he had a child, but when properly asked, he answered that he didn't, but that he wanted to have one, one day.

And then over the years, I started thinking that it was not him but the world that was deficient. The world had not been enough for him, and that was why he chased every one of its tendrils he came across. That was why, as we were growing, he always disappeared and would come back with stories, because it wasn't enough for him to be in one place, and he needed to see all of the word. He had been in a hurry, it would seem, and so now, worry. That was why he was so indulgent in everything he did: in drinking; in dancing when he could; in his love for women – which he explained was because he wanted to find their essentialness, to find the final beauty lodged in all of them.

Like others around us, Motsomi was an aberration. I got to thinking that he didn't belong here, that his making had been an almost unforgivable error, and that he should perhaps have only been imagined. But he was resolute and jealous for himself.

He had never seen the devil. There hadn't been a cat following him. There had not been four black boys, no white hippy man in boots, no lady in a sari, and his pandemic had been his alone. They were all a chimera, and perhaps he *needed* them to allow him to return himself to the world.

Shadow Fever

Sibongile Fisher

I.

Her shadow crept into our home on a school night, unbidden. Amile wobbled past my bedroom, down the corridor, past Mama and Papa's old room and into the kitchen. Mama was making soft porridge, clanking the pots so loud it sounded like our school bell. I hid underneath my bed covers, bit my tongue and wished she would forget about me – just this once. Mama was particular about school attendance. Once, when I was sick, the stomach pangs kind, she looked me straight in my eyes, enveloped me in prayer, and dressed me in my washed-out uniform before spitting me out on the school grounds.

'Go get ready, Amile, there is no time for your antics,' I heard her say in an almost tired voice.

'But I am not well –'

The thud was so loud I got goosebumps. Mama's scream sprung me out of my bed. I raced down the corridor, almost tripping over the server table that faced the kitchen's entryway. A dark mist encased Amile. I shuddered.

Shadow Fever.

Mama said that everyone was born with a shadow, but because they cannot touch small babies, they only appear when we turn thirteen. From then on you stay inside when the sun sets. You are not allowed to peak outside, invite your shadow inside or call on its master's name. If you do this, it will claim your life into eternal sleep. Mama says your shadow controls your body for five days before ferrying you to its land of darkness. Here, you are neither alive nor dead – just stuck in the abyss. She said our town was accursed, and to survive, we do not befriend the night. The shadows howl and claw at our doors and windows until sunrise.

'No more questions, Semi, just do as I tell you.' She'd swat away my curiosity.

Amile knew not to peek out of the window. Or to invite it inside, or to call its master.

We laid her on the bed.

'Fetch me cold water,' Mama instructed me.

I was staring at her, and then at Amile, and then back at her when she tugged my arm.

'Quickly now, Semi.'

I darted to the bathroom, drew water from the tub and into a small waskom. Mama used the water and a facecloth to pat Amile's forehead. She was feverish and mumbling about her wedding day. Something about a ring not fitting her finger. Amile was not old enough to get married – only to wear makeup. First, she had to complete her matric and then go to university and then find a job and then, *only* then, was Mama going to allow her to marry. Next year, for my sweet sixteen, I will also be allowed to wear makeup.

Mama paced up and down while I folded into the corner and stayed out of her way.

II.

She called for the praying warriors of the new church. The women, wearing their regalia, flocked around Amile's bed and began to pray. The dark mist slid beneath Amile's back as though hiding from them.

'*The new god arrived on a boat.*' My grandmother's words swirled above the heads of the praying warriors. Mme had been a firm believer in the old church. The church that she had grown up with and raised her daughter to know.

Shortly before Mme's passing, right after Papa's death, Mama had converted from the ways of the old church to join the praying warriors of the new church. When we ask about him, she defrosts into a puddle. She doesn't speak of him at all. The neighbour's child, Khotso, says Papa died in a mine shaft. Mama told his mother on the week of the funeral. Papa's body was late for its own burial. They say the excavators struggled to get him and other men out of the shaft. Mama is not aware that I know all of this.

'*All things old have passed away*,' Mama always responded to Mme. I watched Mme's words and wished to consult her. To ask how we could heal Amile.

III.

After many hours of fervent prayer and numerous cups of 'miracle' tea, Mmampho swept the other women out of the room. They waddled down the corridor and into the lounge. She turned to face me. For the first time, Mama noticed I was there.

'Leave us be,' she softly commanded.

I pulled the door behind me, knelt on the floor, and pasted my ear against it.

'I am *sure* you can understand the gravity of this situation,' Mmampho pressed.

'Yes.' Mama sighed.

'Then you know that our laws allow us to call for Tomoso.'

Mama gasped. 'Never – not in my house!'

'In extreme cases of strong shadow work, we are permitted to use the methods of the old church,' Mmampho implored.

'But *all things* –!'

'Come now, Mmathuto.' Mmampho sounded irritated. She was not the kind of woman who liked to be challenged. 'You are not a child. Do you really believe *all* things have passed away?'

Mama did not respond.

'We are permitted to use some of their ways, just not to be seen with them.'

The silence swelled.

'Think of Amile. This is the only way.'

IV.

Tomoso arrived carrying a woven basket and a bag full of mixed herbs. His long and heavy green robe exaggerated his small frame. He was light in complexion. His bald head glistened like the skin of the ocean while the imperious sun watched over it. His silver-streaked goatee protruded at a peculiar angle. He wore the back of a leopard over his shoulders. He opened our door without knocking and smirked in delight when he saw Mama's face. Mama posed a sullen pout and pointed him to Amile's room. He hovered over Amile in deep contemplation and then turned to Mama. 'Do you give me permission to do whatever it takes?'

Mama did not respond.

He swiftly glided to his basket, his shadow peeking underneath his robe. He took out a cup with a dark paste in it. 'I will need to consult. She did not invite the shadow or peak outside – it intruded your home and forced itself on her,' he said, as his long fingernails traced Amile's face.

'Can you save my daughter, Tomoso?' Mama's face twisted from a frown into desperation.

'I will return in three days.'

Tomoso gave Mama the mixture with instructions on how to use it. He flew out of the house, leaving imphepho mixed with iswasho wafting about. I studied Mama as she followed the instructions with a dampened heart, wearing the guilt of betraying the all-seeing eye of the new church on her face.

V.

The night hugged our town so tight I suffocated under its dark and stuffy chest while a heavy

rain assaulted our roof. I crawled into Amile's bed. She was cool and clammy. The dark mist was no longer visible, but my bones chilled every time I moved and brushed against her.

I stood on a never-ending body of water. It was placid but not fresh. Green and old in its ways. The moon lazily cast its eyes at me.

I walked on the water for some time. Something pulled me under. I struggled to breathe at first but then grew gills on the sides of my neck. As the breathing became easier, my eyes began to see past the murky water. A glow was sinking to its pits. I rubbed my eyes and opened them again. This time I saw Amile sinking into the depths. I instinctively swam after her.

Before I could grab her arm, Mama nudged me awake.

VI.

The town halted as the news of Shadow Fever advanced with every retelling. Tomoso arrived, his demeanour enlarged. Mama ushered him into Amile's bedroom. He slithered around the room while a bloated silence trailed him. He stopped, turned to face Mama, and in his striking position began to speak. 'In order to wake her, I will need your permission to sleep with her.'

I imagined a dog that ran into a snake. Both were afraid, but only one was poisonous.

'This is why I did not want you here. What do you mean to *sleep* with her?' Mama barked.

'If you want your daughter to live, then this is what we must do,' Tomoso hissed back.

'Not in my house!' Mama's voice almost broke.

'Well then, you better start preparing for a funeral. You know the rules. Five days. That's all it takes.'

The silence bulged into the corridor, pressing me against the wall.

'How do you know that this is it? The only way?' Mama growled.

'I just know. Have you ever heard of me failing?' Tomoso sunk his fangs into the flesh of her desperation.

'But there must be another way,' Mama groaned.

'Mmathuto, I have spent the last three days trying to find *another way.* This is the only one.'

The venom spread across her heart.

VII.

When Tomoso threatened to leave and not help Amile, Mama cowered and agreed for Tomoso to do as he wanted. Tomoso immediately pushed her out of the room. We sat in the lounge and waited. I whimpered while Mama cried in silence.

'The praying warriors of the new church will judge you.' The words leaked out of my mouth before I could catch them.

It was her despair that slapped me when she looked up. 'The new church has failed me.'

VIII.

That night, I slept by Amile's side. She had a strong vinegary scent. I found a lid for my nose. I softly prayed to the old and new Gods to pardon Mama and free Amile from her shadow.

When first light touched her face, Amile moved. She pulled her hand from under my cheek.

'Don't squeeze so tightly,' she whispered.

IX.

Three weeks pleated into one another. The town snapped back into its old rhythm of splashing us out in the mornings and swallowing us in the evenings. The people came in waves to see for themselves the girl who had shaken off her Shadow Fever. Mama had converted back to the ways of the old church, driving a wedge between her and the praying warriors of the new church. She hung her praying regalia in shame outside the wired fence in our front yard. This was required of all baptised members who returned to their old ways.

Every night, she burnt sage, which always gave me a sudden headache. I hated it. Had I not sworn to never speak to her again, I would've told her to stop. No matter what she did, how much of it she burnt, Papa was not coming back. Mme was gone. Nothing could undo what had already been done. What I hated even more was that when they heard how Amile was healed, everyone was accepting of it. Even the praying warriors.

I swam after Amile. The water morphed into crude oil that burnt my lungs instantaneously. 'Keep swimming,' Amile's voice called out to me. The harder it was to breathe, the closer I got to her. Tomoso's hands cuffed her ankles and pulled her further into the darkness.

I woke up afraid. I pressed my body down and closed my eyes. I wanted to go back to the dream. To save Amile.

X.

First light was late. Everyone stayed indoors until it appeared. On its arrival, it spewed us onto the streets. Sonka's mother, our family friend, called for Mama. We walked past the wrinkled houses that frowned at any hint of joy. Our town had a way of masking its strangeness with normalcy. I imagined Sonka's shadow, slinking from underneath her bed, up her thighs and blanketing her. She too fell ill first by fever, and then a mild hallucination, before entering a deep sleep. When we arrived, Sonka's mother opened the door before we knocked and spilled onto Mama's arms, pleading for her help. She did not agree with how Tomoso had healed Amile, but needed reassurance from Mama that the guilt of what she was about to do would be bearable with time.

'This is the only way,' Mama said, to convince herself more than Sonka's mother.

This time, Mama was the one to call for him.

XI.

When Tomoso arrived, he had a youthful bounce to his stride. He sat next to Mama. He told the two women of how he had just returned from saving five other girls who had taken to the same illness. Of how common this was becoming. They nodded like bobble heads, disgust sloppily plastered on their faces. Tomoso spoke of how he would need to take on an apprentice to assist him, if things didn't change.

'I can't have them all,' he said with a sneer before snaking through the lounge and into the bedroom.

He prowled around Sonka's bed. Sonka's mother began to pray under her breath. This rattled Tomoso, who, angered by her hypocrisy, jumped up and began to curse. Mama calmed him. My presence also seemed to disturb him. His shadow scarfed around his neck before sliding back inside his robe. 'What are you doing here? Out!' he shrieked at me.

I squirmed outside and sat with Amile on the porch. Tomoso's presence was draining her. I watched her sway to the dark void; her eyes open wounds that harboured pain. Sweat beads sprouted on her forehead.

'Let's go home.' Amile let out a faint sigh.

The night threw its dark cloth over our heads and drew us closer to its terrors. I wormed into Amile's bed and asked her to tell me the truth about what was happening to her.

Ever since she woke up from her deep sleep, she dreams of a green body of water. She walks on the water towards a gate. When she opens it, there is an aisle with a pulpit at the end and pews on each side. She doesn't know how she gets to the end of the aisle, but once she is there, a dark form, neither man nor anything we have ever seen, stands before her. Our mother sits on the front row, and Tomoso, standing by the pulpit, raises his voice: 'You may kiss your bride.'

She wants to pull away, but the dark form swallows her in a kiss, and she finds herself under the water. She is drowning when she sees my hand appear, but before she can grab it, she wakes up.

Every night.

I replayed the torment in her voice. I had to stop him. I only had three days to do it. Tomoso was to return to Sonka's house and *sleep* with her as he had *slept* with my sister.

XII.

It was the last day of Mama's period of shame. The dull-faced sun sulked above the clouds. She was preparing a fire in the backyard for the praying warriors, who were due to arrive for the burning ceremony. She was smaller and frailer. It was less about Amile and more about Sonka. The guilt of doing Tomoso's bidding had eaten at her.

I broke the silence. "Don't place the big logs on top."

Papa had taught me how to make a feeding fire when I was very small. I don't remember his face, but his stature is stamped on my mind. *'This way, it will burn for longer,'* he'd say while passing me the logs. I wondered, if he were here – would he approve of what Mama had done? Would he agree to this new way of healing Shadow Fever?

'I am so sorry.' She soaked me up with her eyes, then like a wrung waslap, carried on with what she was doing. Placing the bigger logs at the bottom this time and the smaller ones on top. I didn't ask for her permission for what I was about to do, but the apology granted it. In my desire to save Sonka, I was saving Amile and redeeming Mama.

I dashed into Amile's room. She was tired – more tired than yesterday and the day before. Tomoso's presence at Sonka's house had done something to her. She was fading and I was running out of time. 'Do you know any other girls?'

'Just the two.' She named them.

'What happened the day before you fell ill? Do you remember?'

She recounted her day: waking up to the usual noise that Mama made in the mornings; walking with me to school; meeting with her friends at the school gate; daydreaming in class; the cheers that came with the final school bell; walking with her friends after school; Tomoso's son giving her a buddy coke and walking her home; doing her homework; helping Mama with supper; watching TV ... but I was barely listening. I couldn't shake the image of Tomoso's son handing her a buddy coke.

XIII.

I marched to the police station. The gate was closed. I sat outside and watched the people of Donkerstein as life kneaded them. I thought of Mama and the praying warriors. A sadness washed over me. The clouds shrouded the sun, and the smell of rain coming inspirited the soil. I waited and waited for the police officers to return. After some time, one of them sauntered towards the gate.

'We need to do something about Tomoso,' I pleaded.

She was uninterested; she opened the gate and turned to face me. 'Go home. This is how things are done around here.'

That night, when Mama retired to her room, I waited for the sound of her snoring. I tiptoed out of my room and down the corridor. The shadows clawed and squealed. The hairs on my arms ascended the cold chill. My hands trembled as I twisted the doorknob.

My shadow plucked me outside and into the darkness. The stomach of the night was vast. It flung me against the wall and lunged at me. I saw Mama's shadow mauling the open door, unable to go inside. I saw Amile's shadow too. Tomoso had lied to Mama.

The shadows bellowed in hunger. I tried to scream but had no voice. I glued my eyelids shut as my shadow rammed me against the hard ground. My left knee cracked, and a warm red stream slid down my leg. I felt my shadow slowly encase me in a cocoon. I writhed to our doorstep and sat there, frozen.

When dawn approached, my shadow tried to pull me into the house. The others coiled back into the cold earth. I sat there, resisting. It was what I needed to do. First light reached over. I thawed in relief. It caressed my face. I coughed out a small dark cloud that shrivelled into dust before my eyes. I stood up, knowing deeply that things were going to change. That the night was no longer an enemy. I snuck back into the house and crept into Amile's bed.

'I know how to heal you, and Sonka too. And how to free us from the shadows.'

'Really?' she whispered.

I nodded. 'Really.'

Biographies

Chair of Judges

Chika Unigwe serves as a creative writing professor at Georgia State College and University in Milledgeville, Georgia. She is a prolific writer of both fiction and non-fiction, whose works have been translated into several languages. Her notable works include the award-winning novel *On Black Sisters' Street* and the short-story collection *Better Never Than Late.* Her latest novel, *The Middle Daughter,* is published by Canongate Books. In 2023, Unigwe was knighted into the Order of the Crown by the Belgian government in recognition of her contributions to literature.

Editors

Femi Kayode works in advertising and has written for stage and screen. While studying for an MA in Creative Writing – Crime Fiction at the University of East Anglia, he wrote his first novel, *Lightseekers* (Bloomsbury 2021), which won the Little, Brown/UEA Award for Crime Fiction in 2018. *Lightseekers* was selected as a Best Crime Novel of the Month by *The Times, Sunday Times, Independent, Guardian, Observer, Financial Times* and *Irish Times,* was longlisted for the CWA Gold Dagger and was a Waterstones Thriller of the Month. His second novel, *Gaslight* (Bloomsbury 2023) was a Zoe Ball Radio 2 Book Club selection, a Sunday Times Crime Book of the Month and was shortlisted for the Ian Flemming Steel Dagger. Femi lives in Windhoek, Namibia.

Karen Jennings is a South African author whose novel *An Island* was longlisted for the Booker Prize in 2021. Her most recent novel, *Crooked Seeds*, came out in 2024. She is currently writer-in-residence as a post-doctoral fellow at the Laboratory for the Economics of Africa's Past (LEAP), Stellenbosch University, where she explores history through fiction. Karen is also co-founder of The Island Prize for Debut African Novels.

2024 Shortlisted Stories

Tryphena Yeboah is a Ghanaian writer and the author of the poetry chapbook, *A Mouthful of Home* (Akashic Books). Her fiction and essays have appeared in *Narrative Magazine*, *Commonwealth Writers*, and *Lit Hub*, among others. She is currently a Ph.D. student at the University of Nebraska-Lincoln, studying English with an emphasis in Creative Writing.

Nadia Davids is a South African writer, theatre-maker and scholar. Her plays (*At Her Feet*, *What Remains*, *Hold Still*) have been staged throughout Southern Africa and in Europe. Her debut novel *An Imperfect Blessing* was shortlisted for Pan-African Etisalat Prize for Literature. Nadia's short fiction and essays have appeared in The American Scholar, The Los Angeles Review of Books, Astra Magazine, The Georgia Review, the Johannesburg Review of Books and Zyzzyva Magazine. She's held residencies at Hedgebrook, Art Omi and The Women's Project, and was a 2023 Aspen Words Writer. Nadia has taught at Queen Mary University of London and the University of Cape Town and is the President Emeritus of PEN South Africa.

Samuel Kọláwọlé was born and raised in Ibadan, Nigeria. He is the author of a new, critically acclaimed novel, *The Road to the Salt Sea*. His work has appeared in *AGNI*, *New England Review*, *Georgia Review*, *The Hopkins Review*, *Gulf Coast*, *Washington Square Review*, *Harvard Review*, *Image Journal*, and other literary publications. He has received numerous residencies and fellowships and has been a finalist for the Graywolf Press Africa Prize, International Book Award, and shortlisted for UK's The First Novel Prize, and won an Editor-Writer Mentorship Program for Diverse Writers. He is a graduate of the MFA in Writing and Publishing at Vermont College of Fine Arts; and earned his PhD in English and Creative Writing from Georgia State University. He has taught creative writing in Africa, Sweden, and the United States, and currently teaches fiction writing as an Assistant Professor of English and African Studies at Pennsylvania State University.

Uche Okonkwo's stories have been published in *A Public Space*, *One Story*, the *Kenyon Review, Ploughshares, The Best American Nonrequired Reading 2019*, and *Lagos Noir*, among others. She is the author of the debut story collection *A Kind of Madness*: Tin House (2024); Narrative Landscape (2024); and VERVE Books (2025). A former Bernard O'Keefe Scholar at Bread Loaf Writers' Conference and resident at Art Omi, she is a recipient of the George Bennett Fellowship at Phillips Exeter Academy, a Steinbeck Fellowship, and an Elizabeth George Foundation grant. Okonkwo grew up in Lagos, Nigeria, and is currently pursuing a creative writing PhD at the University of Nebraska-Lincoln.

Pemi Aguda is an MFA graduate from the Helen Zell Writers' Program at the University of Michigan and the winner of the 2020 Deborah Rogers Foundation Award. Her writing has been published in *One Story, Granta, Ploughshares, American Short Fiction, Zoetrope*, and other publications, and has been awarded the O. Henry Prize for short fiction in 2022 and 2023. She is the author of a collection of stories, *Ghostroots* (W.W. Norton, 2024; Virago Press, 2024; and Masobe Books, 2024). Pemi is from Lagos, Nigeria.

2024 Workshop Stories

Joshua Chizoma is a Nigerian lawyer and writer. His works explore the themes of family, belonging and place. He has been a finalist for the Isele Prize for Nonfiction, the Gerald Kraak Prize, the Miles Morland Scholarship and has been nominated for the Pushcart prize. His Story, "Collector of Memories" was a finalist for the Afritondo Short Story Prize 2020 and was subsequently selected as a finalist for the 2022 AKO Caine Prize for African Writing. His works have been published or forthcoming in *Isele Magazine, Prairie Schooner, Lolwe, AFREADA, Entropy Magazine, Kalahari Review, Pradhya Review*, and elsewhere. He was selected for the 2019 Purple Hibiscus Workshop taught by Chimamanda Adichie.Joshua has a law degree from the University of Nigeria.

Ekemini Pius is a Nigerian writer and editor who lives in Calabar, Nigeria. His works have been published in the *Kendeka Prize for African Literature Anthology*, the *K & L Prize Anthology, Afro Literary Magazine*, and *Isele Magazine*. His story, 'Time and Bodies' was shortlisted for the 2021 Kendeka Prize for African Literature. He was also shortlisted for the 2022 Awele Creative Trust Short Story Prize. He is an alumnus of the 2019 Wawa Literary Fellowship and was a finalist for the 2022 Guest Artist Space Fellowship. He was also a finalist for the 2023 Caine Prize for African Writing. He is currently working on his debut novel.

Cherrie Kandie is a writer from Kenya whose first published short story 'Sew My Mouth' was shortlisted for the 2019 Caine Prize for African Writing. 'Sew My Mouth' was also shortlisted for the 2017/2018 Short Story Day Africa Prize as part of the *ID: New Short Fiction from Africa* anthology where it was first published. She recently attended the Caine Prize Writing Workshop in Malawi. Ms. Kandie holds an MA in Comparative Literature from Dartmouth College. Her BA with a major in Comparative Literature and minor in African Studies is from the same institution. She appeared on the shortlist for the 2019 Miles Morland Foundation Writing Scholarship and the inaugural 2021 Huza Press/Goethe Institut Writing Gender Residency. She completed the six-month 2021 writing residency at Kenya's Moi University African Cluster Center (Moi-ACC) as affiliated with the University of Bayreuth, Germany.

Erica Sugo Anyadike is a television producer, a writer and a lecturer. She has been shortlisted for the Caine Prize, the Commonwealth Short Story Prize and the Queen Mary Wasafiri New Writing Prize, has featured in several anthologies and been published by *Kwani, Femrite* and *Karavan* amongst others. Whether she's writing for television or writing prose, Erica's stories place African women at the centre of her narratives. She is interested in complex representations of women and is currently writing a novel.

Ndongolera C. Mwangupili (Poet, fiction and nonfiction writer, scholar, culturalist; Malawi) is a writer whose first collection of poems is titled *Fragments of my Broken Voice* (2020). He has also published a short novel titled *Sons of the Hills* (2021). *A Gift to the People: Sr. Beatrice Chipeta's Legacy* (2020) is a short biography he authored as a book project for Lusubilo Orphan Care Centre in Malawi. His literary works have appeared in literary journals such as Southern Humanities Review of Auburn University, Florilege, Open Road Review, The Criterion: An International Journal in English, and Praxis Magazine Online. Others have been anthologized in *Modern Stories from Malawi* (2003), *the Bachelor of Chikanda and Other Stories* (2009), *The Time Traveller of Maravi: New Poetry from Malawi* (2011), *Free Fall: An International Anthology* (2017), *Arbolarium Antologia Poetica Delos Cinco Continentes* (2019), and *Beneath Humanity* (2023). His book *English Language for MSCE: Comprehension, Summary, Note-making and Composition* (2014) is used in Malawi secondary school curriculum as a reference book. He is a founding member of the Malawi Union of Academic and Non-fiction Authors (MUANA) where he served as the Secretary General and the Vice President. In 2004, he was one of the African writers who took part in the Crossingborder Project under the British Council. He mentors several young writers in Malawi and makes presentations at different writers' conferences locally and internationally like Public Lending Right (PLR) International, International Authors Forum, Intanga Hub (Zimbabwe), International Writers Alliance (Kenya), and Heart and Soul Broadcasting Services (Zimbabwe). He currently works as Principal Quality Assurance Officer for the Northern Education Division in Malawi and teaches at the University of Livingstonia as an adjunct lecturer.

Yanjanani L. Banda is a writer from Malawi. She was the 2023 fellow of the Literary Laddership for Emerging African Authors, was shortlisted for the 2023 Kendeka Prize for Literature and the 2022 Bristol Short Story Prize. Her other works have appeared in *Brittle Paper*, *Afritondo Magazine*, *Spillwords*, and *the Quilled Ink Review*.

Foster Benjamin is the author of numerous short stories published in Malawi's leading newspapers—Malawi News and Weekend Nation. He has been writing and publishing short stories since 2002 when he was in secondary school in Mulanje, a tea growing district where he was born; a place which is a fodder for some of his stories chronicling tea estate workers' lives. Foster, soon after secondary school, once worked in the estate as a labourer—a tea picker himself! Some of his stories have been anthologized in *The Conductress & Other Stories* and *The Mandebvu Mistress & Other Stories*, both publications by the Malawi Writers Union, Malawi's reputed literary body. Foster can be contacted on his WhatsApp number +(265)991 78 27 97 and X: Foster Benjamin and Instagram Foster Benjamin173

Beaulla Likambale Ng'ombe: Born on January 29, 1972, Beaulla is a Lecturer in the Business Department at Malawi Adventist University since January 2021. Prior to that she had been working as a Human Resource Manager for the same institution from 2011. Beaulla has a Master of Science degree in Strategic Management from The University of Derby, (UK) and other two Bachelor of Arts Degrees in Business and Management respectively.

Beaulla seriously started the writing journey in 2017, where she has written several (unpublished) novels and other guide books to be used for academic purposes once they are published. The same year (2017), she entered the national writing competition with her story 'Because of His Skin', a story that highlighted the difficult life of a person born with Albinism. She came fourth, and the following year, she entered again with a short story 'Twisted Fate', a plight of an abandoned child and she came second. She has so far authored and published *The Graveyard Meeting*, a collection of short stories which is available on Amazon.

Morabo Morojele was born in Maseru, Lesotho and raised in Ethiopia and in Italy where his father was a UN official. He studied high school in Swaziland, now Eswatini, and has degrees from the London School of Economics and the Institute of Social Studies at The Hague in the Netherlands.

Morabo has worked for the United Nations Development Programme, (UNDP) in Lesotho; as a lecturer at the Graduate School of Public and Development Management at the University of the Witwatersrand in Johannesburg; and as a consultant for governments, for non-governmental organisations and for international organisations including the World Bank, UNDP and UNICEF.

Morabo's first novel, *How We Buried Puso*, was published to great acclaim. His second work of fiction, *Three Egg Dilemma* which was published in 2023 has been shortlisted and put forward for several South African literary awards.

Morabo is a jazz musician and has performed and/or recorded with numerous South African musicians including Abdullah Ibrahim, and the late Sibongile Khumalo and Zim Ngqawana amongst others. He has performed at the esteemed Ronnie Scott's in London, and at the Stockholm, Cape Town and Johannesburg International Jazz festivals. He is currently troubled by the art of short story writing.

Sibongile Fisher is an award winning writer based in South Africa. She is passionate about accessibility to arts and technology in marginalized communities. She holds a BCom in Marketing Management from UJ and a National Higher Certificate in Performing Arts from the Market Theatre.

Her publications include: *Migrations* (Short Story Day Africa); *Between The Pillar And The Post,* (Diartkonageng); *Selves* (Afro Anthology); *Black Tax: Burden or Ubuntu,* Jonathan Ball Publishers; *Joburg Noir* (Jacana); *Hauntings* (Jacana); *Years of Fire and Ash: South African Poems Of Decolonisation* (Jonathan Ball Publishers); and her work has appeared in *Prufrock Magazine; Mail & Guardian; Lolwe* and *Imbiza Journal* to name a few.

PRODUCTION CREDITS

Transforming a manuscript into the book you are now reading is a team effort. Cassava Republic Press would like to thank everyone who helped in the production of *Midnight in the Morgue*:

Publishing Director: Bibi Bakare-Yusuf

Editorial
Copy-editor: Ibukun Olowu
Proofreader: Layla Mohamed

Design and Production
Cover Design: Jamie Keenan
Layout: Abdulrahman Osamudiamen Suleiman

Marketing and Publicity
Marketing and Content Officer: Rhoda Nuhu
Digital Marketing: Nnaemeka Nnam

Sales and Admin
Sales Team: Kofo Okunola & The Ingram Sales Team
Accounts & Admin: Adeyinka Adewole